THE BLUEST NIGHT

Also by Aaron Philip Clark

The Trevor Finnegan Series
UNDER COLOR OF LAW
BLUE LIKE ME

The Paul Little Series
THE SCIENCE OF PAUL
A HEALTHY FEAR OF MAN

Other Titles
GARY PHILLIPS' HOLLIS P.I.
*with Juliet Blackwell, Derrick Ferguson,
Bobby Nash and Gary Phillips*

THE BLUEST NIGHT

Aaron Philip Clark

SEVERN
HOUSE

First world edition published in Great Britain and the USA in 2025
by Severn House, an imprint of Canongate Books Ltd,
14 High Street, Edinburgh EH1 1TE.

severnhouse.com

Copyright © Aaron Philip Clark, 2025

Cover and jacket design by kid-ethic

All rights reserved including the right of reproduction in whole or in part in any form. The right of Aaron Philip Clark to be identified as the author of this work has been asserted in accordance with the Copyright, Designs & Patents Act 1988.

British Library Cataloguing-in-Publication Data
A CIP catalogue record for this title is available from the British Library.

ISBN-13: 978-1-4483-1708-0 (cased)
ISBN-13: 978-1-4483-1868-1 (paper)
ISBN-13: 978-1-4483-1709-7 (e-book)

This is a work of fiction. Names, characters, places and incidents are either the product of the author's imagination or are used fictitiously. Except where actual historical events and characters are being described for the storyline of this novel, all situations in this publication are fictitious and any resemblance to actual persons, living or dead, business establishments, events or locales is purely coincidental.

No part of this book may be used or reproduced in any manner for the purpose of training artificial intelligence technologies or systems. This work is reserved from text and data mining (Article 4(3) Directive (EU) 2019/790).

All Severn House titles are printed on acid-free paper.

Typeset by Palimpsest Book Production Ltd., Falkirk, Stirlingshire, Scotland.
Printed and bound in Great Britain by TJ Books, Padstow, Cornwall.

The manufacturer's authorised representative in the EU for product safety is Authorised Rep Compliance Ltd, 71 Lower Baggot Street, Dublin D02 P593 Ireland (arccompliance.com).

Praise for the Trevor Finnegan Thrillers

"Page-turning . . . S.A. Cosby fans
will hope for a long series run"
Publishers Weekly on *Blue Like Me*

"Gritty, dark, and gripping . . . This series
will appeal to fans of Michael Connelly
and Raymond Chandler"
Best Thriller Books on *Blue Like Me*

"Aaron Philip Clark is a storyteller
of immense talent"
Stephen Mack Jones on *Blue Like Me*

"Trevor Finnegan is the hero our country
so desperately needs"
Eli Cranor, author of *Ozark Dogs*, on *Blue Like Me*

"Racism, fear, lies, and corruption . . . Clark's
ripped-from-the-headlines police procedural
should make readers uncomfortable"
Library Journal Starred Review of *Under Color of Law*

"Gripping . . . This is a smart, suspenseful police
procedural with a timely plot"
Publishers Weekly on *Under Color of Law*

"Extraordinary"
Gar Anthony Haywood on *Under Color of Law*

About the author

Aaron Philip Clark is a native of Los Angeles, CA. He is a novelist, screenwriter, creative writing educator, and former Los Angeles Police Department recruit. Clark is the author of the International Thriller Writers Award-nominated Trevor Finnegan series, inspired by his experiences in the LAPD, as well as the *USA Today* bestselling thriller *The Accomplice*, cowritten with rapper and entertainment mogul Curtis "50 Cent" Jackson.

www.aaronphilipclark.com

For my family, friends, collaborators, and readers who have inspired me to continue writing about Trevor Finnegan. Trevor is a hero and a truth seeker. At a time when truth is under fire, may we all be a little more like Trevor 'Finn' Finnegan.

PROLOGUE

December 2016

I lie on the bed, mulling over the state of our ceiling fan. Darkness does well to hide its dusty blades, but I know the filth that collects there, caked along its edges. Not dusting for a week has invited cobwebs that dangle and sway from the light fixture when air blows from the vents. Housekeeping was once prosaic, dare I say enjoyable—I got lost in the mundanity of it, spinning vinyl records: Nirvana's *Nevermind* and Dr. Dre's *The Chronic*, music of my youth. That was before Sarada left for France to study under a renowned pastry chef whose name I can't pronounce. When she's gone, I don't sleep, consume fast food and too much red meat, and think of all the ways I've let people down, especially Sally Munoz, my old partner in LAPD.

Then Ms. Veronica Dixion arrived at my father's Verdugo Hills condo while I was meeting with a blabby realtor who was convinced she'd get several million-dollar offers for his two-bedroom, sorely outdated abode, which needed mold remediation.

I was worried the gun-toting intruder I killed in the living room during an attempted home invasion days prior would negatively impact the listing's asking price. The carpet still retained blood and brain tissue, which left behind the sulfuric aroma of cadaverine and putrescine. I had scheduled the biohazard cleaning service, BioScrubbers, to remove what remained of the assailant. The cost was $2,000, and they assured me that, once cleaned, it'd be like the man's death never happened. But in a city with unprecedented homicides and deaths, I'd have to wait two days for the cleaning crew.

Ms. Dixion had traveled from Nevada on a mission. She needed my father's help to find her missing son—Pop's missing son. It was information that pressed heavily against my conscience, burdening my soul. In my youth, I knew of my father's dalliances outside of my parents' marriage. Mentions of them would boil to the surface during arguments between Pop and my mother—usually during spats about unwashed dishes, Pop's inability to manage money, and his copious amounts of drinking. The fights were only partly about those things. At their core was mother's resentment and deep-seated disappointment in my father. She existed in a perpetual state of sadness and longing until her death, but neither I nor my mother knew that Pop's dealings with Ms. Dixion had produced Avery, my half-brother. Five years younger than me and raised in Summerlin, Nevada.

I confronted Pop as we sat in the visiting room at his substance abuse treatment facility in Palm Springs. He recalled his tryst with Ms. Dixion. It had begun decades ago, in the early nineties, while he was working out of LAPD's Newton Division. Ms. Dixion owned a late-night café off Central Avenue that served breakfast 24/7. Pop liked the flapjacks, and the coffee was strong. "She loved cops coming in. It kept the riffraff away," Pop said, sitting in an armchair, as he drank iced tonic water with sliced lemon. "But she wasn't a badge bunny. Hell, no—it wasn't like that."

I didn't want to know what it *was* like. Pop might've been sober, but he was still cavalier when it came to my feelings. His detached, matter-of-fact way of delivering earth-shattering information without blinking had been a consequence of providing death notifications for decades, sometimes three or four a shift, and the alcohol only made him more dismissive of sentiments like empathy.

He offered no justification for stepping out on my mother. Only that he was "young and foolish." I didn't press the issue further; instead, I shifted the conversation to Avery, his missing son.

According to Ms. Dixion, Avery was driving to Los Angeles to formally meet Pop and introduce him to his girlfriend, Keisha. There was talk of marriage, and he wanted to make peace with the father he never knew.

That was seventy-two hours ago, and now Avery and Keisha are missing. They were last seen traveling the 15 Freeway headed toward Furnace Creek, California.

My cell phone rings. I answer. Pop is on the other end. "They think they found her in the Malibu Hills," he says. "It's bad, Trevor. My God, it's bad."

"Is she . . . ?"

"Afraid so," he says. "She's dead. Sheriff deputies found her body in the marshlands."

"And Avery?"

"No sign of him, but we need to get up there."

"What about Ms. Dixion? Did you tell her?"

"Not until we know more."

"All right," I say. "You already signed out of the facility?"

"Everything's squared away."

"They give you a hard time?"

"The center's director gave me the standard lecture and advised against me pausing my treatment."

"What'd you say?"

"I told her family comes first."

"You need me to pick you up?"

"Ordered a taxi," he says. "The driver will take me over to my storage unit so I can grab my piece. Then I'm coming to you."

"I'll be ready," I say before ending the call.

The clock on the nightstand reads one a.m. Traffic on the I-10 Freeway should be light at this hour, which means Pop should arrive no later than three a.m., and we should make it to Malibu before sunrise.

It's cold out. I put on jeans, a hoodie, and a quilted bomber jacket. My duffle bag is packed with enough clothes to last a week—maybe two if I wear the same attire more than once.

I chamber-check my Glock, then put it in the gun box before adding it to my duffle bag. I throw in an extra magazine, a small tactical flashlight, and a stun gun, and secure the items with underwear, shirts, and socks.

Pop and I tore each other down for years with words and

actions. I nearly cut him off more times than I can count, but fearing the horror awaiting us in Malibu, I've never felt closer to him.

My gut always tightens before major investigations, especially when there's so much at stake, and I know the next few hours will be consequential. As my training officer, Joey Garcia, once said after we caught a homicide with multiple victims ten minutes from ending our shift: "This might be the longest night of our lives."

ONE

The taxi is a yellow-checkered late-model minivan that parks in front of my and Sarada's condo. The driver hops out and opens the hatch. Pop slides the rear door open and stumbles out as if his leg has cramped. It's a three-hour drive from Palm Springs, and Pop's leg circulation is poor. With a subtle limp, he walks to the rear of the van and grabs his suitcase from the back before the driver can assist him. Realizing the old man doesn't require his assistance, the driver shrugs and shuts the rear gate, then gets back into the van and pulls away. It doesn't matter: Pop always handles his personal effects. He wouldn't have let the driver touch his luggage, believing the courtesy would've entitled him to a tip, which Pop never does.

"Can it get any darker out here?" Pop asks. "All the money Sierra Madre's got, and they can't get more streetlights."

"The car's heater is on," I say. "You should get in. Keep warm."

I've been waiting in the cold for twenty minutes with the Falcon running. Given the long drive ahead, it's best to let the engine warm up.

"You don't have to tell me twice," Pop says, handing me his suitcase. "Let's get a move on."

He's eager to get to Malibu; I feel the same. I place the suitcase next to my duffle bag and slam the trunk closed.

"How long do you think it'll take us?" he asks before getting into the passenger seat.

"At this hour, hopefully not long." I hop in the car and get belted. "You thirsty? I've got water and Gatorade. Might be some granola bars in the glove box."

"Not hungry," he says. "Let's get this thing on the freeway, all right?"

I nod, then back out of the driveway. Once out of the neighborhood, I turn onto Sierra Madre Boulevard and make another turn onto Foothill Boulevard before merging onto the 210 onramp, headed westbound. The GPS says it'll take over an hour to get to Malibu. Pop is silent as he looks out the window, hunched in an oversized hoodie. I've got no words for the occasion, despite spending years comforting strangers after they hear their loved one isn't coming home on account of a drunk driver or someone's violent actions. Often preventable, sometimes not, and now, with my father, I can't form a rudimentary sentence to ease his hurt.

No matter what I think about Avery or how he came into this world, he's still my father's son and . . . my brother. It's odd thinking of him that way, but he's blood, whether I like it or not. And if I'm being honest with myself, I don't like it—a good part of me hates him for no other reason than existing.

Thirty minutes into the drive, Pop sighs and mutters. He isn't a religious man, but it sounds like the Lord's Prayer. We approach 110 North and merge onto the 405; the closer we get to Malibu, the more he repeats the prayer. After a while, I don't notice it over the road noise. Just like the tires thumping on the worn-out freeway, the prayer blends into the background.

I slow down as we approach the flashing red and blue lights ahead. I make out seven or eight sheriff vehicles, an ambulance, and a fire engine. They light up the darkness like a colorful serpent slouching toward moonlit hills.

Dawn is coming, and congestion along Highway 1 will soon thicken. Protecting the scene and mitigating traffic require more deputies. I'm unsure of the number of deputies who work out of the regional station, but they'll need at least twenty more than what I'm seeing.

"How do you know this guy, Cohen?" I ask.

"His father worked at Newton with me," Pop says. "He was a good man."

"Was?"

"Died two years ago . . . cancer, I think."

"And Cohen's the one who called you?"

"I told him to let me know if he finds anything, and he found something." Pop points at the parked vehicles ahead of us. "Pull behind that truck."

I park the Falcon behind a white Tacoma with an exempt license plate. Pop struggles with the seat belt, tugging at the strap and trying to release the buckle while cursing to himself. I reach over to help, but he unfastens it in haste, swings the door open, gets out, and enters a large, overgrown field.

"Hold up a second, Pop," I say, watching him rush toward deputies corralled a few feet away. I get out and quickly follow. Pop doesn't move as fast as he used to. He blames his bad hips and knees on police work, but a good amount of credit can go to a sedentary lifestyle and years of excessive drinking.

I catch up to him. "Pop, take a minute . . . slow down."

"Don't have a minute," he says. "Cohen? I need to speak to Cohen!"

I see a hefty deputy with a lapping belly squeezed into a size-XL uniform from the corner of my eye. He's holding a paper cup steaming like a chimney and notices Pop crisscrossing the field while eyeballing every white man in uniform. Pop still walks like a cop, feet cement-heavy with sturdy heel-toe steps. Even his voice registers baritone, contrary to its usual tenor, mere traces of who he was ten years ago when he wore the LAPD badge. Those days are long gone. Now, he seeks relevance in grocery store aisles, complaining about high-priced canned goods like beans and tuna, his dietary staples. People who encounter him might expect menial chit-chat. Yet these pedestrian exchanges lead to his cantankerous diatribes about conservative politicians plotting to dominate and strip Americans of their freedoms. Even if someone agrees and endorses his ideas, they run. Black men who speak boldly of such things have been called radical or crazy. Pop's been called both.

"Chill, Pop—you've got eyes on you."

"Cohen?" He cuts between two deputies talking and noses up to the taller man. "You Cohen?"

"What?" the deputy says, skirting indignation. "Who the hell are you?"

The hefty deputy closes in with his hot drink and makes his move, taking hold of Pop's sweatshirt. "Hey! This is an active crime scene."

After surviving being shot last month, Pop has lost all tolerance for people putting their hands on him. "Don't fucking touch me," Pop says, jerking from the deputy's grasp.

Pop looks out of sorts. He barely resembles the career officer who kept his hair trimmed, boots polished, and uniform military-pressed. Instead, he looks like he's woken up from a year-long slumber—a Black Rip Van Winkle, balding with sporadic gray patches and a ratty beard.

"This is a crime scene," the deputy says. "You can't be here."

"I just need to speak to Cohen."

"Are you with the press?"

"No. I'm not with the damn press. We're here about my son."

"He's my father," I say, holding up my private investigator's badge. "We're looking for Avery Dixion. His mother hired me to find him. Our understanding is that you may have found his girlfriend, Keisha."

"Hired you? Didn't he just say something about a son?"

"That's right—Avery is family. Now, can you confirm a female victim? Black. Mid-twenties."

The deputy squints at my badge. "Yeah, we've got a female victim that matches that description. No ID, though."

"I'm sure if we can talk to Cohen, we can get this sorted."

"Any signs of anyone else?" Pop asks. "A male who might've been with her?"

"You're supposed to be an investigator, too? Because you don't look like an investigator."

"And what the hell's an investigator *supposed* to look like?"

"Well, even if you were, you're not getting through without authorization."

"Look here, you wet-behind-the-ears . . ." Pop hovers below the deputy's chin. "Let me tell you who I am. I'm retired LAPD Officer Shaun Finnegan, and that girl you found might be my son's fiancée, which means my boy might be out here, too. Instead of standing around with your thumb up your ass, how about you get Cohen over here and stop wasting our time?"

The deputy reaches for the cuffs on his Sam Browne belt

and looks ready to discard his coffee if need be. "You want to say that again?"

"You heard me, *Fife*."

"I could detain you for interfering in a police investigation. I mean, who the hell do you think you are?"

Pop reads the deputy's name tag. "Ortiz."

"That's right. You want my badge number, too?"

"Look, Deputy," I say. "We're just trying to make an ID—that's all."

"Are you a father?" Pop asks Ortiz.

"What?"

"A father, Fife . . . are you a damn father?"

"Yeah, asshole. I'm a father."

"Well, then, maybe you can understand. There's nothing I won't do for my children. So, either you step aside and get Cohen down here or arrest us, because we aren't leaving."

"Easy, Pop." I gently palm his chest to calm what's brewing and feel the heavy pounding as though pistons power his heart. "Do us a solid here, Deputy. We only want to speak to Cohen, and you won't have to deal with us any longer."

Ortiz removes his radio from his Sam Browne. "Cohen to my location. I've got two males who say they might know the victim."

The radio crackles; a voice cuts through the static: "Be there in five."

Cohen arrives in less than five minutes and is slightly out of breath. He's young, with a complexion that reminds me of vanilla custard—smooth, clean, and free of a blemish or wrinkle. His soft features are unexpected. The job tends to wash away boyish looks, but maybe he's one of those cops whose faces withstand the stresses of police work while their bodies go to shit.

Meanwhile, Ortiz's bulging belly tells the story of long, tedious shifts writing speeding tickets to drivers of supercars, arresting drunk celebrities, investigating fatal accidents, warning the public of bear sightings . . . and whatever else happens in the beach town's storied hours.

"Mr. Finnegan?" Cohen extends his hand. Pop gives a firm

shake. "Like I said on the phone, there's quite a bit of trauma to the victim's head."

"Let's see her."

Cohen nods to Ortiz, who steps aside. We begin walking toward the gulley where water has collected. The forensic team works in near darkness using lights powered by a generator. We duck under the police tape. Pop nearly slips, losing his footing in the sodden earth. I hold him steady, and once his feet are secure, he jerks my hand away as Cohen notices.

"Careful," Cohen says. "These marshlands take getting used to."

"You think somebody killed her out here?" Pop asks, scoping the rugged terrain.

"Too early to tell," Cohen says. "Forensics thinks that at least some of her wounds were inflicted here, but we can't be sure of the timeline yet." Cohen directs his hand to the barefoot, brown-skinned woman lying face down, inches from a bloodied boulder. "Let's have her face up." He motions with his hand, and two forensic investigators gently lift the woman's face from a cluster of stones.

It's a ghastly wound; her forehead is crushed, partially inverted—tissue is tucked under a skull fragment. More tissue and bits of bone cover the nearby rocks. Forensic investigators delicately brush the woman's braids, masking a puncture wound, and tilt her head in Pop's direction.

"Is it her?" I ask. "Is it Keisha?"

Pop kneels beside the dead woman and takes out his phone. The locked screen is a picture of Keisha. He looks at the photo, then at the dead woman with eyes as empty as a starless sky. "It's her," he says. He doesn't break from his stare; he can't. I know the look: the creased brow and steely eyes. I've read it on other cops and felt it form on my face, too. It's a cold conversation between the victim and the vindicator—an unspoken promise.

"You say she's your son's fiancée?" Cohen asks.

"Avery told me they were planning a spring wedding."

"I'm sorry."

Pop gets to his feet, crosses his arms, and looks toward the road. "Busy stretch?"

"Usually."

"And her clothes?" I ask.

Cohen frowns. "What about them?"

"Her dress looks homemade."

"My mother still knits me Christmas sweaters."

"Sure, but the dress looks old-timey, colonial. Not something you'd expect a girl like her to wear."

"A girl like her?" Cohen looks uncomfortable. "I'm the wrong guy to ask about fashion."

"Unless Keisha was Amish or belonged to some kind of ultra-modest religious sect . . ."

"Maybe she had a thing for vintage?"

"There's vintage, and then there's provincial."

"The dress does look a little funny on her," Pop says. "What are you thinking, Trevor?"

"We need to get it analyzed. How long will it take, Deputy?"

"I'll try my best to rush it," Cohen says. "But I can't make any promises. Can you two get in touch with her family?"

"She didn't have anybody," Pop says. "Dead parents. No relatives to speak of. The way Avery tells it, it's been them against the world for years now."

"We'll find your son, Mr. Finnegan." Cohen sounds like most cops—assured to a fault.

"Who's the primary on this?" I ask.

Cohen looks toward the road where an unmarked sedan has parked behind the Falcon. A woman gets out, a slim brunette in civvies: cargo pants, tactical boots, and a field jacket.

Cohen pushes a button on his radio, opens the channel, and says, "Have Brennan meet me at the scene."

Ortiz confirms over the channel: "Copy."

"Brennan?" Pop asks. "Has she been an investigator long?"

"A few years. Originally from Iowa, I think."

A wind whips through the marsh. Pop puts his hands in his hoodie pockets. "Is that where they eat cheese curds for breakfast?"

"I believe you're thinking of Wisconsin."

"Ah, right—knew it was one of those flyover states."

"She looks young to be an investigator," I say, studying her as she approaches. "Maybe she's good, squared away."

"Or it's nepotism," Pop says.

"No family on the job from what I hear," Cohen says. "She's a transfer from the Crescenta Station. We've worked a case or two . . . a little green in areas, but she's sharp."

"Crescenta? She's more than green."

"Give her a chance, Pop."

"Like we've got any say . . ."

Brennan smooths untamed strands of hair near her temples and works them into a ponytail. She has a downhome look—stud earrings and no makeup, which is what I'd expect of a Midwestern girl.

Cohen straightens up. "Gentlemen, this is Detective Beatrice Brennan."

No one bothers to shake hands.

"This is unprecedented," she says, circling the body. "Civilians trampling a crime scene."

Pop glares. "Trampling?"

"They aren't civilians . . . exactly," Cohen says. "Retired LAPD Officer Shaun Finnegan and his son, former LAPD Detective Trevor Finnegan. The victim is the fiancée of Mr. Finnegan's son, Avery. He's missing as well."

"They were on a road trip," Pop says. "Traveling from Nevada to California."

"You know this, how?" Brennan asks.

"They were coming to see me."

"I see," Brennan says. "Any particular reason?"

"Family stuff." Pop clears a lump in his throat. "Cohen did us a favor by notifying us of what he found. We came to . . ." He struggles to compose himself. "I thought I could provide a positive ID."

Brennan shines her flashlight into Keisha's cratered skull. "Well, I don't have to tell you the importance of protocol and scene integrity."

"We aren't here to complicate things, but my son Avery is still out there, and we want to help you all find him."

"You're presuming they were traveling together for the entire trip."

"What are you saying?"

"It's possible they weren't in each other's company the entire time, correct?"

"Why would they not remain together?"

"Who's to say they didn't separate by choice or circumstance?"

"I'm going to need you to make it plain," Pop says. "Separated? Meaning what exactly?"

"Could mean nothing, or it could mean everything. That's why it's an investigation."

"Avery wouldn't have left Keisha somewhere alone. Something had to have happened to both of them."

Brennan kneels next to the boulder. She concentrates on Keisha's micro braids, partially affixed to the rock with blood and brain matter. "So intricate," she says, putting on a pair of blue nitrile gloves. "Sometimes people argue. I remember my father putting my mother out of the car during a family trip in Tennessee. It took her over an hour to walk back to our motel in the rain."

"That's terrible," Cohen says.

"Like I said, people fight."

Pop's face starts to show grief, then anger. "Sounds like you're already making up your mind about the type of man Avery is."

"We should get going," I say. "Protocol and all."

"I'll keep you updated," Cohen says. "If Avery's out there, we'll find him."

I take Pop by the arm and nudge him away from the scene toward the Falcon.

"What the hell was that?" he asks.

"Can't say . . . She's different, that's for sure."

"Of all the detectives, we get some kind of *freak show*."

"Maybe it's just how she works."

"She was looking at Keisha's body like it was roadkill and touching her hair like that. *Intricate*? And you saw the wheels turning. She's already thinking Avery had a hand in this."

"We can't focus on all that," I say. "Not until we find him."

"What do you think people like her see when they look over our dead bodies?"

"People like Brennan?"

"You know what I'm saying. I couldn't tell you the number of times I heard 'NHI' thrown around at a scene where the victims looked like us. *No Human Involved*? Can't get much more fucked up than that. I mean, who thinks of that?"

"I don't know, Pop. I just hope Brennan sees what I see. Someone who needs justice."

"Yeah," Pop sighs. "That's what you're hoping for, but we'll never know what goes through their heads. As much as we want to believe it, some victims will never be victims in their eyes."

"Better to give her a fair shake. All she needs is to solve this. She doesn't need to love us."

We get into the Falcon. I start the car while Pop scrolls on his phone. "We need to stay close to this mess," Pop says. "Set up shop somewhere local so we aren't trekking back and forth from Sierra Madre."

"Agreed."

"You think we should get a motel or something? Maybe one of those Airbnbs."

"I know a place."

"How much a night?"

"Pretty sure it's on the house."

Pop looks up from his phone, frowning. "On the house? Don't get me in any situation."

"It's all good, Pop."

I put on my seat belt, flick on the headlights, and pull onto the road. "What's that you got there, Pop?"

"Hot damn," he says, looking wide-eyed at his phone's screen. "Like I said, a freak show."

"What is it?"

"Googled the *missy*."

"You mean Detective Brennan?"

"I need to know who we're dealing with, and it's a good thing I took the time. You'd be surprised what people put on the internet. Don't they know that shit lives forever in cyberspace?"

I quickly glance at his phone, then put my eyes back on the road.

"Did you see it?" he asks, holding up his phone. "You get a good look?"

On the screen is the picture of a woman who resembles Detective Brennan. She's slightly younger and blonde, but it could be a wig or a poor dye job. She has unnaturally pouty beet-red lips, blue eyeshadow, and thick makeup with lots of contouring. She's posing in a shiny American flag bikini, holding an M60E3 machine gun.

"I mean, what the hell is this?" Pop asks. "She's packing heavy artillery."

"It's her social media account. Looks like she models on the side . . . or used to."

"I know that," he says. "But I mean, what's the point? Is she selling the gun or the bikini?"

"Probably both."

"And how the hell can she do this when she's sworn?"

I take a closer look. "It's a magazine cover from three years ago, Pop."

"Cohen said she's been an investigator for at least two. That means she was running and gunning back when she took this picture." He continues to scroll. "Over one thousand followers. She even has sponsorship. A burger chain and sporting goods store."

"A burger chain? Which one?"

"You really want to know? I'm pretty sure you like their milkshakes."

"Doesn't matter," I say, wanting to forget the machine gun and Brennan's barely covered breasts. "We only need her to do her job. She needs to work the case, figure out what the hell happened to Keisha, and find Avery. Aside from that, what she does in her free time isn't my business."

"There used to be a time when departments wouldn't allow

shit like this. Brennan's a deputy, not auditioning for Rambo . . . *Birdie Brennan, the Patriot Hottie*. Hashtag *Sexywithabadge*. Hashtag *Cutebutdeadly*. It's the kind of shit that puts cops in a bad light. You'd think the sheriff department would be more aware of that."

"What can I say? Times they are a-changing, Pop."

"Damn, if I don't know that. They're changing all right, just not for the better. A gun-fanatic deputy built like a Playboy bunny. She's a right-winger's wet dream. What's next?"

A streaking figure steps into the road. I slam on the brakes; the person freezes. The Falcon skids to a stop, inches, maybe less, from hitting what appears to be a man in torn, bloodstained clothing. His face is battered and caked with blood.

"Oh, shit!" Pop screams, seizing the grab handle.

Smoke emits from the undercarriage and rear, and smells of scorched brake dust and heated rubber.

"Ah, hell, did you hit him?" Pop asks.

"Don't think so." I open the door and step into the road. "Call Cohen. Tell him we're about two miles north of the crime scene on Latigo Canyon Road."

"On it."

I walk to the front of the car; the man is sprawled on the pavement with his arm stretched across the double-yellow line. He's a bald man with a face like pounded meat. There are plenty of bruises along his cheeks, neck, and forehead, and his eye is swollen shut. There are cuts on his hands and wrists—deep lacerations.

"Sir? Can you hear me?"

The man moans.

Pop hits the hazards, then gets out of the Falcon. He walks gingerly toward the injured man. "He's taken some damage," Pop says, squinting as he investigates the man's face. "Cohen's sending help. Where do you think he came from?"

"No telling. Maybe down from the canyon . . ." I crouch near the injured man. "Sir, can you hear me?"

More moaning.

Pop crouches for an even closer look. "Injuries are severe. You sure you didn't hit him?"

"Check the hood," I say. "There's not a dent or scratch."

The man's face is pressed against the pavement, and dirt and gravel speckle his cheek. His complexion is fair, like mine and Pop's, and his perfectly round head has a moderate neck slope, something common with Finnegan men.

"I think it's him," I say. "It's Avery."

"What?" Pop says. "Hand me your flashlight."

I give him the small LED flashlight I carry in my pocket. He adjusts the beam so that it isn't blinding and shines the light on Avery's face. "Kid?" Pop asks. "That you?"

Avery tries to retract his arm. It demands more strength than he can spare, and he surrenders with a weary sigh. "Help me."

Pop's shaken, barely able to dial Cohen again on his phone. "It's Shaun," he says, talking fast. "We found him. We found him, and he's alive, by God—he's alive!"

TWO

I've spent too many hours in hospitals not to be in the healthcare profession. I dread having to sleep another night in a waiting room. I'm not sure my back can take it. Usually, long car rides and knotty mattresses are to blame, but sleeping on vinyl hospital chairs has put me in traction before. Doctors say I've reached the peak—no amount of rehab will repair the damage my back sustained when a three-inch knife entered it. Hazards of being a cop, they say—there are days I regret ever putting on the badge.

"He's still getting evaluated," Pop says, sitting down beside me. "Nurses say they'll update me when they've got something."

"Been thinking," I say. "About that deputy who was giving us the runaround tonight."

"*Fife* . . . what about him?"

"What you said to him about being a father . . ."

"Yeah?"

"Did you mean it?"

"What the hell kind of question is that?" Pop asks.

"I always saw you as a cop first, then my dad. So tonight, when you said there was nothing you wouldn't do for your children . . ."

"Get to the point, Trevor."

"It's just that I didn't see it coming, that's all."

"Is this about Avery? You think I abandoned him?"

"I'm not saying that."

"But you're thinking it, aren't you? Probably been on your mind since Veronica showed up in LA wanting me to find him."

Pop is right. The word *abandonment* has bounced around in my head since I learned of Avery's existence, but when I think about anyone's abandonment, it isn't only his. My father treated my mother and me either as ghosts or burdens, and now, after all these years, I understand why. He was trying to manage two families, which is impossible to do equally, and from what I know of Avery's upbringing, Pop provided the bare minimum—no phone calls or visits, only letters and checks in the mail.

"I'm not saying it was right. I don't deserve your compassion or understanding, even," he says. "But know this: I chose you and your mother because that's where my heart was. I'll never say Avery was a mistake, but . . ." He leans in closer, his eyes bloodshot and glossy. "I did my best to look after him, but clearly, it wasn't enough, and I'll regret that for the rest of my life."

"Did you ever think to . . ." I pause. *Is there any upside to my questioning? Or am I only wounding Pop further?*

"Go ahead," he says. "Ask me."

"Nah, forget it, Pop—it's nothing."

"OK, then." Pop gets up from his chair with a grunt. "I'm getting a coffee. Want something?"

"I'm good."

"You sure?"

I nod, and Pop walks droopily toward an automated coffee and hot cocoa machine in the corner of the waiting room. It's hard to see him this way, but part of me, an enraged part, knows he brought this madness on himself. He's always been inscrutable. Sometimes indecipherable, but for the past few days, he's been unusually transparent and vulnerable. Avery's disappearance seems to have affected him more than being shot in his home weeks ago; on that fateful night, despite the risk of bleeding to death on his living-room floor, Pop appeared unaffected, casually indifferent to his plight. Maybe he thought he deserved it. After all, the hired killer had come to enact revenge on Pop for an investigation that sent an innocent man to prison. The inmate later developed a terminal illness and expired in his cell.

If Pop had his way, he would've carried the secret to his grave, but fate had other plans. Perhaps it was the drinking that numbed the guilt over the years and kept him from thinking about his time as a street cop—busting heads, usually Black and brown suspects—or just people who happened to be in the way of the police. Pop has plenty of regrets; that's for damn sure. No less than mine, I guess, and while I found solace in cheap sex, Pop used liquor to mask his suffering. But his journey to sobriety means he's receptive to every thought, no matter how depressing. With Avery being near death and Keisha succumbing to it, that familiar darkness stirs in him—it's what pushed him to drink those many years ago.

My cell phone rings. It's Sarada calling. I get up and walk to a small alcove near the restrooms. "Hey, baby."

"Trevor. How are you holding up?"

"We found them."

"Are they . . ."

"Keisha didn't make it. The Sheriff's Department is investigating, but it's too early to tell what killed her."

"My God . . ."

"It's bad. I keep thinking about how we found her—the body, it was so . . ." I try to articulate the brutality. "We just have to get to the bottom of it," I say. "That's what we need to focus on."

"And Avery? How's he?"

"Alive . . . but barely."

"And how's your father taking all this?"

"I don't know," I say, watching Pop stand aimlessly in front of the brewing machine. There are six beverage choices, but he's been fluctuating for five minutes as if the possibilities are infinite. "I think he's in bad shape, but he won't say it. I'm worried he might drink."

"Have you tried to talk to him?"

"Tried, but it didn't go well."

"I know you're angry, Trevor. I can hear it in your voice, but there's a time and place. And right now, you need to be there for your father. Can you do that?"

"Yeah, I can do that."

"Good."

"How are things going with you?" I ask. "Weather still shitty?"

"It's France," she says. "Sunny days are few and far between. Coffee-shop owners make a killing this time of year."

"Imagine if LA had a consistent winter. We'd be able to visit your family every year off coffee sales alone."

"Yeah, but it wouldn't be LA anymore. It'd be Seattle or Portland."

"Screw that," I say. "And the baking—how's it coming along?"

"Things are . . ." She pauses; it feels cryptic. "Let's just say I regret not taking French as a language in high school."

"Shit, Sarada. I'm sorry."

"It's fine," she says. "Don't worry about it, OK? You've got enough going on. Besides, the master baker is helping me out."

"Master baker?"

"He's taken me under his wing and is teaching me a lot."

"OK—well, you got this."

"I made it this far, right? No use in giving up now."

"That's right, Chef. Everybody knows your scones are the best in LA."

She giggles. "The best, huh?"

"Without a doubt. You won't catch me eating anyone else's scones, muffins, cookies—nothing that doesn't come out of *your* oven."

Sarada laughs hard. I'm grateful she still finds me humorous. It's how I know she's keeping her spirits up, hanging in there, staying strong. "I miss you, Trevor," she says. "I can't wait to see you."

"Christmas will be here before we know it," I say, wondering if we'll have much to celebrate.

"Don't worry about getting me anything, all right? All I want is to see your smiling face when I step off that plane."

A woman calls over the intercom, "Shaun Finnegan to the nurses' station . . . Shaun Finnegan to the nurses' station."

I look toward the brewing machine. My father shuffles toward me, holding two cups. "Got to go," I say. "I'll call when I can."

"I love you, Trevor."

"Love you, too."

I end the call as Pop hands me a coffee. "Got you something anyway. You still take it black, right?"

"Yeah," I say, accepting the dark brew. "Thank you."

"C'mon, I think Avery's awake."

We walk to the nurses' station, where a thin-lipped woman with sunspots plucks away on a keyboard. She looks up from the screen and, in the same grating tone that rang over the intercom, says, "Are you Shaun Finnegan?"

"Yes," Pop says. "I am."

"You can see the patient now." She points to a room down the hall. "Room six on the right."

I follow Pop into the room and stand under the TV mounted on the wall. The room is colder than the rest of the hospital. A tall nurse wearing an unzipped purple hoodie over her scrubs injects something into Avery's IV line. "It's for the pain," she says, looking at Pop. She continues pushing buttons on the infusion pump. "I'll be back to check on him . . . The doctor should be in shortly." As she walks toward the door, I read the print on the back of her hoodie. Embroidered white words read: "Golden Hills' 34th Annual Marathon."

Ordinarily, a hospital with a namesake marathon seems overindulgent, but Golden Hills is a well-funded hospital with a reputation for treating celebrities and upper-echelon types, mainly because of its location. It's a few miles from the mansions perched on the cliffsides, with expansive views of the Pacific—multi-million-dollar homes secluded in gated communities patrolled by paramilitary-looking guards in golf carts. Twenty-four-hour security has always been a symbol of opulence in Southern California, especially in cities like Beverly Hills, Calabasas, and Malibu, which celebrities call home. But Avery isn't a celebrity or a wealthy local. He's an "everyday Black man" receiving care, and the best we can hope for is that the care is adequate.

"Kid, it's me," Pop says, setting his coffee on the bedside table. He takes Avery's hand as though it were a delicate flower. I noticed them before, but I see them more clearly now: dirt under his fingernails; cuts and bruises cover his knuckles. Some are old. Others look fresh. Judging by the scabs, the older cuts might've happened a day or two ago, but I can't be sure. Avery struggles to open his good eye, managing to raise the lid to a slit. Liquid drains from the eye's corner . . . a yellowish tear with a hint of blood. I've seen common injuries on domestic abuse victims, and once, an unhoused man attacked with a metal rod outside a Seven-Eleven. But the eye isn't the worst of Avery's injuries. Someone beat him badly over days and with more than their fists. The wounds on his arms resemble lash marks.

"Can you hear me?" Pop asks. "I've got someone with me I'd like you to meet."

I step closer and stand where Avery can see me best. "I'm Trevor . . ."

Before I get the words out, Pop says, "He's your brother, and he's been wanting to meet you for a long time."

Pop's lie doesn't bother me. I know whatever he says has little to do with me and how I feel. He'll say whatever he has to for Avery's benefit. It's like Sarada told me: right now, Pop needs support, and if that means faking that I've wanted to meet my half-brother for years, so be it. And while I'm choosing not to condemn Pop, it's damn hard smiling through his bullshit. It's as if I'm forcing rotten meat down my throat and trying not to choke.

"I'm very sorry we're meeting under these circumstances," I say.

Avery stares at me out of his good eye.

I continue, "I'd like to ask you some questions. We should get them out of the way before the sheriff's investigator arrives."

Pop elbows my arm and whispers, "What are you doing? This ain't the time."

What does Pop know about time? He hasn't worked a case in decades, and the second Birdie Brennan shows up, she'll shut us out because we're spectators at her investigation or complications. Either way, the result will be the same, and we need her to see us as assets.

"I agree with *our* father. It isn't the best time, but we don't have any other choice. We need to know what happened tonight, and that means you sharing as much information as you can remember."

A cop's instincts might fade, but they never die. Pop may

not agree with my timing, but he knows this is our best opportunity to question Avery. He reluctantly asks, "Can you remember anything, Avery? Whatever it is, you can tell us. We're here to help."

A sticky white substance coats Avery's lips, and crusted mucus forms around his nose, which is likely caused by the constant flow of oxygen into his nasal cavity. He prepares his mouth to speak, slowly pursing his lips. Blood has collected between his lower teeth; his tongue is a wine-soaked cork, deep red and swollen. "It's all right," he says, words shaky. "Go ahead. Whatchu want to know?"

"Let's start at the beginning," I say, taking a notepad and pen from my pocket. "You and Keisha drove from Nevada to California, correct?"

Pop looks on in disgust. I know he doesn't want me to bring up Keisha so soon, but there's no time for sensitivity. Avery is a potential witness, and what he's able to tell us will set the course for this investigation. Coddling him would only hinder our progress.

"Nevada?" Avery says, surprised. He acts as though the word is foreign. "What about Nevada?"

"Isn't that where you and Keisha were traveling from?"

"Yeah, maybe," he says. "Me and Keisha have been on the road a good while . . ."

Pop whispers, "Can't you see he's confused? I told you it was too soon to question him."

"You were traveling to see Pop . . . to meet him, correct?"

Avery exhales, and mucus secretes from his nose, collecting above his lip. "I . . ." he stammers, and then his good eye shuts. "Can't keep it straight in my head," he says. "We might've left Vegas a few days ago, but it feels like it's been months now. It's all in pieces like a puzzle, and I can't connect them."

"Connect them how?" Pop asks, unable to keep quiet. "What's the puzzle supposed to be?"

"Pieces of time . . ." he says. "It's all pieces of time. Some things feel like they happened yesterday. Other things feel like months have passed, and I can't put it right in my head."

"OK," I say. "Let's focus on Malibu. Do you remember

coming here to the Lost Hills area? Is there a reason you didn't meet with Pop first?"

"I don't know," he says. "Keisha probably wanted to see the beach, ya know? Dip her toes in the water. Otherwise, I've got no idea why we'd come here."

"We found you and Keisha near a canyon, about five miles from the coastline. Is there a chance you know someone in Malibu that you might've come to visit?"

"Nah," Avery says, growing agitated. "I don't know anybody in this place. Not you . . ." He looks to Pop. "Not him, either. We never should've come here . . . never."

Pop looks panicked. "What do you mean you don't know us?"

"Strangers," he says. "Both of y'all . . ."

"We've been talking on the phone, Avery. You don't remember why you came here? It was to see me," Pop says. "You saying you don't remember any of that?"

"I know who you two say you are . . . that we're supposed to be family and all. But I can't remember no conversations happening before this one." Avery squeezes Pop's hand.

"It's going to be all right, Avery . . ."

"What's happened to me? Why the hell can't I remember?"

I've never seen Pop look so aghast. "We better get the doctor to evaluate him," he says. "He needs a full workup—an MRI or something."

"Must be some kind of amnesia," I say. "I've seen something similar in other victims, but never this severe."

"Where's Keisha?" Avery asks. "I want to see her." He squeezes Pop's hand tighter.

"I'm sorry, son." Pop lays his other hand on Avery's shoulder, trying to comfort him as much as possible in the confines of a hospital bed. "She's gone."

"Gone? Whatchu mean? Gone where?"

"They don't know what happened, exactly," Pop says, "but they found her."

While Pop struggles to explain, I consider what Brennan said. Suppose Avery and Keisha were separated and lost sight of each other while fleeing from whatever danger lurked. If someone was pursuing them, they might've gotten to Keisha first, killing her in the marsh, giving time for Avery to escape.

"Someone better tell me where Keisha is," Avery says, grimacing as he worms his way up the pillow, barely able to straighten his back.

"She's dead," I say bluntly. Pop looks like he wants to slug me. Maybe if I were ten, I'd care, but right now, his feelings are inconsequential. If we're going to get a decent lead, I need Avery to keep talking—I need him to remember, so I put it plainly: "Keisha was attacked. Someone killed her, and we need to find out who. Was there someone else out there with you? What were you running from?"

"No, Keisha . . . not my baby . . . She can't be dead . . . can't be." Avery flails his arms and tries to remove the oxygen from his nose. Pop holds his hand, but Avery bucks his body, shaking the bed.

"Ah, hell," Pop says. "We need to get someone in here!" Pop struggles to hold on to Avery as a vein bulges in his neck, but each attempt at controlling his arms is met with Avery's unyielding strength, surprising for a man in fair but stable condition. Pop snaps, "I told you it was too soon, dammit! You've got him all worked up."

Avery seethes, gushing saliva and dried blood onto his gown. "Let me up! I need to get out of here . . . let me loose. They're going to kill me."

"Who's trying to kill you?" I ask. "Tell us something—anything—so we can help you."

"They're coming," he says. "They're out there, and they're coming."

"Who's out there?" Pop asks. "What's going on, son?"

I look toward the door. The commotion alerted Avery's attending nurse in the purple hoodie, who signals for assistance. We're down to minutes, probably seconds before the nurses barge into the room. "Who did it, Avery? Who killed Keisha?"

Avery grabs Pop's sweatshirt and pulls him closer. "You have to help me. It's not safe here. I feel it." His body starts to tremble. "All around me. There's something wrong with this place. They're evil, I tell you. Mutherfuckin devils and they want me."

"Ease up, Trevor," Pop says. "Or he's going to crack."

"How about the clothes?" I ask. "Tell us about the clothes. Do you remember where you got them?"

"I said he's had enough, dammit," Pop says, clearly losing the contest of wills. Avery swings his leg over the side of the bed. His foot dangles, almost touching the floor. If he's able to get some stability, he could lift himself out of the bed.

Three nurses enter the room and rush to Avery's bedside. "What's going on in here?" A fit Asian man asks us. Before Pop can answer, the nurse nudges him out of the way and tends to Avery. "Let's get him something to settle him down," he orders the nurse in the purple hoodie.

Pop frees himself from Avery's hold and latches onto my bicep. "We're leaving."

"But Pop . . ."

"Go. Let the nurses do their jobs."

He pushes me toward the door as the male nurse draws the privacy curtain. "He's hiding something," I whisper, which further infuriates Pop.

Pop opens the door and forces me into the hallway, which is filled with heightened chatter and squeaky sneakers. I traipse on a shellacked floor that appears to dull by the hour.

"What the hell is wrong with you?" Pop asks. "Have you lost your ever-loving mind?"

"There's something he isn't telling us."

"He doesn't remember shit, and hammering him like that isn't going to change it. The poor guy is probably concussed or something. With the ordeal he went through, there's no way to know why he can't remember. That's why he's getting treated by the doctors—they're the professionals. Not you and not me. If something is wrong upstairs, they'll detect it."

"And if they don't?"

"What the hell are you trying to say?"

"Memory loss is convenient."

"For God's sake, the boy's girlfriend is dead. What the hell has gotten into you?"

"You don't see it, do you? Or maybe you do and can't admit it."

"See what?" Brennan asks, coming up from behind Pop.

"Sheriff Brennan," I announce her arrival, causing Pop to stop speaking and snarl at me.

"Had the wrong floor," Brennan says. "I took the stairs."

"I bet if it were a photoshoot, you would've found it," Pop says, choosing not to abandon his warlike mien.

"Excuse me?" She postures like she's taken shit from men before, surely from ones in her profession. "Something you want to say to me?"

"I just said it . . . You should've been here an hour ago."

"I don't answer to you."

"I pay taxes, so yeah, you do," Pop says.

"So, it's true what they say about you Finnegans," she says. "You're a real couple of assholes."

"How about we all cool down," I say, trying to defuse the situation. In the police academy, we called it *verbal judo*—the art of de-escalation. Some cops used it. Plenty didn't. "It's been a long night, and I think we're all worked up."

"Uh-huh," Brennan says. "Need I remind you that your involvement in this investigation is a courtesy? No, better yet, it's a fucking gift. One I can rescind at any time."

"Duly noted," I say. "And we are appreciative."

"Then I'd expect your father to show me some respect."

"He's sorry, Sheriff Brennan." I look at Pop who is too angry to show anything except contempt. "Aren't you, Pop?"

"I spoke out of turn," he says. "Apologies. As Trevor said, we appreciate the courtesy."

"We're all a little on edge, given what's transpired tonight," I say. "My inkling is that we can help each other, but we have to remember we're on the same team."

Brennan puts on like a punchy quarterback. "All righty, teammate. Can you tell me if Avery is awake? I'd like to interview him."

"He was," Pop says. "Got a little worked up earlier. I think the nurses in there are giving him a sedative."

"What riled him?"

"He's dealing with a lot," Pop says. "As far as I can tell, it's all rattling upstairs." Pop pokes his temple. "He probably needs to rest before he'd be any good to you anyway."

"So you spoke to him without me present?" She cranes her neck like a dog picking up a scent.

"Briefly," I add.

"What did he say?"

Pop and I are quiet.

"Really? Are you clamming up now? You fucking guys . . ."

Pop settles on a lie by omission. "We told him Keisha was dead—thought it was better hearing it from a family member."

"Keep at this, and you'll be iced out by morning."

I cave under the threat. "He doesn't remember anything about Keisha's murder or what happened to him. He's not even sure how or why he's in Malibu."

"Amnesia?"

"Extreme trauma can do that. Manifest in missing blocks of time, paranoia, disorientation . . ."

"I guess we're both familiar with manifestations of victimology. I see that's one training you didn't sleep through in the LAPD."

"I approached every training with seriousness."

"But you can't speak with authority because you're no doctor, am I right?"

"Well, Avery's condition is nothing definitive. We're still waiting for the physician's report, but his chart indicates broken ribs, multiple facial fractures, and contusions on his torso. Enough internal injuries to send him into shock."

"All the more reason I should speak to him now while he's stable."

I peruse the sea of people in lab coats, hoping someone will break from the herd to check on Avery. "I'm sure his doctor will be by soon and we can get a clearer picture of what's going on with him," I say. "Like most things around here, it's a waiting game."

"So you actually believe he's experienced memory loss?"

"I'm only stating what I've observed."

"Right," she says, "I'll take it from here." She brushes past me and enters Avery's room.

"You're just going to let her go in there?" Pop asks. "He's not fit to talk to her."

"What do you expect me to do?"

Pop draws in his bottom lip and bites hard. "Damn, you're spineless."

"Yeah . . . and I'm beginning to wonder how much of the alcohol is really to blame for you being an insufferable ass—"

Pop checks me with a look. There's no point in finishing the sentence. The damage is done. He drops his head, eyes fixed on his shoes. I've never called my father a derogatory name . . . at least not to his face.

Pop looks up from his shoes as if something has broken in him. "Got yourself a mean streak, don't you? Suppose you got it honest, though." He steps away, headed toward the elevator.

"Where are you going?"

"To call Veronica. Let her know our boy's alive and Keisha's not."

Pop hasn't had to make a call this difficult in years. While Ms. Dixion will be relieved her son is alive, her joy will likely dwindle when she learns about Keisha's death. It'll take Pop a little while to explain what we know, which is hardly anything.

"I'll meet you back at the car," Pop says, continuing down the hallway.

I'm ashamed. I shouldn't have insulted my father. He might've deserved it, but not from me. I should be supporting him, like Sarada said. I'm all he's got, and while we bicker like children, he needs to know I have his back.

Brennan exits Avery's room, frustrated, still holding her notepad. "Fuck," she says.

"Get what you needed?" I ask.

"As you said, amnesia. He doesn't remember much and whatever drug they gave him is starting to kick in. He stopped making sense halfway through."

"So, you got something out of him?"

"Whatever I got is of no concern to you. I shouldn't involve you any further."

"But you're working this case alone."

"And your point is what, exactly?"

"When was the last time Malibu had a crime like this? Decades, probably. A homicide of this scale and a surviving victim. Once word gets out, people will draw their own conclusions and panic. You know what this looks like, Brennan—it's the kind of case that scares people, keeps them off the streets when night falls."

"And how is that a bad thing if there's someone out there killing people?"

"It's a beach town," I say. "It runs on tourism. If those vendors start closing their doors at sunset, their businesses will dry up."

"The media hasn't even gotten wind of it yet. We could have this thing solved in forty-eight hours."

"Wishful thinking. And if you don't?"

Brennan tucks her hands into her pockets, considering the conundrum I've laid before her. She might've gone to detective school, but they don't teach the economic impacts of homicide in affluent communities. Murder is bad for business, especially in places like Malibu, where crime is well below the national average, and people expect safety and tolerate little else. Fear keeps the tourists away and makes the locals stay inside at night and lock their doors. No dinner reservations. No bonfires on the beaches. It's a domino effect that Brennan hasn't weighed, and it could all contribute to the PR crisis the Sheriff's Department is currently facing. In the past few years, scandals have marred the department—narcotics and guns stolen from evidence lockers, deputies openly using racial epithets on duty, sexual harassment claims, and department gangs that routinely assault citizens and terrorize minority communities—all of this has eroded public confidence and brought the scrutiny of the Department of Justice, along with the *LA Times*.

"Consider what we know," I say. "The evidence suggests that Avery and Keisha are victims who may have been abducted. I'm guessing for days. Two or three."

"You're jumping to conclusions."

"You think Avery beat himself up?"

"No, but I wouldn't be so quick to call him a victim."

"Don't tell me you believe he and Keisha willingly dressed in those strange clothes?"

"My point is, it's too early to determine the reasons behind any of that."

"Fine. Let's say the evidence starts pointing in one direction, suggesting that the person or persons responsible are members of this community. What then? It'll be hard for you to see this town as a harbor for the types of people who would commit such acts against other human beings."

"So that's what this is about. You think I can't be objective?"

"I know you can't. It's not because you don't want to, but when you look at people around here, you see your family members—grandparents, your mother and father, uncles, aunts, cousins. They're all your neighbors and friends. Not murderers."

"This is all assumption, Finnegan. You don't know anything about me, and you've got no idea how I work."

"Maybe, but I'm certain of one thing—you've never faced an investigation like this one, and you're working it alone. I've been in your shoes, Brennan. Someone—and I'm guessing a superior—wants you to fumble. And when you do, they're going to boot your ass to some dead-end beat like Lancaster. They're betting against you. But you can even the odds."

"And how do I do that?"

"My father and I have experience working these kinds of cases. You can keep us on the bench or let us help you."

"My goodness, just when I thought you couldn't be any more condescending. I'm no greenhorn, Finnegan. I've been around the block," she says. "And I don't need you or your father's help."

"Fine, but the offer stands."

"OK, then I respectfully decline in perpetuity."

"Tell me, Brennan. Why are you alpha on this?"

"What's with you thinking I need a partner to do my job? You think a woman can't work a case alone?"

"That's not it," I say. "But I study law enforcement organizations for a living. I know their tactics, and if things were copacetic between you and the department, you'd be talking to your partner instead of me. What reason did they give for you working alone?"

"I haven't had a partner in years," she says.

"Budget cuts?"

"That's the reason they gave."

"Didn't the sheriff order a fleet of new cruisers last month? It's funny how budget cuts only impact certain aspects of a department."

"I just do my job. Budget issues are above my pay grade."

"Right, right. You keep your head down and toe the line, is that it? Valiant strategy, but it rarely works in your favor."

She's apprehensive, eyes shifting from the floor to the ceiling. Either she tells me to kick rocks or she recognizes Pop's and my usefulness.

After a moment of staring at her boots, she says, "You don't give up, do you?" then opens her notepad and holds it up for me to see. It's a drawing of an insect—folded wings, an oval body, a large head, and prominent eyes. "Avery drew this."

"Didn't know he could draw. What is it?"

"Looks like a flying beetle or something. He said it's the only thing he remembered."

"The only thing? Weird. What'd he say about it?"

"Nothing. Doodled it and dozed off to sleep."

I snap a picture of the drawing with my phone's camera. "Well, it's something . . ."

"You're an asshole, but you're right," Brennan says. "I might not be a favorite in my department, but I'm a good cop who closes cases without a partner, and that proves I'm a better detective than most."

"If only people could ignore the thongs and machine guns."

"So you looked?"

"My father did."

"What I do in my personal life shouldn't matter. I'm the best detective out of that station, and I don't give a damn what they think."

"You get no judgment from me, but I can see how it can be distracting for the department."

"Give me a break," she says. "This department has far greater issues than my fucking Instagram."

"Fair enough."

"I looked into you, too, *Mr. Lawsuit*."

"No revelations there. It's all public record."

"Yeah, but that settlement. You could've retired in Costa Rica for what you pocketed."

"I don't like humidity, and it rains too much."

"Nova Scotia, then."

"LA's my home."

"I get that, but still . . . you could've been someplace cleaner, nicer, safer."

"You mean like Malibu," I say. "Don't kid yourself. There's no such thing as paradise because certain people will always resort to murder as a solution to their problems."

"I've always thought this place was pretty damn special, and I intend for it to stay that way."

Pop appears at the end of the hallway, looking how I'd imagine Orpheus did after returning from Hades. I can just about smell the brimstone.

He announces, "I told her. Now, I need to sleep."

"OK, Pop. We're about to head out," I say, then ask Brennan, "How long do we wait for Keisha's autopsy results?"

"Give it forty-eight hours," she says. "Maybe sooner. We don't get many autopsy requests, so it's being prioritized."

"That's one thing Malibu has going for it," I say. "If you do happen to die here, your autopsy goes to the front of the line." I hand Brennan my business card, the first of a new batch: weightier paper stock, classier font, and the same details. "I know you don't want our help, but can you call me if anything comes up? Even if you think it's insignificant."

She slips my card into her pocket.

I join Pop, who's standing a good distance from Avery's room, probing my and Brennan's exchange. I'm certain he's reserving judgment for playing nice with the *enemy*. Before he can say anything offensive within ear-shot of Brennan, I swiftly redirect him toward the elevator.

"You getting all chummy with *America's Next Top Cop?*"

he asks. "Before you know it, you'll be exchanging recipes for potato salad. Bet she puts some unnecessary shit like raisins and pineapples in hers."

"She's trying her best, Pop."

"Just don't forget what we're doing here," he says. "We find out who hurt Avery and killed Keisha. Then I'm going to—"

"Stop talking like that. We aren't vigilantes."

"Speak for your damn self. I ain't got shit to lose."

"You're tired," I say as the elevator doors open. "You don't know what the hell you're saying."

"I know exactly what I'm saying."

We step into the elevator, and I press the button for the lobby.

"But you're right: I could do with a minimum of six hours of shut-eye," he says. "Now, will you tell me where we're supposed to sleep tonight?"

"I told you, it's taken care of."

"It'd better not have bed bugs or be swarming with hookers."

"Far from it," I say. "There's even a butler."

"Get the hell outta here," Pop says, breaking from his sullen disposition. "Is this some five-star Shangri La outfit?"

"What do you know about the Shangri La?"

"Not a damn thing because I don't have five-star money."

"It's all good, Pop—like I said, it's been arranged . . ."

THREE

The Falcon's high beams illuminate the canyon road. My eyes are weary—dry and throbbing—but I must stay alert: there are plenty of dangerous curves, and wild animals sprint across the roads at night.

Pop is slipping in and out of sleep, mumbling between snores. I roll down the window and let the cool air into the cabin. It whistles through the small opening and sounds like a tea kettle, but it isn't jarring enough to wake my father.

He's had a long night. Even his demons are tired.

Despite suffering the physical effects of fatigue, my mind is churning, processing everything we've learned about Keisha's death, though it isn't much. I'll experience insomnia and broken sleep for the next few days until we get a break in the case. Being unable to sleep is the opening act to enervation. It comes on like a virus, draining everything out of me and leaving me hollow. Pop and I are no good to the investigation if we get that way, so rundown that we can't function, can't think straight.

We're close to where we'll stay for the next few days. Considering the early morning hour, I hope the offer of gratis lodging is still good.

High beams burn in the rearview. A vehicle—maybe a truck or SVU—is approaching fast. Headlights angled high flood the Falcon's interior. The tinted windows do little to diminish their luster. I accelerate, closing in on sixty miles per hour. The speed limit is forty, and a sign says the roads and byways are patrolled by aircraft. I'm doubtful a plane or drone is flying above monitoring vehicles' speeds. Most departments, especially Highway Patrol, are experiencing budget constraints like those of the Sheriff's Department and LAPD. They prioritize officers making traffic stops and reserve their aerial resources for well-traveled roads during holidays like Memorial Day and the Fourth of July, when incidents of drunk driving are more frequent. Then again, Christmas comes in a few days, and some people can't resist getting blitzed on eggnog . . . it could be the impairment of the driver behind me.

The last time I was speeding through a canyon was in pursuit of LAPD Officer Joey Garcia. I was convinced he was responsible for the murder of recruit officer Brandon Soledad. It was a heinous crime and the most difficult investigation I had ever faced, and it led to the end of my career with the LAPD. Garcia died that day, but I often wonder how things would've turned out had he lived to face justice . . .

Focus, Trevor . . . Focus. Stay sharp.

I take a turn too fast and apply the brakes. The car banks hard near the rocky hillside. There's play in the steering wheel. Too much. Something isn't right. There's a popping sound coming from the left wheel well. I brake gently. More shrills and squeaks.

Pop begins to stir. "The hell are you doing?" He braces his hands against the dashboard.

"We have a tail."

He looks out the back and is momentarily blinded. "Damn, those are bright."

"Whoever it is wants us to lose control."

"I remember this stretch," he says. "There's a sharp bend up ahead."

"On it . . ."

"Keep her steady."

"Doing my best."

The truck comes closer, rides my bumper, and comes shy of ramming us.

"Someone's been messing with the suspension," I say, wrestling with the wheel.

A sign warns of the sharp curve ahead and falling rocks. I decelerate, and the truck taps my rear. We nearly lose control, but I'm able to keep the car in line.

"Son of a bitch." Pop reaches toward his ankle. I hear the unfastening of Velcro.

"What are you doing?"

"Getting my piece."

"We can't shoot at them."

"The hell we can't. They're trying to kill us."

"We've got no idea who's behind that wheel. Put the gun away. I've got it under control."

Pop hesitates, looking back at the vehicle. "Who the hell is this mutherfucker?"

"Put it away, Pop. Trust me."

He slowly returns the snub-nosed pistol to his ankle holster and holds the grab handle as we enter the curve.

"Hold on," I say, slowing down to enter the curve safely and then accelerating. I come out of the curve faster than our pursuer can manage, and their vehicle is forced to brake hard, nearly skidding off the bluff.

Once out of the curve, I floor the Falcon downhill, reaching eighty and putting more distance between us and the tail.

"We need off this road," Pop says.

"Working on it."

The GPS says we're half a mile from our next turn. I push the Falcon to ninety, then slow down as I make a hard right, followed by another right and left, and drive until we enter a well-lit neighborhood of mansions.

"Looks like we lost them," Pop says, gazing into the sideview mirror. "Dry-clean a bit more, then put us back on the main stretch."

"I'm not dry-cleaning," I say, observing the five-mile-per-hour speed limit. "This is where we're supposed to be."

I accelerate to the top of a long driveway where floodlights illuminate a box-shaped mansion, and two Teslas are parked. The Falcon smells of burning oil and grinds to a stop.

"Whose house is this?" Pop asks.

"Sit tight. I'll be back." I get out of the Falcon, walk to the front door, and ring the bell. A surveillance camera is positioned above the threshold. I look up and smile.

Moments later, the wrought-iron door opens. Cassandra Boyle stands in gold strappy stilettos and a cream-colored nightgown, sheer enough for me to see the red-laced bra under it. She's wearing three gold bracelets on her left wrist and chandeliers for earrings. A jade amulet matching the flicker of color in her smoky eyes lies in the crease of her breasts.

Most men would froth at the mouth and kowtow before the statuesque brunette, but I see past Cassandra's frilly adornments. I'm only reminded of my ex-partner, former LAPD Detective Sally Munoz, who's wasting away in a state penitentiary after pleading guilty to felonies incurred during a botched investigation into Cassandra's marijuana dispensary business. I won't say Sally's incarceration isn't warranted, but she shouldn't be the only one sporting a prison jumpsuit. Cassandra deserves to be in a three-by-five cell more than anyone I know, but she's also been an asset to my investigations and a loyal associate. Despite speculations about her lawlessness, I trust her.

"Took you long enough," she says, squinting from the glow of the porch light.

"We had some trouble coming down the mountain."

"*We?*"

I point to my father sitting in the passenger seat and beckon him to get out.

"Is that . . . ?"

"My father."

"I see," she says, folding her arms across her chest, hiding her cleavage. "I didn't realize you had a companion."

"I hope it's all right . . ."

"Of course," she says, blinking too much. Her false lashes cage her wide eyes. Her lips have grown plumper, the residual effects of an allergic reaction or fresh filler. "I had Nigel prepare the guest room. I hope two queen-sized beds will suffice."

"That'll more than suffice." I look back to see my father taking the luggage from the trunk.

"Should you give him a hand?"

"There's nothing he hates more than help."

"Independence," she says. "A noble trait."

"Or an annoying one, depending on the hour." I cringe as Pop struggles to put my duffle bag over his shoulder. "I was expecting Lurch at the door."

Cassandra's smile belongs in a toothpaste ad; it's most beguiling when paired with her charming giggle. "I gave Nigel the evening off. He's out camping with friends and will be back at sunrise."

"Nigel has friends?"

"Some hippie gathering. Lots of hard kombucha and folk music."

"How's he with cars?" I ask, recalling his ingenuity with compactor motors.

"Excellent. I haven't been to a mechanic in years. Why?"

"I've got a suspension issue."

"What type of issue?"

"The life-threatening kind."

"Making enemies already?"

"Nah, everyone loves me."

"I'll leave a note for him to inspect it when he gets back."

"Thanks."

"Guess this makes us even?"

"Sure," I say. "We're square."

Pop approaches the entryway carrying our luggage. "Hello," he says. "Name's Shaun Finnegan."

"Cassandra Boyle . . . Now I see it."

"What's that?" Pop asks.

"Where Trevor gets his regalness."

"Regal? Can't say I've heard that before." My father's face turns flush, and he nearly drops the luggage. "He's never told me about any Malibu friends."

"That's not surprising. I'm often a man's best-kept secret."

I take my duffle bag from Pop. "We should sleep."

"Certainly." Cassandra moves aside, and we enter the Spanish-tiled foyer adorned with orchids and colorful flowering plants. "I'll show you to the guest room."

The house still looks staged as it did the last time I was here, and it smells of fresh paint. The photos of Cassandra with politicians that once lined the hallway are gone, replaced with photos of her and her daughters. We walk upstairs and enter a room to the right of the staircase. Cassandra flips the light switch. The room is tastefully decorated. Modern furniture—a dresser, two nightstands, and two stone-colored headboards match a textured accent wall.

"This is it," she says. "Usually, my daughters sleep here, but they moved to Colorado—got themselves a cute place in Boulder."

"How are they?" I ask.

"Living their best lives, thanks to you. A mother couldn't ask for more, right?"

I place my duffle bag and cell phone on the bed. "I think we're good, Cassandra. Don't let us keep you."

"It's fine," she says, toying with her amulet. "I'm well rested. Suppose I was anticipating a long night."

"*Right* . . ."

"Nigel prepares breakfast around seven, but if you happen to rise early, help yourself to anything in the kitchen."

"We appreciate the hospitality," Pop says. "Not sure what my son has done to earn it."

I look at Pop disapprovingly, the same way he grimaced when I was a kid and said something embarrassing in front of his friends.

"Uh, Trevor," Cassandra says, "can we talk a moment . . . in private?"

"Sure." I follow Cassandra into the hallway while Pop looks on, baffled. "So, is everything cool with us staying here?" I ask.

"Yes, of course," she says. "Though I must confess that I'm surprised you called."

"I am, too."

"I've had the sneaking suspicion that you've been avoiding me."

"Not exactly," I say. "Just been busy."

"Are you sure that's it? I left three voicemails."

"Four, actually."

"So you listened?"

"You know the deal, Cassandra. I'm involved—"

"Yes, with the baker," she says. "Or is it chef?"

"Her name's Sarada."

"I'm not one to pine over things I desire but can't have."

"No revelation there . . ."

"And while some might think me cold-hearted inside," she says, placing her hand over the amulet. "I am more . . ."

"I'm flattered, Cassandra. Really, I am—"

"But you're in love with the pie-maker," she says. "I suppose I've made a fool of myself?"

"I wouldn't say that."

"Then what would you say?"

"I'm thankful you're allowing us to stay, but if me being here presents an issue . . ."

"Please, Trevor, you aren't casting any spells. I'll manage just fine in your presence."

"OK . . . so, we're good?"

"Yes," she says. "Do me a favor and delete those voicemails."

"I don't know about that. The one where you recite Gibran is sweet . . . *When love beckons to you, follow him . . .*"

"I had way too much wine that night."

"Sure you did."

"Look, don't make me shoot you," she says in jest. "Delete it."

"All right, I'll delete them."

"So, about this investigation you're working on—"

"Probably best we don't get into that," I say. "Remember our agreement? Don't ask. Don't tell."

"Yes, you're right," she says. "You don't ask about my dealings, and I won't ask about yours. The less either of us knows about the other's business, the better."

"Makes it easier to pass a polygraph," I say, though the stale look on Cassandra's face lets me know my drollery has fallen short.

"Sleep well, Trevor."

I go into the room, and she shuts the door before going downstairs. When her footsteps are silent, Pop asks, "Care to tell me what all that was about?"

"What do you mean?"

"You see the stems on her? When did you start hanging with Malibu beauty queens?"

"She isn't a beauty queen. At least, I don't think so."

"How's it you know her, then?"

"Helped her daughters out of a jam."

"What kind of jam?"

"Sexual exploitation," I say. "Two of LAPD's finest had her daughters held up in a seedy motel. They promised no jail time for solicitation in exchange for sex. Cassandra needed her girls out of the situation. I made it happen."

"That's some serious shit," Pop says. "Bet she paid you well for that."

"It's confidential."

"Well, judging by this place, she's loaded. What's she do?"

I remove my dopp kit from my duffle bag. "Inheritance."

"Figures. That's how she can afford to walk around here without a care in the world."

"I don't know about that," I say. "What's that Christopher Wallace said—*Mo money, mo problems?*"

"Yeah, but rich people's problems probably aren't even problems to the rest of us common folk."

If Pop knew where most of Cassandra's money came from, he'd ask, "What have you been smoking?" and curse me from now to Sunday. While Cassandra inherited a fortune from her grandfather, a movie mogul who reigned supreme in the 1960s and 1970s, most of her revenue is believed to come from money laundering, drug trafficking, and blackmail, though there's little evidence to prove it. Pop wouldn't be wrong for asking what I'm doing getting involved with someone like Cassandra, but I'm a private detective now, and if it's taught me anything, it's that things can't always be delineated clearly into categories of right and wrong. Wearing the badge made seeing the world in black and white easier, but it's never been that. The world isn't a parable, and Cassandra's resources are vital to this investigation. Her centrally located home is close to where Cohen found Keisha's body. It's well fortified, and she knows the community. Her tradecraft is gathering intel on anyone and anything that might threaten her business operations, which is a helpful skill when trying to identify a murderer who could be anyone.

"I'm going to get washed up," I say, entering the adjoining bathroom. I run warm water in the pedestal sink, wash my face, and brush my teeth. There's a set of decorative towels with seashells that are so nice I don't want to sully them with toothpaste. I spit in the sink and wipe my mouth on my sleeve.

The monotony of my nightly routine helps me concentrate, particularly on our death run down the mountain. Whoever tampered with my car would've done so while we were at the hospital. The only person who knew we'd be there and for how long was Detective Brennan. She was late getting to Avery's room, but was that enough time to weaken a control arm or coilover? And if she did, how'd it go unnoticed? What purpose would she have in impairing my car? And who the hell was tailing us?

Pop bangs on the door. "Hurry up in there. Nature calls."

"Give me a second." I wash my mouth out with a mint-flavored rinse and spit into the sink. "Coming out."

I open the door to Pop standing in his boxers and nothing else. "'Bout time," he says. "Your phone's been blowing up."

"Probably Sarada."

"Tell *Good Genes* I said hello."

"You know she hates that name. Why keep at it?"

"She knows I'm too old to change."

"Or too stubborn," I say under my breath.

My phone displays text message notifications over the locked screen. I slide my thumb up, revealing three texts from Tori, my daughter's mother. We were never officially an item—our relationship fell between casual dating and a series of hookups. Tori isn't the easiest person to get along with, but she's a good mother to our daughter, Simone, and has recently moved to LA from Vancouver, to allow me to co-parent.

I read the first text: Tori thinks I'm in Rungis, France, which is how I prefer it. I was supposed to accompany Sarada on her culinary excursion to learn from France's most eminent pastry chefs. My presence would have been solely for support, though I considered taking a painting class to keep busy. Instead, I nearly died hours before I was due to drive Sarada to LAX. Believing I'd stood her up, she took a car service to the airport and got on the plane. I don't blame her—it was for the best— but as her plane was taxiing the runway, Officer Joey Garcia's accomplice, an ex-LAPD officer turned fugitive, Amanda "Boston" Walsh, had lured me to the law firm where I worked, shot my employer, David Bergman, and then turned the gun on me. I fought her with everything I had, and in the melee, a fire broke out, and Boston burned to death. I made it out, but not unscathed. It took weeks for me to recover from smoke inhalation, and when I was finally given the clearance to fly, I bought my ticket to join Sarada in Rungis, but I didn't make that flight either because that was the day I learned of Avery's existence and that he was missing.

David Bergman is never far from my mind. Our mission was to expose police wrongdoing wherever we found it. I led the investigations, uncovering all manner of criminality among law enforcement officers, and David sued the hell out of the officers and departments. Even though we routinely disagreed on tactics, we both recognized our cause was noble and necessary in the wake of police corruption and the killings of unarmed citizens.

These days, I question if I can continue the mission without him. I've lost so much trying to do the righteous thing, and when I recount all this misfortune, it feels like a Shakespearean tragedy where I'm subjected to one misadventure after the other. My father likes to say, "Finnegans court disaster," but Sarada cautions me from indulging in such thoughts . . . something about the power of manifestation. "Believe it, and it will come to be," she says. I'm not sure I agree with her. Some stories are prewritten. Etched in time, destined to come to fruition. I can no more outrun fate than I can outrun a bullet.

Tori's next message reads like a standard check-in, asking how things are going and if I'm indulging in plenty of wine and cheese, which she told me was all she thought France offered. She includes a photo of Simone.

The last message is the longest. Tori writes that she hasn't slept well in more than a week, and the costume design job her friend promised her fell through. She doesn't ask for money, but I presume she could use it. Interpreting the tone of a text message requires a forte I don't possess. Maybe she's venting, a cathartic moment, or is more going on? I'll call her, but I can't predict when.

"I still can't get over that woman having kids?" Pop says,

coming from the bathroom trailed by a funk. "Cassandra popping out babies and ending up like that. If that doesn't show you the power of money, I don't know what does. I bet she has one of those celebrity trainers or got that liposuction."

I cover my nose. "Damn, Pop. Did you crack a window or something?" Nobody's stool should smell as bad as my father's, but decades of alcohol abuse caused gastritis. His doctor said it'll likely go away if he remains sober.

"All I'm saying is, if that woman has kids, I've never wanted to see stretch marks so bad in my life. And what's with her answering the door looking like a Victoria's Secret model?"

"Didn't think she was your type."

"I'm pushing seventy, kid. In the dark, a soft body is a soft body."

"Give it a rest, Pop. Besides, her kids are adopted."

"That explains it."

"We almost get creamed on the highway, and you want to talk about Cassandra Boyle's legs and possible stretch marks. Someone's on to us. It means we're close to something."

"Or maybe it was just some peckerwood who saw two brothers on a dark road and decided to take a run at us. Shit like that happened all the time when I was coming up."

"In Goldsboro, but this is Malibu."

"Don't be so naïve. Look who this country elected as president. I bet ninety percent of this town voted for that trifling-ass con man."

"And what about my car?"

"I don't know," he says, stretched out on his bed. "An underlying issue. Bad timing going down that mountain."

"My ride is solid . . . was solid. And we're investigators, remember? We can't afford to believe in coincidences."

"I'm just saying, you go looking for conspiracies, and you're guaranteed to find one."

"That's funny coming from you."

"What'd you mean by that?"

"Nothing," I say, too tired to argue. "Forget it."

Pop fluffs his pillow, positions his head in its center, and closes his eyes. "Better get some sleep," he says, putting his back to me. "We're fixing to have a long day. Better get a few good hours of sleep before that sun comes up."

I turn off the light and use the glow of my cell phone to find my way to bed.

After ten minutes, Pop is snoring, and my mind is toiling in the dark. Cassandra was the distraction he needed, titillation for a horny old man. While his chauvinism runs deep, it isn't uncommon, especially in cops from his era. After shootouts and nearly dying in high-speed chases, cops like Pop find consolation in strip clubs, drinking booze, and distracting themselves from the realization of being so close to death. They shove dollars in G-strings to get their "heads straight," then go home to their wives and children and avoid talking about their harrowing experience.

Tonight, Cassandra took Pop's mind off Avery and Keisha, if only for an hour or so, long enough for him to ignore reality and sleep. I'm envious because the only thing that'll settle my mind is Sarada and her sultry whispers in my ear. I force my eyes closed and envision her in my arms, snug in our bed, as the cold winds from the San Gabriel Mountains stir the fallen leaves outside our window. In those moments, I'm home, and I've never longed for it more than I do now.

FOUR

I wake up to Pop looking out the window, his face dulled by ashen light. "How'd you sleep?" he asks.

"Decent," I say.

"Well, it's a hell of a mattress, that's for sure," he says, scratching his curly gray chest hair.

"What are you looking at?"

"The barefoot hobo fiddling under your car. Should we go out there?"

"Pretty sure you're not supposed to say *hobo*."

"Says who?"

"Never mind," I say. "That's Nigel, Pop. He works for Cassandra. I told you she had a butler."

"That's more than a butler. He's got an entire toolkit out there."

"He's a jack of all trades."

"Seems to me he's more of a manservant."

"Hearing you call him that gives me stomach pains. Pretty sure I tasted a little bile in my throat."

"Well, that's what she's got. Do you think they have a *thing* going? Like, is he providing full service? Know what I mean?"

I yawn and taste the sourness that won't leave my throat. "I don't know, and I don't care."

"Bet she gets lonely in this big house, especially with her daughters gone . . ."

"Can we talk about something else?"

"What? Is it making you uncomfortable?" He takes a cotton swab from his pocket and digs wax from his ear. "All that chatting in the hallway last night seemed a little inappropriate to me. Does Sarada know about you and *Miss Green Eyes*?"

"Chill, Pop. Nothing is going on between me and Cassandra Boyle."

"OK, I hear you," he says. "Maybe she'd like the original version?"

"I'd vomit if my stomach weren't empty."

"I'm hungry, too," he says. "It's after nine. We should get a move on things."

"Agreed," I say, getting out of bed. "Almost forgot . . ." I scroll on my phone, searching for the photo I took of Avery's insect drawing and show it to Pop.

"What's that?"

"Meant to show it to you before," I say. "I was hoping you'd have an idea of what it is." I hand him my phone; he studies the drawing closely. "According to Brennan, Avery drew it while she was questioning him."

"Kinda looks like a cicada," he says, holding the phone centimeters from his nose.

"Is that like a beetle?"

"Not quite. Came up with them as a boy in North Carolina. It was comforting hearing them sing. Besides rain on a tin roof, listening to those bugs knocked me right out. Best sleep in my life."

"Never heard of cicadas in California."

"Me either, but Nature Boy out there might know. He looks like the type."

Pop goes into the bathroom to shower. I type "cicadas in Malibu" in my phone's internet browser. It's a quick hit—a nature preserve and research center on St. Catherine University's campus, three miles from Cassandra's home. The preserve is open to the public, and according to reviews, the cicadas' habitat is a favorite for visitors.

Downstairs, in the kitchen, platters of food and carafes of coffee and orange juice are set on a marble counter. There's a Viking stove, stainless steel with eight burners, and a refrigerator with a touchscreen in the door.

Pop grabs a chocolate-glazed donut and spoons scrambled eggs with chives onto his plate. I opt for a plain toasted bagel and walk outside to the driveway.

Nigel is on his back, flashlight in hand, inspecting the Falcon's undercarriage.

"Morning," I say.

Without greeting me, he slides from under the car and stands barefoot in a shabby tunic. Despite looking as though he doesn't bathe regularly, he smells of patchouli and sandalwood. It's hard to estimate how much Cassandra pays him, but judging by his hand-made attire, I'd say it's in the high seven or eight figures. There's a premium price tag for being bohemian chic these days, and while his clothes may look ragged, they're likely handspun vicuña wool or cashmere purchased from a boutique in Malibu Village.

"Someone loosened your control arm," he says, placing his flashlight in his toolbox. "Perforated it, too. I think with a drill bit."

"Well, that wasn't nice."

"It will take some time to repair." He wipes his oily hands on a rag and lowers the car off the jack. "Perhaps Cassandra can lend you one of her cars. I believe the Model S is fully charged."

I consider the two Teslas shaped like bar soap and weigh other options. I recall a sign advertising a car rental lot off the 101 near Calabasas. I can take an Uber or Lyft there.

"Don't be absurd, Nigel." Cassandra marches through the garage in a cream long-sleeve sweater dress, almost identical to one in Sarada's closet. "Trevor favors high-octane."

Pop emerges behind her, still smacking on the donut and licking frosting from his fingers. He stands next to me and mutters, "Was the Jolly Green Giant about to have you driving one of these smartphones on wheels?"

"Not in this lifetime."

"Follow me, boys," Cassandra says. "I have something that should fit the bill."

She leads us into the garage, a structure twice the size of my first apartment, and draws our attention to a car hidden under a satin cover. "Now, this is a piece of history."

Nigel removes the cover, revealing a BMW E28 M5—black on black, stanced, but not annoyingly low, and Alpina wheels and Pirelli racing tires—a German larker with soul.

"They don't make them like this anymore," I say, drooling over the lines and shark-nose profile. "You're a Beemer enthusiast?"

"No, it was my ex's car," she says.

"He gave this baby up?"

"Wasn't much use to him."

"Why's that?"

"He's dead."

Ordinarily, if a woman tells me her boyfriend is deceased, I might inquire how and offer my condolences, but with Cassandra Boyle, I keep my mouth shut.

"It was accidental," she says, reading my dismayed expression. "A mishap while spelunking two years ago."

Before I can change the topic, Pop asks, "Is that like skydiving?"

"Cave exploration in Iceland."

"Damn—hell of a way to go," Pop adds.

"When was the last time you started her up?" I ask.

"I take it out every weekend," Nigel says smugly. "It's something I look forward to."

"Nigel has grown fond of the car, but it's a gas guzzler," Cassandra says, motioning dismissively at the sports sedan. "And if anyone from his cult of tree-huggers were to see him, he'd be promptly excommunicated."

Nigel sighs. "I keep to the back roads."

"I bet you do." I open the driver-side door and inhale the vintage leather horse-mane-filled seats. It's an immaculate time capsule.

"I considered selling it but feared Nigel would kill me in my sleep."

The odometer reads over one hundred thousand miles. It's not a collector's piece; the car has been driven and enjoyed.

"Keys are in the glove box," Nigel says. "It's freshly waxed with a full tank."

"Get in, Pop!" My father wipes traces of frosting onto his pants, gets into the car, and sinks into the passenger seat.

"And please, Mr. Finnegan," Nigel says, "bring it back without a scratch."

"Don't get your chakras out of whack. This baby is in good hands." I push the key into the ignition, turn, and let the engine warm. "One more thing, do you know anyone working at the nature preserve?"

"The one on St. Catherine's campus?" Nigel asks.

"That's the one."

"Talk to Cree," he says. "Tell her I sent you."

"Cree, you say?"

"Yes—she's a good friend."

"Nigel, don't tell me you're still bothering with that girl," Cassandra says. "I thought you were done with all that."

Nigel sulks, looking away in humiliation. It isn't the first time I've witnessed Cassandra visibly annoyed by Nigel, and at times, she flirts with cruelty when speaking to him. He usually seems unbothered, but this time I see a flash of fury in his eyes.

"We should be going," I say, giving Nigel a thumbs-up like Maverick in *Top Gun*, something I never do, but the car's 1980s aesthetic is turning me into a nostalgic gearhead.

"What is it with you and this car?" Pop asks.

"Sarada's father bought one after he sold his Benz. He'd take us joyriding through the Palisades."

"I don't remember that."

"You wouldn't," I say. "Put your seat belt on."

Pop pulls his seat belt across his chest as I shift out of neutral into first. I come off the clutch too fast, and the car stalls. "Give me a minute."

"Take your time," he says, retracting the moonroof. "I'm sure only Nigel's judging you."

Nigel looks anxious, and Cassandra chews her thumbnail like she's quelling the urge to laugh.

Once I determine how much pressure the clutch needs, I drive forward into the sunlight. The engine is quieter than the Falcon's but runs strong. Nigel has done well to preserve it.

I shift and gas the car, turning away from Cassandra's street. Pop waves "goodbye" through the moonroof. "You know that hippie will kill you if something happens to this car," he says, toying with his power seat controls.

"It'll be fine."

"You're sure this is the way to the cicadas?" Pop asks.

"We passed the entrance to the university just before that truck tried to run us off the road."

"All right, then," he says, enjoying the fresh beach air on his skin.

The E28 mounts a hill with ease. I taste the salty air and glimpse the twinkling shoreline in the distance. I know why Brennan called it a paradise. There's tranquility here, away from LA's seediness and infirmity, as if time has no bearing. But even Satan began in heaven, and this town may be masking a secret . . . something vile.

Seagulls circle the university's flag pitched on a forty-foot-high pole: a peace dove with an olive branch. It may be the most placatory mascot I've ever seen, though, admittedly, I pay little attention to schools that don't compete in the Rose Bowl.

"Does Tori know you aren't in France?" Pop asks.

"Why do you ask?"

"Figured she would have called by now asking for money."

"She's Simone's mother. You don't have to talk about her like that."

"I want to know why she really came back. I mean, she took off without even telling you she was pregnant. Only to pop back up out of the blue, and for what?"

"She came back so Simone could know her father. Why's that so hard to believe?"

"Sure, that's what she told you, but I don't think that's the only reason."

"Now who's being paranoid?"

"Tori bears watching, that's all. You and Sarada have a good thing, and I don't want *Little Miss Spray Tan* messing things up for you two. Take it from me; losing sight of a good thing is easy."

"Losing sight? Mom and I were right in front of you."

"That's my point . . . You can get so wrapped up in other things that you drift away without noticing."

"You share these moments of reflection with Avery? I'm sure he'd love to know why he grew up without a dad."

"Jesus, man . . ."

"What?"

"You might be angrier than I was at your age, and that's saying a lot."

"I'm not angry for no reason. Do you think I like being this way? Feeling how I feel. It's exhausting."

"Make a right," Pop says. "Before you miss it."

"What?"

"You're passing it." Pop points to a sign for the Nature Preserve and Research Center. I slam on the brakes, sending him forward, his arms outstretched like Superman taking flight. I reverse and turn down a dirt road leading to a building next to a glass dome.

"Easy," Pop says, swaying as the car maneuvers over craters.

I park beside the entrance, secure the windows, and leave Pop inside, trying to unbuckle himself.

When he's finally out of the car, I lock it, and we walk through the building's double doors. It smells old, with poor recessed lighting and a floor tile pattern common in museums and galleries.

Collections of preserved butterflies, moths, and beetles are showcased in illuminated boxes on the walls. Display cases of insects and arachnids are positioned throughout, identified by plaques showing scientific illustrations and diagrams.

A young woman comes from behind a bookcase dressed like Nigel: a popover shirt, maybe linen, tweed cargo pants, and ankle-high boots. A gold butterfly pendant hangs from her neck, and her name tag reads "Cree."

"Hello," she says. "Welcome."

"Cree?"

"Do I know you?"

"Your friend, the male version of the Barefoot Contessa, sent us," Pop says.

"Who?" she asks.

"Nigel," I say. "He thought you might be able to assist us."

"Um, OK, and you are?"

"Trevor, and this is my father, Shaun."

"Cree Makaya," she says. "How is it that you know Nigel?"

"He sold us some shoes once," Pop says flippantly. "I don't think he was using them much."

Cree proffers a smile, which does little to relieve the awkwardness. "OK, so what brings you to the preserve?"

"We're hoping to see the cicadas."

"The next tour begins in thirty minutes. You're welcome to wait in the gift shop."

"Is there any way we might take a peek now?"

"That's not really how we do things."

"Not even for friends of Nigel?" Pop asks.

"Our practices are equitable, Shaun."

"Mr. Finnegan is fine," Pop says. "We're both Finnegans, actually. And while I understand your policy, this is a criminal matter."

"Criminal? I think you should speak to our director."

"Or maybe you can help us. We have reason to believe someone may be planning a heist."

"A heist? Like a robbery?"

"Exactly."

"Are you guys serious?"

"Very."

"Do you have identification?"

"Go ahead, show her, son."

I show her my PI badge. She studies it briefly; then I return it to my pocket when she appears leery. I continue Pop's fabrication: "We're investigating the recent theft of rare insects from a sanctuary in San Diego. We think your cicadas may be the next target."

"Hold on. People are stealing bugs?"

"People will steal anything when incentivized, and these insects fetch a pretty penny on the black market."

"Why have I never heard of this?"

"That's why it's the black market, miss."

"I really should consult our director about this."

"We only need a minute of your time," I say. "We'd just like to see the enclosure where the bugs are kept."

"I don't know . . . This whole thing is making me uncomfortable."

"Oh, we don't want that," Pop says. "But imagine these helpless bugs. What might they be feeling when they're sold to the highest bidders?"

"And what do you think people are doing with them?"

"They're being consumed," Pop says, straight-faced. "Without a doubt. Stir-fried with lemon and garlic is popular."

"That's terrible," she says. "These bugs should be protected."

"Yes, and we'd like to protect them, Cree," I say. "A few minutes of your time, and I promise we'll be on our way."

She looks at her watch. "All right, what do you want to know?"

"Did anything odd occur recently—say, in the last forty-eight hours—that might've involved the cicadas?"

"I mean, not during my shift, but I overheard Travis saying someone had entered the cicadas' dome."

"A break-in?"

"I think so . . ."

"When?"

"Two nights ago, he found people sleeping in there."

"Did he call the sheriff?"

"Yeah, after he chased them off. He said they were baked. Looked totally strung out on something."

"Any idea how they got in?"

"Broke one of the panels," she says. "We lost some cicadas before Travis was able to seal it."

"Can we take a look?"

Cree checks her watch, "OK, but the tour will be starting soon. I really should prepare."

"We'll be quick . . . You have my word."

She huffs and walks toward the double doors leading outside. "Watch your step," she says as we navigate a stone path leading to the large glass dome. She opens the door to an air tunnel. It's loud, and the cranking turbines cause my eyes to water. "This will be important later," she says. The air batters Cree from above, blowing her hair wildly. "Sometimes the cicadas try to hitch rides out of here in our clothes and hair. The air pressure is gentle but strong enough to knock them off."

Clearing the air chamber, I see the shattered panel and walk toward it. Travis covered it with cardboard and sealed it with electrical tape. It's large enough for someone to crawl through, but not without risking injury. Upon closer inspection, I see blood traces on the metal frame that once held the glass in place.

"Careful where you walk," Cree says, standing near the door. "Some of the cicadas are emerging."

"Emerging?"

"They live in underground burrows for most of their lives. Recently, we've had some come up."

"We'll be mindful," I say, examining the blood's placement.

"One of them hurt themselves climbing in here," Pop says, noticing the blood. "You think it was Avery?"

"That would explain the cuts on his hands." I turn to Cree, who is staring at her watch. "Do you know if the sheriff collected any evidence, maybe took pictures?"

"No idea."

I take snapshots of the blood with my camera phone and record video of the broken window.

Cree hums, growing more annoyed, until I turn around. "Sorry, guys, I need to get set up for the tour."

In the corner of the dome is a surveillance camera. "Just one more thing . . . Do you have the surveillance footage from that night?"

We stand in a cramped office filled with boxes of textbooks and supplies. Cree plays the break-in footage on a laptop sitting on a dusty desk. "And all of this footage is stored in the cloud," she says. "We archive three months at a time."

The footage is grainy and purple in hue. The recording would have benefited from more light, but I can tell that the only measure comes from the light pole outside the cicadas' dome. The timecode passes a minute. Then, at 1:30:15, a rock shatters the glass panel. Two figures crawl through the opening, moving strangely, unable to walk straight, and they seem frenzied. I understand why Travis presumed they were under the influence. They wander the dome for two minutes, then huddle in a corner, squeezing each other, maybe keeping warm. When Travis enters with a flashlight, they're spooked, crawl back through the opening, and disappear into the night.

"That's it," Cree says as the video cuts to black. "Hope it helps."

"Thank you."

"Don't mention it, but if you happen to see Nigel, tell him he owes me dinner."

"Guy's twice your age," Pop says, more intrigued than disgusted.

"So?" Cree says.

"Pop, mind your own business," I say. "Let's go."

Outside, Pop mumbles to himself. I catch words here and there—*Keisha . . . drugs . . . fucking Malibu*—but my mind is on the footage.

"Keisha and Avery might've been cold and drugged," I say, "but they were afraid, too."

"Of what?" Pop asks. "If they were under the influence, maybe they were fleeing from whoever doped them?"

"Why wouldn't they ask Travis for help? He was right there, and they ran. They could've tried to explain their situation or waited until the sheriff came. It doesn't make any sense."

"No telling what they were thinking. Brains might've been scrambled from whatever they were on. Without knowing what they took, we can't judge a damn thing. The only thing I know is that someone had to have dosed them."

"Someone?"

"Yeah, Trevor, that's what I said—*someone*."

"What if they came here to see the ocean, score some dope, and—"

"And what?"

"We have to look at every possibility, Pop. It could've been a bad trip. People get high and do things they don't remember."

Pop begins pacing. "That's not Avery."

"How can you be so sure? Having a few conversations on the phone doesn't mean you know him like the back of your hand."

"Well, it doesn't matter if he took something or if somebody forced it on him," Pop says. "We both read his chart at the hospital. According to the tox screen, there was nothing in his system. He was clean."

"Enough time might've passed for the drugs not to be detected."

"What about your car? Someone tried to drive us off the road. You said it yourself: no coincidences."

"And you said it was probably a drunk asshole."

"Well, now I'm thinking maybe it wasn't," Pop says. "I've got the freedom to change my hypothesis."

"We need to talk to Avery again," I say. "See what else he can remember."

Pop's cell phone rings. "Hello?" He listens attentively. "OK," he says, nodding, then ending the call.

"Who was it?"

"Keisha's autopsy results are in. Cohen will meet us at the Coroner's Office."

"We should leave now," I say. "Beat the traffic."

Pop doesn't respond. He stands by the passenger-side door and waits for me to unlock the car . . . When things weigh heavy on his mind, he becomes withdrawn, and I anticipate a silent drive.

"I wanted to call you earlier," Cohen says, standing in the hallway under a ceiling of fluorescents.

"You said Brennan has already been here?" Pop asks.

"That's why I couldn't call sooner. Brennan and the prosecutor were here, and I thought it better to listen in."

"Prosecutor?"

"They came together."

"Dammit," I say.

"So much for cooperation," Pop says.

We walk the taupe corridors, dingy and cold, until we reach a large, refrigerated room called a "cooler" in cop-speak. Inside, rows of bodies on tables and stretchers line the walls, some covered with bleached white sheets; others are fully exposed: gunshot and accident victims—varying degrees of burns and crushed limbs.

Once the flesh is mangled and charred, it doesn't look real, but there's an odor that cuts through the redolence of disinfectants and detergents and demands recognition. It's a reminder that these people existed—they held space and, in an instant, they were extirpated to nothingness.

"Keisha," Pop says, finding her on a slab. "Such a shame."

A Black man in a lab coat, whom I take to be the medical examiner, approaches. "Are you family?" he asks.

"Friends, but we could've been family," Pop says. "She was my son's fiancée."

"My condolences."

"This is Dr. Iyo," Cohen says. "He performed the autopsy."

Pop steels his nerves, "What was it that killed her, Doctor?"

As if to read a menu, Dr. Iyo pulls a pair of glasses from his lab coat, puts them on, and skims notes in his binder. "The internal bleeding was significant, but it's not what killed her. She was struck in the head by a large object. Based on the tiny fragments we pulled from her skull, it appears to have been a rock or boulder."

"And what caused the internal bleeding?" I ask.

"Trauma . . . lots of trauma. She was beaten." Dr. Iyo rolls the sheet to Keisha's waist, exposing her breasts and rib cage. "See this contusion?" He points to bruising along her flank. "She was struck with a piece of metal. Likely steel or aluminum."

"Something like a pipe?"

"Possibly, or a flashlight," he says. "A heavy-duty kind."

"Like the ones cops carry?" I ask.

Dr. Iyo looks at Cohen as if to acknowledge the dangers of my implication. "Well, if she hadn't received the blow to her head, she would have succumbed to her injuries in hours . . . maybe days."

"Are you saying she wouldn't have survived?" I ask.

"Not exactly," he says. "The conditions needed to be right. But say the victim was given immediate medical attention that stabilized her, and she was transported promptly to a trauma unit, then, yes, she might've lived."

"She could've survived," Pop says, looking at me. "If only

they didn't run at the cicada dome. That would've been their chance to get help."

"Like you said, Pop, they probably weren't in their right minds."

Pop wrestles back tears, vigorously wiping his face when he senses moisture. Perhaps his tears are not solely for the girl he barely knew but for the girl he won't have the opportunity to know. "I told Avery to come," Pop says. "I put the idea in his head about a road trip to see me, and look how they ended up."

Pop had never communicated with Avery or Keisha by video call. When I asked him why, he said it was too much of a bother to learn how to use the feature on his phone. Instead, they conversed a few times a week, and Avery texted photos. A road trip to California seemed fitting after Avery confessed he'd never been outside of Nevada. The picturesque drive was supposed to be an adventure and a chance for him to experience a mild winter, soaking up the sun on soft, sandy beaches far from the frigid desert.

Pop continued, "They seemed happy. I thought maybe, despite everything—me not being there for him—that he still turned out OK, you know? He still managed to find some joy."

"You can't blame yourself," I say, hoping to ease his guilt.

"Then who's to blame? He sought me out because he didn't want to make the same mistakes I did. He said the only way not to was to forgive me. As if I deserved forgiveness."

"There's no way anyone could've known this would happen, Pop. It's all chance—wrong place, wrong time."

"I'm afraid there's more," Cohen says, nodding to Dr. Iyo. "It's all right, Doctor. Tell them."

"We collected tissue from under her fingernails and ran a DNA analysis."

"Did you get a match?" I ask.

"Yes, to Avery Dixion."

"Ah, hell," Pop says.

"Hold on a second, Pop. Let's hear what Dr. Iyo has to say."

"I don't need to hear anything else," he says. "They're going to arrest him. I see it plain as day."

"Mr. Finnegan is right," Cohen says. "The DA plans to file

homicide charges tonight. His office wants to move quickly, and Brennan's on board."

Realizing what Avery is facing, I pity him. I hold dear very little, knowing so much can be taken away. There are days I'm convinced humans are capable of nothing but death and destruction, and we're hellbent on seeing the planet in ruin. Then, while looking at Simone or laughing with Sarada, I'm smitten by the richness and beauty in life. And in those moments, I exalt love and humanity—I indulge in the gift of living.

Pop doesn't want Avery to be guilty, but it isn't about what we want to believe. Investigations should be dispassionate, governed by reason and facts—and the fact is, Avery is a stranger to me and Pop. Aside from sharing genetics, he's no more akin to us than Cohen. And while I can't speak to the malice that may reside in his heart, I know when things don't fit. This case deviates from expectations and logic. Brennan and the prosecutor may believe they are working from neutrality, but they aren't looking deep enough.

"The boy didn't do this," Pop says angrily. "I know it in my bones. He's no killer."

"We won't be able to talk to him now," I say, working the nape of my neck. "They'll move him to a secure wing—he'll be on lockdown."

"I'll call a lawyer," he says. "Unless you think Kimber can recommend someone from David's Rolodex."

"I don't know, Pop. It might be a little soon . . ."

"We have to get a jump on this," he says. "Can't just sit around waiting for them to bury Avery in charges."

"I understand that, Pop, but I think it's time we investigate Avery's life. Maybe whatever was going on in Vegas spurred their trip to Malibu. It could be directly connected to Keisha getting killed. We need to figure out why they went to Malibu and didn't see you first. If we can understand Avery's motivations, we can start making sense of things."

"OK, then we're going to Nevada."

"We can fly out first thing in the morning."

"Take me back to Cassandra's," Pop says. "I need to pack."

"Give me a second, Pop."

"Fine. I'll be outside. Don't be too long. I don't feel like sitting in traffic." Pop leaves the morgue.

"I can escort you and your father back to Malibu, but I'm afraid that's it," Cohen says. "With Avery's potential arrest, my involvement could be seen as—"

"Interfering," I say. "I get it. We owe you for all you've done, Cohen."

"No, you don't," he says. "Your father didn't tell you the story, did he?"

"What story?"

"He saved my dad's life once. Even on his deathbed, all my dad wanted to talk about was how Shaun Finnegan kept him from dying in a gunfight. He called your dad a hero."

"I didn't know . . ."

"Well, you know how parents can be," Cohen says. "The best we get sometimes are snapshots of who they truly are, their whole existence. It isn't until they're dying that we finally see the full picture."

Cohen leaves the morgue. I stay behind, nagged by a thought. "One more thing, Dr. Iyo."

"Yes?"

"Did you run a toxicology report?"

"We did."

"Anything shown in the screening? Narcotics, maybe?"

"There were faint traces of lysergic acid diethylamide."

"LSD?"

"Yes, but with a small amount present, it's difficult to gauge its effects on the victim leading up to her death. She may have ingested the drug days prior or received a small dose hours before her murder."

"Thank you."

"Certainly," he says. "I didn't want to say this before in front of your father. He seemed quite affected by the girl's passing, but there was evidence of previous injuries."

"Like what?"

"Long-term abuse," he says. "Small bone fractures and bruising consistent with moderate prolonged physical violence."

"What do you mean by moderate?"

"Attacks that wouldn't put a person in the hospital per se, and the injuries likely healed on their own. I typically see this kind of trauma in victims of domestic violence, where their partners avoid injuring them to the point of hospitalization. It keeps the police at bay."

"Thank you, Doctor."

Prolonged injuries? Possible domestic violence? Was Avery harming Keisha, or did she sustain the injuries some other way? There's no way to be sure without knowing how long they were dating. The abuse could've occurred before they became involved, at the hands of someone else—a previous romantic partner, or a family member. It could be that Avery saved Keisha from a life of torment. Even if I could convince myself Avery was Keisha's savior, the principles of Occam's razor would suggest he was the sole culprit. But I have to keep off the path of judgment, at least for Pop's sake.

I step outside the cooler and into the hallway, leaving Dr. Iyo to examine a female cadaver with stab wounds. My father may be right: we should be shopping for a lawyer for Avery, and Kimber could provide a reputable recommendation. After David Bergman's death, Kimber, his legal assistant and unwitting confidant, assumed his belongings, including his treasured Rolodex that, astoundingly, wasn't incinerated in the office fire. David was something of a throwback, preferring to write contact names and details on the small cards that he kept alphabetized in the plastic housing.

I text Kimber, asking to meet, but avoid telling her what it's regarding. She's been through enough lately with David's death, and I don't want to appear insensitive. It's better to sit face to face, gab a little, and then solicit her help.

It's getting to be late afternoon. I need to book our flight to Vegas, and hunger is setting in. I need to find Pop, who I fear may be slipping into darkness. He's always been a solitary creature who's faced his demons alone, but that was in the past when he had the bottle to lean on. Now that he's sober, all he has is me.

FIVE

Pop didn't say a word the entire drive back to Malibu. I thought being cut off by a semi-truck near Ocean Park would've elicited a swear or two, but nothing. My father seems shattered, and for the first time in my life, I can't blame it on my mother's death, cop trauma, or drinking. It's a new kind of hurt, that of watching his child in peril and not being able to apply an instant fix.

We park in Cassandra's driveway, get out of the car, and walk toward the front door.

"Rough day?" Cassandra asks, greeting us with a cocktail in hand.

Pop says nothing and walks upstairs. Not even the "bohemian beauty queen with the stems" can take his mind off today's defeat.

"Mind if I watch the news?" I ask.

"OK."

We walk into the entertainment room. A flat-screen TV mounted on the wall is in front of a cream leather sofa with curved edges and a low back.

I sit down, feasibly, on the most comfortable sofa my ass has ever graced. Cassandra stands, flipping channels, and finds Channel 7 *Eyewitness News*. We watch a bit—the weather report calls for rain in the coming days, and a star Lakers player was found unresponsive in a Las Vegas brothel.

"I'm not sure the last time I watched TV in here," she says. "This room was my girls' domain."

"Missing them a lot, aren't you?"

"More than I realized I would. But kids have to fly the coop. At least, I think that's the saying."

"When did you talk to them last?"

"Oh, I don't know," she says. "Maybe last week. You know,

they're always on the move—going, going, going. I'm sure they'll call when they've got a moment."

"This is it," I say, recognizing aerial footage of the marsh where Keisha was found. "Mind turning it up?"

Cassandra turns up the volume. The veteran reporter David Ono delivers the story with an earnestness demanding of the tragedy: "A suspect in the homicide of a young Nevada woman has been arrested this afternoon and is expected to be charged with murder . . . *ABC 7 Eyewitness News* is on the scene outside the Malibu Courthouse." Brennan appears in uniform and delivers talking points, ending with: "This case has rocked this community, and we're relieved to have a suspect in custody."

"You can turn it off," I say. "I know what comes next."

"*Rocked the community*? I haven't heard anything about this." Cassandra presses the power button; the TV goes black. "Trevor, what's this about?"

"The man in custody is my brother—half-brother."

"And he's going to be charged with murder?"

"Charges are imminent."

"Where is he now?"

"The hospital, for the time being. But he's the prime suspect, and now that he's been arrested, they'll move him to a secure wing. Post guards outside and monitor him around the clock. Come morning, he'll be transferred to the Towers in downtown LA, where he'll receive moderate care. Once well enough, he'll be placed into the general population."

"Gen pop? He won't make it in there," Cassandra says. "Those guys would kill him the first chance they get."

She's never set foot inside a jail or prison cell, but I know she's thought about what life would be like if she were incarcerated. Protection doesn't come cheap on the inside. While she'd have the money to buy a degree of protection, some inmates make names for themselves by killing prisoners with high profiles. If they're successful in their attempts, they become jailhouse celebrities, earning respect and bragging rights. Out of the many senseless reasons to die, being murdered for clout is one of the more asinine. Still, she's right: Avery doesn't stand a chance.

"It wouldn't take long for word to spread of Avery's charges," I say. "Inmates watch a lot of news. He'll be an easy mark, and those with mothers, wives, and daughters will take what he's been accused of personally and target him first. He'd be lucky to last a week."

"But you don't think he did it?"

"I don't know, but if I'm going to get to the truth, I need to start connecting as many dots as I can."

"I take it your father isn't handling this well."

"He'll be OK."

"I can't imagine what you all are going through. First David Bergman and now this."

"I'm beginning to wonder if my father's right about the Finnegan curse."

"You don't actually believe in that sort of thing, do you?"

"No, but the alternative explanations are that my life is a lightning rod for bad shit, or I'm being tested . . . a crucible."

"Tested by what exactly?"

"God . . . a higher power. The purveyor of the universe."

"I think the idea that you're cursed is more plausible than some figure in the heavens playing with your life as if it were a game of chess."

"You don't believe in God?"

"Seriously, Trevor?"

"Can't say I'm surprised, but I thought maybe, given the meditation and Kabbalah . . ."

"More like exercises to focus my mind. I don't have to believe in a spiritual world for the practices to work."

"Then what *do* you believe in?"

"Myself," she says without taking a beat.

"And that works for you?"

"It has so far," she says. "I'm sorry you're having to deal with all of this. It isn't fair to you. Nothing ever is, though."

"Don't take this the wrong way, Cassandra, but I didn't think someone like you could feel sorry for anyone."

"You're suggesting I can't relate to what other people are going through?"

"No—not fully. Empathy isn't something you embody. You mimic it fine."

"I may not feel in the same way most people do, but I do feel things, Trevor."

"Like what?"

"Distress for what you're experiencing, the same as if a hawk plucked a koi fish from my pond. It'd start as a pinch, an increasing annoyance, and likely grow into anger."

"Anger?"

"Yes, having been wronged and inconvenienced. Then, depending on how upset I felt, I'd get another fish or hunt the hawk down and kill it."

I'm dumbfounded and without a rebuttal. It's hard to see how Nigel and Cassandra coexist—he loves nature and desires to protect it, while Cassandra holds disdain for all things that might inconvenience her.

"I understand and accept the unfortunate things in life," she continues. "I don't have to like it, though. And if I can do something about it, I do, but I know, in the end, it's all up to chance."

"Chance? Sounds a lot like a deity playing chess."

"Well, sometimes it's chance, but more often than not, people are what you think they are from the moment you meet them. It's a waiting game to see how long it takes until they prove you right with their actions. I don't know your brother, but I know men. And given my time as a woman in this world, men have an intrinsic penchant for harming us."

"Not *all* men."

"*Beware of the man who wants to protect you; he will protect you from everything but himself.*"

"Who said that?"

"Erica Jong—a novelist and poet. She's brilliant, which is why I know you'd love her."

"I do appreciate brilliance," I say. "I'll look her up."

"You should."

"If Avery did kill his girlfriend, then he's where he's supposed to be," I say. "But if he's innocent, I'm the only one who can prove it."

"Trevor Finnegan: the valiant righter of wrongs."

"Not all wrongs. You're still in business, aren't you?"

"You can't turn that cheekiness off for a minute, can you?"

"Relax. I'm not building a case against you. Sally made that mistake. Look where it got her." I get to my feet and shake out my legs. "And I'd rather not spend the rest of my life in witness protection."

"Is that the only reason?"

"No." I move toward her slowly. "I'm holding out hope that you'll have an epiphany, see how this lifestyle has trapped you, and leave it all alone one day. Find something that'll make you happy."

"Setting any allegations about my businesses aside, how do you know I'm not happy?"

"We both know you're not."

"Well, maybe there isn't enough happiness in the world for me to give all this up," she says. "This lifestyle is all I know. Whether it makes me happy or not is insignificant."

"You won't know unless you try," I say. "If you look hard enough, maybe you'll find something with staying power . . ."

"Oh, is that right?"

"Sure."

"How insightful of you," she says. "The many facets of Trevor Finnegan, with so much wisdom to disperse . . . but what do you care? How does my happiness or what I do in this world have any bearing on you?"

"Because if you can change, then it'll prove we aren't all damned to repeat our follies. See, my father made mistakes, and despite seeing how it made his life hell, I made similar choices. Avery, too."

"That's your half-brother's name?"

I nod. "I've fought against making the same mistakes as my father, only to make different ones that were equally damaging. The things we do, our actions, only demolish relationships with our loved ones and harm them in ways we can't fathom. We force them to endure the pain we inflict, and they carry the scars for their entire lives. I need you to understand, Cassandra, your daughters will carry what you've done in this life like a corpse on their shoulders, and worse even, if they follow in your footsteps."

She's silent for a moment. Baffled, maybe. Then, she says, "Wow . . . I mean, OK. I wasn't expecting to sojourn in the existential no-man's-land with you, but I understand, Trevor. Finding something you love enough that you'd change your life for it is respectable. Is that what you did in order to be with the baker?"

"I made necessary changes so that Sarada and I could be happy."

"And are you *happy*?"

"Yes, I believe I am," I say. "Sorry. I didn't mean to get so worked up. Not being a cop has given me more time for self-reflection."

"And reflection you have achieved." She begins walking toward the kitchen. "I'm going to fix myself another drink. Would you like one? I can fix just about anything, thanks to my daughters; they taught me how to manage a wet bar."

"Bourbon on the rocks."

"A drink that manages to be simple and sophisticated—that I can do."

My phone chimes and I look at the screen. It's a response from Kimber—she's free to meet in an hour and provides an address for a location in the Hollywood Hills. "I'll have to take that drink another time," I say.

"Oh?"

"Something's come up."

"Another time, then," Cassandra says, much to her chagrin.

SIX

I wasn't savvy enough to Google the address Kimber texted me before driving to the location, but the GPS directed me to Forest Lawn Cemetery. It looks like a sprawling park or golf course. I get out of the car and begin walking toward Kimber, who stands wearing a black coat, too long and cumbersome for her petite stature.

"I should've seen this coming," I say, leaning in to hug her. Our embrace is brief but meaningful, considering how much Kimber despised me when we first met two years ago. I was a besmirched cop, the antithesis of Kimber's ideological views of law enforcement, but over time, she warmed to me and I to her, and I'd like to believe we're friends.

"It's good to see you, Trevor," she says, slipping from my arms.

"So this is where you've been spending your time?"

"I put fresh flowers on his grave once a week," she says. "Carnations."

"Didn't think David cared much for flowers."

"Laying legal briefs on a gravesite wouldn't go over well with the groundskeepers."

"It's definitely not where I imagined him being buried," I say, walking a flight of stairs alongside Kimber. "Seems posh for a man who only owned three suits."

"David might've come from money, but it wasn't who he was," she says, slightly out of breath. Grief manifests in everyone differently. In mere weeks, Kimber has become replete. No doubt, stress eating and indulging in her predilection for sweet wines. She pauses a moment, breathes steadily, then continues. "His parents bought the plot when he turned eighteen, so he'd recognize, as they put it, his 'ephemeral existence.' They said preparing for death and voting were the first steps in adulthood . . . What is it you were expecting?"

"I don't know . . . His body was donated to research. Maybe his remains were turned into fertilizer for endangered trees."

"He was Jewish, Trevor. Most of us don't buck tradition," she says. "Not being buried in a Jewish cemetery was defiant enough, but David preferred to rot in a simple biodegradable box six feet underground."

"Didn't realize . . ."

"Well, he was, more or less, Jewish in spirit."

When we reach the top of the staircase, we're met by elegant sculptures, a spire twisted and folded in mesmerizing ways, and an unvarnished bronze obelisk—a visceral beauty starkly imagined by its creator. "It's a lovely place," I say, admiring the art and groundskeeping.

"His grave is right over there." Kimber points toward a small tree less than a yard away, washed in the sun's gilded light. "You want to come with me?"

I look at the tree, slender and bare with crooked branches, near a marble headstone—David's final resting place. "All right," I say, joining her.

We walk down a grassy mound across a concrete path to the gravesite.

Kimber lays the flowers at the base of the headstone engraved in Hebrew: קדצהו קדצה תא חכשת לא םלועל.

"What's it say?" I ask.

"Never forget righteousness and justice," she says. "It's what kept David going all those years. It was written on an index card he kept taped on the wall in his office. If he had last words, I thought those would be it."

I heard David's last words before Amanda Walsh put a bullet in his head, and those weren't it . . .

"I noticed the card," I say. "Just never bothered to ask what it meant."

"He wanted me to give you this." Kimber reaches into her coat pocket and hands me a letter envelope. "He said if anything ever happened to him, you'd know what to do."

I open the envelope. Inside is a folded document. I begin to read it—it's a deed to a property.

"David bequeathed his assets to various charities. Everything except this," she says. "It's a small office building."

"What do I need with a building?"

"David purchased it in the 1980s. Last time he saw it, squatters had made it their home," she says. "It'll need work, but he felt you'd find good use for it."

"Why the hell would he leave me a building?"

"Don't know," she says. "David didn't provide any instructions."

"But the firm was nearly bankrupt. It doesn't make sense. Why wouldn't he have sold this when times were tough? And they were plenty tough, weren't they?"

"Things were never as bad as David made them out to be. He often erred on the side of doom, but he always had a plan, and this is part of it."

"What plan, Kimber? I watched the man die in front of me. Not even on his worst day could he have planned for that."

"I believe he wanted us to carry out his work," she says. "Continue to fight for the people of this city."

"I'm not a lawyer."

"No, but I will be," she says. "And I want to reopen the firm."

"This is why you had me come out here? David's only been dead for a few weeks, and we're talking about reopening the firm?"

"I'm carrying out his wishes, Trevor."

"I get that, but I can't think about this right now. Not with what's hanging over my head."

"I'm sorry," she says. "It wasn't my intention to lay this on you . . ."

"Then, can we table it for now?"

"All right," she says. "So, you want to tell me why you wanted to meet?"

"I need you to search David's Rolodex for a good defense attorney."

"More referrals for Sally Munoz?"

"Not this time," I say. "It's a new case I'm working on. I'll need an attorney with an open mind."

"How open?"

"The accused is claiming amnesia."

"And the evidence?"

"Circumstantial . . . mostly."

"I'll get some names for you," she says. "You know, you could've asked me this over the phone."

"I wanted to see you . . . make sure you're doing all right."

"I'm getting by. Some days are tougher than others. What about you?"

"Working. Keeping busy."

"I see that, but are you taking time to grieve? You know, processing what happened is impor—"

I quickly cut her off. "I'll take time when I can," I say, choosing curtness over having to contend with what she's broaching. There's no time to mourn David's passing, and he wouldn't want me to, considering what's at stake for Avery.

"Trevor, you can't ignore what happened."

"I'm not ignoring anything, but life doesn't stop because David's gone. People need my help."

"What about what you need?"

I look off in the distance at the setting sun; its amber light washes over the gravestones and plaques. If I were the type to seek out heavenly signs, I'd think David was trying to remind me that even when surrounded by death, there can be light.

"I should go," I say.

"Please, don't be a stranger, Trevor. I'm always here if you need me."

"I'll give some thought to the office building."

"I know you'll make the best choice."

I reach in for another hug. Kimber rubs my back the way my mother did when things were heavy on my mind. She could always sense when things troubled me, and maybe Kimber has the same intuition.

"See you later," I say, leaving her and walking back the way I came.

I ring Cassandra's doorbell. I'm surprised when she answers, having expected Nigel.

Red wine residue is on her lips. "You look like you could use that drink now," she says.

"Perceptive as always," I say, entering into the foyer. "Is Pop awake?"

"Still upstairs. I peeked in to check on him. His snore sounded like a freight train. The poor man was exhausted."

"Must be the stress . . ."

"You hungry?" she asks.

"Without question."

I follow Cassandra to the kitchen, where I wash my hands in the sink, and she fixes me a bourbon on the rocks. I down the drink fast, and she's ready with another. This time, I sip it, appreciating the smooth body and subtle sting in the back of my throat. My palate has been ruined by cheap liquor. I don't ask about the brand, but it tastes expensive.

My stomach growls loudly. "I get the hint," Cassandra says, taking out an oblong Pyrex dish from the fridge and serving me spaghetti leftovers from the night before. "Nigel's specialty—extra garlic, fresh parsley, and grated Romano."

"Looks delicious." I take a seat at the table.

While it seems odd to be dining with Cassandra alone, I'm too hungry to overanalyze the situation. After two bites, I understand why she's crowned the meal an achievement.

"Pretty good, isn't it?" she asks.

"What can I say? The man can cook. Hopefully, he's as good at car repairs as he is making pasta."

"Tired of the E28, already?"

"Oh, I don't think that's possible," I say. "The Falcon and I have history, that's all."

"Men and their cars . . ."

"So tell me, does Nigel prepare all your meals?"

"I'm halfway decent at making eggs, and I can boil a hotdog," she says, "but that's about it. I'm not sure what I'd do without Nigel."

"Get a personal chef? Isn't that a perk of being a one-percenter?"

"One-percenter? You're lumping me in with those assholes?"

"Which assholes do you prefer I lump you in with?"

She laughs. "Well, aren't you catty tonight?"

"Sorry, I usually reserve my angst for my punching bag." I twirl the pasta around my fork. "Can I ask you something a little personal?"

"Personal-personal or business-personal? Because we agreed we'd keep everything above board."

"Don't ask, don't tell—I got it, but this isn't that."

"OK."

"Why'd you agree to let me stay here? A former cop staying in your house. You must admit, it's risky."

"Should I not trust you?"

"I might be the only person connected to law enforcement that you can trust. Last time I was in Pacific Division, officers used your face as a dart board."

She bubbles over, giddy, shielding her laugh with her palm. "Glad I left an impression."

It's the most jovial I've seen her, and it only took a glass or more of Cabernet.

"Since we're getting personal, I have a question for you." She touches my hand; her fingers graze my dry knuckles. It's silly—an impetuous gesture—but I feel guilty.

"We should probably stop while we're ahead," I say, getting up from the table. "I shouldn't have asked . . . and it's getting late."

"You didn't even finish your food."

I pat my stomach. "Pasta tends to bloat me . . ."

"Don't blow me off," she says. "I want to answer your question, but I've got a legitimate one of my own."

"Not the best idea. We've been drinking."

"Don't worry, Trevor. I can handle my booze."

"Fine," I sigh. "Shoot."

"How come you aren't as torn up about your brother's plight as your father seems to be?"

"Like I said, I don't know Avery. Neither does Pop. He only thinks he does."

"Well, that's my point," she says. "Seems like he was willing to open up his world to a stranger, but you're far less trusting. Why is that?"

"What are you getting at, Cassandra?"

"I think a part of you"—she points at the center of my chest—"some tiny part is so used to being the only son that you can't fathom having to share your father with another. Even if Avery wasn't facing prison time for murder—say, he was the model human being—something tells me you'd still find fault with him."

I chuckle at her failing attempt at psychoanalysis. "That's what you've deduced from this conversation?"

"Makes sense to me . . . It's been you and your father for so long. And sure, it's been rocky, but he needs you, and I think you like to be needed—the only one he can turn to. It's your drug, Trevor. Might even be the closest thing to love you've ever received from him."

"Hell of an assessment."

She sips more wine; the ruby color matches her freshly polished fingernails. "And to answer your question . . . had I known you were working a case this awful, I might've suggested you stay at a beachside motel."

"You're worried it'll bring police attention?"

"Malibu works best when its law enforcement spends its time writing traffic tickets and organizing beach cleanups."

"I always appreciate your honesty, Cassandra."

"There's more where that came from," she says, toasting her glass. "Here's another tidbit: you should take time for self-care."

"I've got all the self-care I need right here," I say, drinking the last of the watered-down bourbon. "But thanks for the therapy session."

She holds out her hand, palm flat, and wiggles her fingers. "That'll be five large."

"You take checks?"

"Cash only."

"How about IOUs?"

She holds a devious smile. "All right. I know you're good for it."

"I've got a flight in the morning. I should sleep."

"Commercial?"

"The only way to fly on my salary, which is zero for this job. I did spring for business class, though. More leg room."

"Ridiculous. Take my jet."

"Say what now?"

"It's at Santa Monica Airport. Hangar Five."

"Of course, you have a jet . . ."

"I can have a pilot ready to go by nine."

"I don't know . . . I'm pretty sure you're under surveillance."

"Not funny," she says, wagging her finger. My ego reverts to boyhood. It's like being chastised by my sassy aunt.

"What if someone sees?" I ask. "I've managed to keep our dealings low profile."

"It's aircraft, Trevor. Not my bedroom."

We're frozen in awkwardness, but my ego rebounds when I consider her proposal, and I instantly want to text Sarada.

"Offer stands," she says, tracing the mouth of her wine glass with her finger. "No pressure."

I don't inquire which offer. "Need help cleaning up?" I toss my sauce-stained napkin into my plate and prepare to take it to the sink.

"Leave it. Nigel will take care of it when he comes home."

"Where is *The Grateful Dead* this evening?"

"Reiki session."

"Thank you for dinner." My voice cracks into staccato. I'm becoming a pubescent teenager. "It was . . ." I search for the most innocuous phrasing. "Enjoyable."

She laughs; this time, it's more endearing, underscoring something invaluable: Cassandra Boyle's complete trust.

"My pleasure," she says. "Have a good night."

Upstairs in the guest room, Pop lies across the bed, shoes still on, snoring. I remove sweats from my duffle bag to change into and go into the bathroom.

It's been a while since a woman who isn't Sarada has looked at me with *bedroom eyes*. If I tell Pop about tonight, he'll marvel at my self-control. Then he'll spend the next decade recounting to anyone who'll listen how I turned down an offer of pleasure from the alluring yet murderous Cassandra Boyle.

My breath reeks of garlic; I should've repelled her like a vamp. I brush my teeth and remove my shirt, which smells vaguely of her perfume. One dinner and her redolent scent attaches to me . . . Maybe there's a parable in that?

The liquor is taking its toll. My thoughts are scattered, my chest's warm, and my eyes are heavy. I welcome a good night's sleep. I set my phone alarm for four o'clock, preparing for my seven a.m. flight to Las Vegas.

I text Sarada, I **love you**, and close my eyes.

I dream I'm floating in a tank. The water is warm but cools the deeper I sink. My mother's voice calls to me, but I can't reach the surface. She's up there, somewhere, and I know it. I have to reach her, but something is holding me down, tight around my ankles. I'm losing air. Pressure builds in my ears. It's getting dark.

Darker.

So dark . . .

Then . . .

I wake up out of breath, wet and hot around my neck. I reach for my phone on the nightstand. It glows brightly. I stare at the screen until it comes into focus. It's after two a.m.

I get out of bed and look over at where Pop was sound asleep, but he isn't there. I turn on the bedroom light and notice the bathroom door is shut. I don't remember closing it. Pop might be inside.

"Pop?"

Silence.

"Pop, are you in there?" I leave the bed, walk to the bathroom door, and knock. "You in there?"

No response. I open the door . . . empty.

I go downstairs; light spills from the kitchen. I round the corner and see Pop sitting at the dinner table, his face buried in his arms and the wine bottle beside him. The plates of discarded pasta are still on the table, along with Cassandra's wine glass and my tumbler that held bourbon.

"Ah, dammit . . ." I touch Pop's shoulder. "Pop? Let's go, Pop."

He grumbles, still tired but mostly drunk. "I'm sorry," he

says, bloodshot eyes. "I couldn't go back to sleep. Thought I'd eat something."

"It's all right . . . c'mon, Pop." I help him up; he can barely stand. He's finished the entire bottle of wine. "Let's get you cleaned up." I wet a tea towel and wipe the wine residue from his face.

Cassandra comes downstairs and enters the kitchen wearing a sherpa-lined robe and matching fuzzy slippers. "What the hell's going on?" she asks, pulling a small-caliber pistol from her robe pocket.

"You don't need the gun, Cassandra."

"It's damn near three in the morning. I'll be the judge of that."

"He's drunk."

"What?"

"The wine from last night."

"But Nigel was supposed to clean, same as every night."

"That didn't happen. I want to talk to him."

"He should be in his quarters."

"His *quarters*?"

"The basement."

I help Pop to the entertainment room and sit him on the couch. "I'm sorry, Trevor," he says. "I didn't mean to . . . I just—"

"It's going to be all right, Pop."

"God dammit, Nigel," Cassandra says, still holding the gun. "Perfect time to slack on the job." She pulls a recessed handle from the wall built under the staircase and opens a door camouflaged by wooden panels.

"Is that a panic room?" I ask, noting the freshly painted panels.

"It was, until Nigel convinced me to turn it into his live-in man cave. It's completely soundproof with a separate HVAC."

I follow Cassandra into the cubby, down a short flight of stairs, and into a large room. She flicks a light switch so we can see our way. The carpet is orange shag, something I haven't seen since my grandmother's house, and it smells of marijuana. An acoustic guitar rests next to a bean-bag chair; tie-dye tapestries and shelves of vinyl records decorate the walls. The only thing absent from Nigel's psychedelic fantasy is a lava lamp.

A king-sized bed with extra-large pillows is at the far end of the room. Limbs poke out from underneath a comforter, too many to only be Nigel's.

"Get up, Nigel!" Cassandra demands. "Now, dammit!"

Is this how she sounds when she chastises her daughters? I've always struggled to see her as a mother. Is this a taste of what it's like having Cassandra as a parent?

"I said, get up," she says, tugging at the comforter.

Nigel begins to wake, shifting and turning. A girl appears next to him—I immediately recognize her. It's Cree from the university's nature center.

"What is she doing here?" Cassandra asks.

Nigel is slow to respond.

"You might want to get out of here, Cree," I say.

Cassandra throws the comforter to the floor. "Trevor, you know this girl?"

"Met her at St. Catherine's. I'm guessing she and Nigel were reconnecting."

"Please, Cassandra," Nigel says. "She was going to be gone by sunrise."

"You must be crazy bringing her here."

"Um, hello?" Cree says, nude and barely lucid. "Can someone please tell me what's so wrong?"

"Get her out of here," Cassandra demands, still holding the pistol. "For crying out loud, is she even old enough to drink?!"

Nigel is in his fifties, yet he appears far younger than men his age, with his shoulder-length hair and rubicund skin. Cassandra once called him a testament to plant-based living and, I'd add, a healthy libido.

Cassandra shows no signs of calming down. "How could you be so stupid?" she asks. "Fucking amateur hour."

"You should put the gun away," I say, gently taking her wrist. "You're angry and don't want to risk a discharge."

"I've never shot anyone in my life, Trevor . . . accidentally."

Cree starts to get dressed, fastening her bra. Nigel finds

more of her garments on the floor, buried in the bedding, and frantically tosses them to her. There's something pathetic about the whole ordeal, emasculating even. I didn't see it before. Nigel isn't an employee; he's—as my father put it—a manservant in every sense of the word.

Cassandra stands in judgment at the base of the stairs. "We'll discuss this later," she says, hands on her hips. "And she'd better be gone in ten minutes if she knows what's good for her."

We leave the basement and walk into the entertainment room, where Pop has fallen back asleep on the couch.

"Are you going to kill him?" I ask.

"Nigel?" She laughs. "I can't. He's the best. Besides, I know why he did it."

"You mean aside from the obvious?"

"It's not easy dedicating your life to being in service to someone. It doesn't matter how much they're paying you, but I do wish he sowed his late-in-life oats somewhere else."

"And the girl?"

Cassandra is quiet, brooding. "Hopefully, Nigel isn't one for pillow talk."

"That's not an answer."

"Her presence in the house jeopardizes my operations."

"Find another way . . . She's a kid that didn't know what she was doing."

"You mean, *who* she was doing?"

"Let her be, Cassandra. We both know she won't be any trouble."

"I don't know anything about her except that she was in my home."

"Dammit, I'm telling you that she doesn't pose a threat."

"Well, aren't you a bleeding heart?"

"Give me an answer."

"All right, Trevor. I won't go near her." She places her hand over her heart. "Now, what are you going to do about your father?"

"I've put him in a bad spot. Being here jeopardized his sobriety. He needs to return to the treatment facility."

"How can you manage that? Your flight leaves in a few hours."

"Guess I have to take you up on that jet offer."

"OK," she says. "I'll make the call. And don't worry about checking your gun. The crew doesn't screen luggage or ask questions."

"Good."

"As for your father, I'll arrange his transportation."

"You don't have to do that," I say. "He can take a taxi."

"I left the wine out," she says. "It was my mistake."

"Really, it's no bother. He can manage in a taxi."

"No, Trevor. It's the least I can do. Besides, the last taxi company operating in Malibu went bankrupt two months ago, and it'll take hours to find an Uber driver willing to take your father to Palm Springs."

"Fine," I say. "But only because you insist. I've asked enough of you just by being here."

"Don't overthink it," she says. "What's a little help between friends . . ."

Friends?

She's caught me off guard again—it's best to pretend I didn't hear her.

It's seven thirty a.m. Pop has sobered up but refuses to get out of bed. I've packed his luggage and notified the Palm Springs facility that he'll be returning. It was reckless for him to abandon his treatment in the first place, but he needed to be a part of this investigation. Now, it's up to me to solve it for both of us.

"Let's go, Pop. The car will be arriving soon."

"Can't believe you're sending me away."

"It's for the best, and you know it."

"It was shitty Cabernet, not even whiskey. I should've gone for the whiskey."

"Doesn't matter, now. We've got to deal with it."

"Who's going to watch your back out there?"

"I'll be fine; don't worry about me," I say. "You only need to work on getting better."

"You're making a mistake." He scoots to the edge of the bed and stands with a groan. "I'm back to day zero. It doesn't matter now. You should let me go with you. We should finish this together."

"I can't do that . . . and backsliding is normal for the first few years. Remember, Pop, it's a disease, not a choice."

"Where'd you read that?"

"The pamphlet."

"Can't believe you read that drivel."

"Every word."

"Food is terrible in that place."

"Says the man who was eating canned tuna for every meal." I zip his suitcase shut and place it by the door. "You're still in your clothes from yesterday. Are you going to change?"

"To hell with it . . . I'll shower when I get to the facility."

"Fine, Pop, but you smell like the morgue."

A limo pulls into the driveway. I watch from the window as Nigel directs the driver where to park. "Your ride is here."

"Take this," Pop says, removing the pistol from his ankle and handing it to me.

"You were sleeping with your pistol?"

"I always do," he says. "I won't have time to put it back in storage. Can you hold on to it?"

"You sure?"

"Might come in handy," he says. "I wish the facility wasn't so strict about firearms."

"Guns around recovering alcoholics—what could go wrong?"

I carry his suitcase downstairs, and we meet the limo driver outside; he's all business in a black suit, tie, and loafers. I hand him Pop's suitcase, and he places it in the trunk.

"I thought this was supposed to be a taxi," Pop says.

"Cassandra got you a chauffeur. Says it'll be a more comfortable experience."

Pop peeks his head inside the stretch sedan. "There's a wet bar in here."

"Stocked with sodas and flavored water. Chips, too."

"She didn't have to do all this," he says.

"Maybe she's grown fond of you?"

"Would you tell her I said 'thank you'?"

"Yeah, Pop, I'll tell her."

"Welp, then," he says, extending his hand. "I guess I'll see you when I see you?"

I step in for a hug, wrapping my arms around him tightly. "I love you, Pop." The words come out without much thought. We continue to hold each other, and when we break, there's a semblance of tears in his eyes.

Without another word, he gets into the limo and shuts the door. I watch as the driver makes a three-point turn and heads down the driveway.

I turn to see Cassandra on the porch, still wearing her robe. "The jet is ready," she says. "You should go."

SEVEN

I land at Henderson Executive Airport shortly after ten o'clock. I'm freezing in my hoodie and jacket and regret not packing a heavier coat. A pallid sun peaks from behind the clouds, and soon it'll banish the pewter morning.

A Town Car is waiting outside the hangar, as Cassandra said it would be. The car's rear seats are heated, and the driver is cordial. "I can drop you wherever you'd like," he says. "Here's my card. Call the number on the front, and I'll come get you. No matter the time or place."

I pocket the card and have him drop me off at an apartment complex on Dean Martin Drive, the last known address for Avery and Keisha according to Pop, which he'd gotten from Ms. Dixion. The letters A, B, and C mark the three buildings across from a small leasing office with drawn shades and a closed door. It's Saturday, and there's no office staff on duty.

I walk to Building B and go upstairs to their second-floor unit, number 106. Grocery store ads and newspapers are piled on the welcome mat, and taped over the peephole is a yellow document with "FINAL NOTICE" typed at the head. There's a date for the upcoming eviction proceeding.

I feel eyes on me . . .

An older woman, wrapped in a knit shawl and carrying grocery bags, is perched on the stairs and watching.

"Good morning," I say. "Need any help with those bags?"

"Question is, do *you* need something?"

I show her my PI badge, but it looks as though she's unable to read it from afar. "Trevor Finnegan," I say, pointing to the name on the badge. "I'm a private investigator. Can you tell me anything about the people who live here?"

"Private investigator?"

"Yes, ma'am."

"Who hired you?"

"I can't divulge that information."

"You mean you won't," she says. "Is it like an oath thing?"

"No, ma'am. It's only to protect my client's privacy."

"Sounds like hogwash to me," she says. "Especially if you're snooping around, wanting to know about those two?"

"Anything you can share would be helpful."

"Not a whole lot to tell. As you can see, they're behind on their rent and facing the boot. Come next month, their asses are gone."

"You don't sound displeased."

"The man who lives there has been a problem since day one, and the pretty girl—well, she's sweet but dumb as rocks if she's with him. I'm telling you, he's no damn good."

"When did you see them last?"

"Two weeks ago, maybe . . . the fella was standing outside his door having a cigarette. Mind you, there's no smoking outside the designated areas near the dog run. Anyway, he must've had too much to drink because he was real chatty, which is unlike him. He was going on about some big opportunity in California and how he'd never set foot in this town again."

"Did he say what the big opportunity was?"

"No, and I didn't care enough to ask." She holds the bags like anchors; her arms will be wet noodles soon. "But it sounded like a get-rich-quick scheme. The kind of idiocy that ends with the feds raiding your apartment."

"Why do you say that?"

"I know his type—always looking for an angle. Anything to avoid getting an honest job. Three months ago, he said he'd made a fortune in Bitcoin. Whatever the hell that is. The fool can't even pay his rent," she said, adjusting her grip on the grocery bags. "Fortunes don't come to people like him. Even if he got lucky and won the lottery, he'd burn through every cent in a week."

"Has anyone come by looking for them?"

"Nobody except you," she says.

I turn the knob and press against the door with my shoulder. It's locked but gives a little. Whoever installed the door likely used shorter screws to fasten the strike plate, which loosened over time. With enough force, I should be able to break through with minimal damage.

"You shouldn't be doing that. You'll ruin the door," she says. "Management isn't going to like that one bit."

"I heard someone inside. It sounded like a scream."

"I didn't hear a damn thing!"

"Yep, it definitely was a scream." I rear back and drive my heel into the door. The strike is unsuccessful, and I stumble.

Alarmed, the woman shuffles behind me. "I'm going now," she says. "You're crazy."

"Fifty bucks, and you don't call management or the police."

She stops squawking—I've got her attention. "Make it one hundred."

I dig into my pocket, pull out a few bills. After a quick count, I hand her a stack of twenties. She snatches the cash and continues to her unit.

I plant my foot, ready for another attempt. I'll need to concentrate my power near the handle. I drive my hips forward, raise my knee, give it a slight cock, then drive it into the door. The door explodes open. I haven't kicked in a door since my days in uniform, and it's as satisfying as I remember.

The apartment is dark, musty, and smells like an ashtray. It has all the markings of a couple struggling to stay afloat—a small TV on a precarious tower of milk crates, a card table with two folding chairs, and a couch that looks as if it was plucked from an alley.

I switch on a floor lamp in the corner of the room next to a bookcase lined with computer coding manuals, comic books, and photography and graphic design books for beginners. There are sketches of faces taped on the walls, made with charcoal and colored pencils. There are portraits of Keisha in various stages of dress, and what I presume is an aerial view of the Grand Canyon, along with a drawing of Pop from his days as a beat cop . . . These are Avery's compositions. The penciling matches that of the cicada he drew in the hospital. I suppose he's an artist, too. It's probably the only thing we have in common, and neither of us made a profession out of it.

I spent four years at an elite arts high school in Santa Monica.

As one of the only Black students, bullying was a daily occurrence. Mostly from upper-echelon white kids who knew I was a scholarship recipient and, in their eyes, poorer than dirt. The only good thing about attending Pershing Arts Academy was befriending Sarada, which changed my life in ways I couldn't have imagined.

I notice a shoebox shoved in the corner and open it. Inside is the photo of Pop in uniform that inspired Avery's drawing, along with written letters from Pop bound with rubber bands. Some date back to the early nineties. I consider the invasion of privacy but convince myself that reading the letters might assist me in the investigation. The more I know about Avery, the better.

Many of the handwritten letters are short, less than a page. Pop's stoic tone feels as if Avery's a pen pal or past acquaintance. His words are rigid and lack warmth, and the sentences are pared down, only focused on facts, the way he'd write a criminal incident report. There are paragraphs in which he describes his life as a police officer and complains about how little he gets paid for carrying out a challenging and dangerous job. He even suggests that the acquittal of the LAPD officers who beat Rodney King not only spurred days of violent riots but also made the streets far more dangerous. He considers resigning if things don't get better, something he's never told me. Pop's *hard life* theme spans multiple letters. At times, he lays it on thick, suggesting that the long hours and stress have caused him to be a neglectful father and husband, and that Avery is better off without him. After the fourth letter, Pop's purpose for writing becomes clear. He was never trying to bond with Avery; rather, his tactic was to deter him from seeking him out and asking to live with us in LA.

He concludes the last letter with:

This place is not what people think. Raising a son here is the hardest thing I've ever had to do. You'd have to watch your back. Dangers exist on the street. Not just the gangs but those wearing badges, too. Every day, I pray Trevor doesn't encounter the wrong kind of cop.

I put the letters back the way I found them and direct my attention to a leather-bound binder on the coffee table. I open it and turn the pages—all photos of Keisha, at least fifty or more, some bordering on professional; others, clearly taken by an amateur. I'm not prudish, but I wouldn't call them tasteful. There are hints at BDSM: a topless Keisha with a studded collar around her neck. In another photo, she wears a leather mask without eye holes, and a zipper covers her mouth, only partially unzipped so she's able to breathe. The shots give the impression of violence and defilement. There are too many pictures to suggest that she models as a hobby. This is Keisha's professional portfolio, and Avery might've been the primary photographer.

A hallway leads past the kitchen to the rear of the apartment. Across from the bathroom is a bedroom. I flick the room's light switch to see strewn clothes and a toppled dresser. Someone shredded the mattress, and there's broken glass from a shattered mirror. Was there an altercation before they left? I see no blood evidence, and the bedroom is the only part of the house that's ransacked. Someone probably entered after Keisha and Avery left. They were looking for something important.

I check the closet: more clothes, muddy sneakers, a tripod, glamour lights, and a laptop bag. I pick up the bag; it weighs a few ounces. People usually don't leave laptops behind unless they intend to return. I unzip the bag and look inside. There's no laptop, but there is an external hard drive labeled "2015–2016."

I hear voices outside, strong accents, and they're getting louder.

"Watch the door," a man's voice commands. "I'mma check it out."

I peek into the hallway. A hefty, bald white man dressed in a peacoat faces the front door, talking to someone outside. He looks in my direction. I keep out of sight. Leaving the closet door ajar, I duck behind the ripped mattress.

When the man is outside the bedroom, I grip my Glock, release the safety, and wait. Heavy footsteps enter the room. The man walks to the dresser and pivots to the closet. He swings the door open. I spring up from hiding, my gun at his back. "Let me see your hands," I say. "How many more of you are there?"

He calmly raises his hands above his head. "Just one other outside."

"Who are you?"

"Nobody."

"Everybody's somebody."

"You don't want to know me."

"Why are you here?"

"I was just about to ask you the same thing," he says. "Put the gun down, and we can talk."

"What's there to talk about?"

"Your life . . . and how it will end unless you drop the gun."

I pat him down and find a 9mm semi-automatic pistol in his waistband. "Nice piece," I say, releasing the magazine and tossing the gun aside. "How'd you know I was here?"

"The old lady told us she saw somebody come in here."

"What's she care?"

"She doesn't," he says, keeping his hands up. "We told her to keep an eye on the apartment in case anyone showed up. We pay her, and she does what we ask."

"Guess I should have doubled what I gave her."

"Don't feel bad; she hustles everybody."

"Who were you expecting?"

"We were hoping for Keisha and Avery. The old lady said you were a private detective. Is that true?"

"What do you want with Keisha and Avery?"

"C'mon, man, drop the gun. This is pointless—"

"Answer me."

"We just want our money. That's all."

"Sergei!" the other man calls from outside. "What's taking so long?"

"Tell him you're fine," I say.

"You're making a bad decision, my friend."

"Do it."

"It's fine—everything is fine," Sergei yells. "I had to take a shit. I'll be out in a second."

"OK," the man says. "Just hurry up!"

My cell phone alerts me to a text. Dammit. I forgot to silence it.

"Sergei?" The man waiting outside sounds increasingly worried. "What is happening?"

Sergei chuckles. "You're fucked now, *brother man*."

I discharge my stun gun into his back until he falls face first into the closet. I never had any real intention of shooting him. I'm a private citizen now, and not wearing a badge makes firing a gun far more complicated. As my firearms instructor in the police academy used to say, "You better be sure the law's on your side before you pull the trigger."

Looking at my phone, I see another text from Tori—long with lots of emojis. Besides having terrible timing, she leans heavily on the digital pseudo-language that resembles more what cavemen used to communicate than the King's English. I'm often unsure of what she's talking about. This time is no different, although the numerous sad and crying yellow faces are troubling.

But I can't tend to her crisis now. I'm behind the door, figuring out the best way to get out of the apartment. Sergei's comrade is moving down the hallway quickly; his voice is frantic. "Sergei! What the hell are you doing, man?"

The stench of clove cigarettes wafts through the hall. The odor preludes him as he moves closer, and I'm able to see him more clearly. He's shaggy-haired and lean but not in a physically fit way—more like he consumes junk food and chain smokes, which keeps the weight off. If he exercises, it's just enough to keep him agile.

The man's right fist is balled tight, and his knees are slightly bent. While he doesn't look intimidating, I contend every man can land a punch when it counts and kill if pushed to the verge.

I dive for his legs and snatch them where his knees crease and pull him to the floor. He lands on his back, reaching for the pistol on his waist. I disarm him, throwing the gun into the bathroom, and hammer-fist his jaw—two solid strikes, and he's out.

Sergei might awaken soon . . . I leave the apartment and go downstairs. When I'm near the leasing office, I pull out my phone and the driver's business card and start dialing. I'm two digits in when a black SUV pulls up. Men with pistols, better dressed and far larger than Sergei and his comrade, get out and bookend me with their guns pointed at my sides.

"Get in," one man says, jabbing the gun's barrel further into my ribs.

One man opens the SUV's rear door, and the other bashes me in the back of my head with his gun butt. I collapse inside the vehicle, striking my face on the seat buckle. As much as I try to stave it off, everything gradually turns black, and soon there is only silence and darkness.

I wake up in an apartment nearly as dirty as Avery's, strapped to a chair with bungee cords. Despite the frigid temperature, the windows are open. A man in a charcoal turtleneck is in the kitchen. He drizzles olive oil over a chicken, seasoning it with salt and massaging it with dried herbs. Next, he opens a bottle of red wine and, between sips, douses the bird. "Very nice. Very, very nice . . ." he says.

"Where am I?" I ask.

"Oh, hello," he says, flipping the chicken onto a roasting pan. "Do you require ice for your head? Some aspirin, perhaps?"

"No."

"Are you sure? Head injuries can be very painful unless you can reduce the swelling."

I'm sure I have a knot, but I don't want anything this man is offering—not ice or aspirin. "What is this place?"

"An apartment—what's it look like?"

"OK, but why am I here?"

"I didn't think you'd mind being in a stranger's apartment, given that's where my men found you."

"Your men?" Man, who are you?"

"Chakhokhbili . . ."

"Who?"

"The dish I'm preparing is called Chakhokhbili. Roasted chicken with pomegranate seeds and herbs. A special recipe."

"Look, I don't know who you are, but I'm going to need you to cut me loose."

"I can't do that. Not until we talk." He wipes his hands on a towel and removes his apron. "My men say you attacked them."

"Before they could attack me? Damn right, I did."

"You presumed they were there to cause you harm."

"They had guns."

"Well, my friend," he says, standing before me. "It's Vegas—everyone has guns."

"Are you going to tell me who you are and whose apartment I'm in?"

"Sure—it's my son's place. I'm preparing a meal for his birthday. Normally, I wouldn't do this sort of thing in his . . . what do you call it?" He contemplates for a moment. "Ah, yes, that's it . . . *bachelor pad*—but I prioritize family over business. I told my men to bring you here so we could talk. I apologize for the terrible smell. My son is turning twenty-two and still hasn't learned to clean up after himself."

The place reeks like a high school locker room, a salty musk. The fresh air from the open windows makes it bearable, but it cuts to the bone, giving me the shivers. "You only answered one of my questions. Tell me who you are and what business you have with me."

"I'm only a man looking to have a meaningful conversation," he says. "My name is not as important as what I do."

"OK, then tell me what you want."

"For starters, you injured Sergei and Dimitri."

"You want an apology?"

"I want to know why you were in that apartment."

"I'm investigating a crime."

The man sits across from me on the brown leather couch piled with laundry and rests his hands on his knees. "A crime, you say?"

"It involves the people who live there . . . or lived there."

"Do you know these individuals?"

"Yes—in a way, I do."

"Then you speak of Avery and the woman, Keisha?"

"Yes, but I never met Keisha, and I never will."

"Why do you say this . . . never?"

"She's dead. Murdered . . . I'm here to find out why."

"Her killer is unknown?"

"There's been an arrest."

"Yet you're looking for someone else who might've done this?"

"I'm looking for anything that doesn't fit."

"Now I understand," he says, picking a chin boil. "It is Avery . . . You are his relative, no?"

"I am."

"A brother," he says, fixated on my forehead. "Same head. Same arrogance."

"Avery didn't do it. I'm here to find out who might've wanted him and Keisha dead."

"So much certainty," he says. "What makes you think Avery didn't kill her? I mean, forget that he's family. If you are an investigator, as you say, there must be evidence to the contrary if they've arrested him."

"Evidence doesn't always tell the full story."

"Because full stories are unachievable, my friend. Impossible to obtain. The best you can hope for is getting enough information to make some sense of a story—not always *the* story," he says. "But Avery's situation does present a problem for me."

"What kind of problem?"

"Avery owed me a great deal of money."

"For what?"

"Gambling. Cock fights, mostly."

"He bets on chickens?"

"He loses money on chickens," he says. "And football and boxing and MMA and so on and so on."

"How much does he owe?"

"Fifty thousand. Plus interest."

"He's in jail and can pay you when he gets out. His debt has nothing to do with me."

"I wish it were that simple."

"And why the hell isn't it?"

"You committed violence against my men and, in doing so, caused an injury to one of them."

"No one died. They'll heal."

"Yes, of course, but while they are recovering, they aren't working. If they aren't working, I'm losing money, and if I'm losing money, it's bad for my business."

"So, those men in the apartment were debt collectors?"

"Yes, among other things, and since the debt did not belong to you, they would've left you alone."

"Why don't I believe that?"

"Believe what you will, but you've involved yourself in Avery's affairs."

"I was protecting myself. The way I see it, your men involved me."

"Tomayto, tomahto," he says. "Avery owes it. You are here, so now you can pay."

"You think I'm going to pay you fifty thousand dollars—"

"Plus, ten percent interest."

"Not going to happen, buddy. So cut me loose."

"OK, Mr. Finnegan." He gets up from the couch, returns to the kitchen, takes a cleaver from the butcher's block, and examines the blade.

My pocket is lighter; the PI badge is missing, along with my cell phone. If these men have my name, it won't be long before they know everything about me, including Sarada and Pop . . . if they don't already.

"I can't imagine it," he says, hacking the chicken into pieces. "It will be so hard for your father to lose both of his sons—one to prison and the other to pride."

"Look, I don't have that kind of money."

"Really? But Los Angeles City paid you a great sum, did they not?"

"That lawsuit was years ago. The money's dried up."

"A big spender like your brother? How unfortunate."

"Killing me would be a mistake. You don't want that kind of heat."

"Complicated, yes . . . but not a mistake."

"You still wouldn't get your money."

"As you say, if Avery is innocent, he'll be freed, and I can collect. Perhaps your death would show him how serious I am. Or if you have life insurance, your family could use that."

Laughter builds in my gut and spills out loud and wild. I regain composure, not wanting to pass out from the constricting bungee cords around my chest.

"What is funny?" he asks. "I didn't tell a joke."

"Your logic is flawless, but let me educate you: Avery is guilty until proven innocent. Not the other way around. I'm his only chance. Without me, he'll be on Death Row this time next year."

"The Black man's plight? Is that what you are suggesting?"

"Not just Black folk these days."

"In my motherland, these things happen often. We expect corruption. The police, the judges, the politicians. No one denies it, but we never speak about it. Instead, we do our best to stay out of the policeman's way and not speak ill of those who govern. But here, in America, you march and rally for every offense—and for what? What do you gain? People say corruption exists and that the police do great and terrible things and go unpunished. But these people you fight for are criminals, are they not? None of them are innocent. Otherwise, they wouldn't have had dealings with the police."

"Whether they have a rap sheet or not, it doesn't mean they deserve to be executed or imprisoned on false charges. There are good, honest cops out there, but the way I see it, one corrupt cop is one too many."

"You were police, yes?"

"That's right," I say, "and when it comes to wearing a badge, there's no room for anything except honest policing."

"And you were an honest cop?"

"I tried to be . . . never took anyone's freedom that didn't deserve it. I protected the public. Kept communities safe."

"Sure, sure, but this belief that police are targeting Black people. It's like a conspiracy, no?"

"It's because I was a cop that I know it's not a conspiracy—it's how it is, and it's probably going to be that way forever. Plenty of offenders of all skin shades deserve prison, but if one innocent person is locked up, it means the system has failed."

"Nothing's perfect, Mr. Finnegan. I'm sure you know that."

"Would you say that if most of the innocent people dead or in prison looked like you?"

"And you think you can save Avery from this fate?"

"I can try."

"And if you fail, you will pay me. Otherwise, I will have to do things—far more terrible things than you could ever imagine. Not only to you but—"

"I get it."

"Good," he says, coming from the kitchen with the cleaver in his palm. "Then, we are in agreement . . ."

"Either Avery pays you, or I pay you. If no one pays you, you start hurting people. Pretty sure I've got it."

He runs the well-whetted blade across the bungee cords; they snap and fly across the room. "You can go," he says before whistling loudly.

A barrage of men enter through the door. First, a man in a puffer coat, followed by others, each with a severe look, as if murder is never far from their minds. The man in the puffer coat pulls a black hood from his pocket and throws it over my head. Someone puts my badge in my pocket, along with my phone and the stun gun. They never found my switchblade, having failed to search my right ankle.

I'm forced to walk.

Outside, we enter an elevator. It's a short ride down, then more walking in what feels like a windy corridor. I hear the opening of a gate, and after a few more steps, I'm ordered to stop. I recognize the squeaking brakes of the SUV I'd been forced into, and again I'm thrown across the leather seats. The man removes the hood, and the door slams. The tinted windows are obsidian and coated in a film that blurs everything. It's difficult to know where I've been, but the unique odors of pomegranate and tarragon fanning in the air means it's likely the ethnic enclave called Russian Town.

"What about my gun?" I ask, digging in my pocket and ensuring the hard drive is still there. "I'm going to need my piece back."

The driver turns around and smiles; his gold-plated teeth are encrusted with letters spelling "Suck it." His teeth are as ridiculous as his shearling hat—we aren't in the middle of a Serbian winter. "You'll get your gun when you're dropped off," he says.

He pulls away from the curb and begins driving. After a series of turns, we merge onto the highway.

"You would've been great in the last *Die Hard* flick," I say. "Russian Bad Guy number one. Straight out of central casting."

"Ethnic jokes? Really, Mr. Finnegan?"

It's an unexpected retort, and while the man and his comrades are bonafide assholes, he's right. "Low blow," I say. "Not my usual style."

"Let's keep things professional," the man says, his eyes like daggers in the rearview.

Pop's insensitive musings are rubbing off on me. "The movie was shit anyway."

"Ordinarily, I'd beat you until your eyes bled," the man says, "but I respect what you're doing for your brother. It is admirable. Family is everything."

I correct him: "Half-brother, and how'd you hear us talking?"

"We are always in communication." He points to a small radio in his ear. "Avery is an idiot, but you seem decent and wise," he says. "Keisha did not deserve that kind of ending. What will you do if you find this mysterious person who is responsible?"

"I don't know."

"Yes, you do," he says. "Men like us always know."

"Men like us?"

The SUV stops hard, and I'm rocked forward. "Shit, man! Easy on the brakes."

"Get out."

"With pleasure."

He hands me my pistol and magazine. "You have no bullets. I removed them."

"Are you going to give them back?"

"No. Shut the door and walk away."

I curse him under my breath as I get out, then slam the door. The SUV speeds off, cutting in and out of lanes until I can no longer see it in the distance. It takes me a minute to get my bearings—I'm on Las Vegas Boulevard, near the Palazzo with hordes of tourists. I've always hated Vegas, more so after this visit. I used to be able to stomach a weekend here, but after this trip, I have no intentions of ever returning.

The Strip stinks of desperation and soulless consumerism. I wonder if having a gambling addiction is a consequence of living here, or if people seek out this coruscant dumpster fire of a city because of their addictions.

Avery was raised not far from the casinos' golden lights and syncopated fountain. He probably frequented the Strip, walked its sticky boulevard, and saw things that a child shouldn't. Nothing like me growing up sheltered in the LA burbs—it was boring, but for a kid, especially a Black one, boring is good. Boring means you stayed out of the criminal justice system, far from juvenile hall, and I have Pop to thank for that. Even though living under his roof caused emotional trauma I'm still recovering from, having a father present made all the difference. And for Avery, not having one did, too.

My cell phone rings—Sarada's calling. "Hello?"

"Hey, Babe! What's going on? I haven't heard from you," she says, her voice taut with fervency. "I was getting worried. Where are you?"

"Vegas."

"What are you doing there?"

"Making headway in Avery's case. He's been arrested for Keisha's murder."

"What? I don't understand. How?"

"The physical evidence was enough to bring charges, but it's far from delivering the full picture of what happened that night. I still have more questions than answers."

"My God," she says. "They really think he did it?"

"For now," I say. "Until I get to the truth."

"You sound exhausted."

"I'm working against the clock. Have to sleep when I can."

"I don't like the sound of that."

"Everything's under control, Babe."

She sighs, and I imagine her purging precarious thoughts from her mind. "Just, please, be careful, Trevor."

"Always."

"How's your father handling things?"

"About that . . ."

"Don't tell me—"

"He drank."

"How'd he manage to get alcohol?"

"Long story, but it's under control—everything's under control."

"You keep saying that . . ."

"I'll call you when I'm back in LA."

"Please remember to pick me up from LAX."

"How could I forget?"

"I know how things can get in your way."

"Those were emergencies, babe. Out of my control."

"I get that," she says. "And I don't hold it against you."

"I'll be there—I promise."

"I know you will, but give yourself enough time. Traffic could be bad on Christmas Day."

"Don't worry. Everything will be fine."

"I love you, Trevor."

"Love you, too."

Sarada hangs up, and I dial the driver. "It's me," I say. "I need a ride."

"Where are you?"

"I'm sending it to you now." I use the phone's "Share My Location" feature to send him my whereabouts. "You got my coordinates?"

"Confirmed. On my way."

I end the call and wait. Ten minutes later, the sedan arrives, and I get in. The driver examines my face. "Sir, may I ask what happened?"

"A minor abduction," I say. "More of a misunderstanding."

"Ms. Boyle will not be pleased."

"Last I checked, it was my face."

"I had explicit instructions to make sure no harm came to you."

"Really? Why's that?"

"It's what Ms. Boyle requested. She was very clear that I was to keep you safe." He repeats, "She will not be pleased."

"It's not your fault, man," I say, tapping the lump in the back of my head to gauge its firmness. "I've had worse concussions."

"Sir, you're bleeding above your right eye."

I touch a gash near my eyebrow and flinch. Blood collects on my fingers. "Damn."

The driver hands me a tissue. "Would you like me to kill them?"

I nearly choke on the air. "Kill who?"

"The men who harmed you," he says blankly. "Would you like them dead?"

"No, I don't think that'll be necessary. Wouldn't know where to find them, anyway. They did the old hood-over-head bit."

"We have resources."

"It's OK, really. Don't worry about it." Realizing I never got the driver's name, "What do I even call you?"

"Driver."

"Of course, Driver," I say, dabbing more blood with the tissue. "Let's skip the killing, and you drive me to the jet hangar. I've had enough Vegas to last a lifetime."

"Yes, sir," he says, shifting into drive and pulling into traffic.

I keep the tissue pressed to the gash. The warm red steadily soaks through the single-ply until I'm forced to ask for the entire box. It takes a handful of tissues and firm pressure before the bleeding stops.

If Avery is dimwitted enough to get mixed up with the Russian mob, finding trouble in Malibu isn't a stretch for him. But what could he have possibly gotten involved in that would've ended in Keisha's death?

"On second thought," I say. "You think the pilots can fly me to Chino?"

"Where's Chino?"

"It's about thirty miles outside of LA."

"Let me check with Ms. Boyle," he says. "One moment." The driver dials and takes the call over his wireless headset. Minutes later, he says, "The pilots will be notified of the itinerary change."

EIGHT

I haven't visited Sally Munoz at the California Institution for Women in weeks. After our last conversation, she refused to see me. She was angry and bitter, and rightfully so. The persistent threats from other inmates and harassment from piggish guards had brought out the worst in her. All prisons are dens of suffering, but ex-cops are condemned to Dante's lowest circles of purgatory. While Sally did everything to put herself here, I abandoned her—something a partner should never do—and I've been trying to make up for it since her incarceration.

The visitation room is full of inmates and their families. Children's laughter does little to conceal broken hearts. Christmas is coming, but for many inmates, it's another holiday away from their loved ones, and no amount of tinsel and garlands will make them see anything except the brick and metal that keep them caged.

A guard unshackles Sally. She sits down and stares across from me. Both of her eyes are puffy and borderline swollen. It could be from poor sleep, but more likely they're injuries from a fight. I don't ask. Considering the gash above my brow, I shouldn't be questioning her appearance, and I prefer she doesn't question mine.

"Looks like the toy drive is picking up," I say, noticing more gifts around the artificial tree. "That'll put some smiles on kids' faces."

"What are you doing here, Finn? We had an agreement."

"I need your help."

"This isn't really the place people come to for help."

"It's about a case."

"I'm sure there's someone else you can call on." She readies her hand to signal the guard to end our visit. "I'm going back to my cell."

"Sally . . . will you listen a second?"

"I've got shit to do," she says. "I'm halfway through Connelly's latest paperback, and I want to finish it by Christmas, so find someone else to pester."

"Please, Sally," I say. "Hear me out, and if you've got no answers for me, then I'll leave."

"You'll fuck off, you mean."

"Sure, Sally, whatever. I'll fuck off."

She huffs and looks at the clock on the wall. "You've got five minutes."

"It's my half-brother. He's been arrested for homicide."

"Didn't think you had siblings. Then again, there's a lot I didn't know about you, isn't there?"

"It's a long story."

"Always is, with you . . . So, what do you need from me?"

"It happened in Malibu."

"That's a twist. What's their murder rate—one per decade?"

"There's a narrative that's shaping," I say. "The sheriff and DA think Avery and his girlfriend were under the influence of narcotics, running around Malibu at night in rags. There was a sighting of them near a university campus. Hours later, his girlfriend, Keisha, is dead with her head bashed in a marsh near the canyons. And I find Avery bloodied and disoriented on the highway."

"You found him?"

"My father and I."

"What's Avery say happened?"

"His mind is all jumbled. There's no way to know what caused it, but he recalls things as slivers in time. He drew an insect. So far, it's the only thing he recollects."

"A bug?"

"Cicada."

"Didn't know they had those in Malibu."

"Me either. They were being housed at a nature preserve that Avery and his girlfriend broke into. I think they were running from someone."

"You said the female was found near the canyons?"

"Yeah, in a marshland."

"And the clothes . . . what do you mean, rags?"

"I'm still waiting on the analysis, but they looked like costumes for a production of *Les Misérables* or something."

"So they were rags or just meant to look like it?"

"Definitely not rags. Aside from the blood, dirt, and some fraying, they looked new."

"Strange."

"No kidding," I say. "Have you ever heard of anything like this happening up there?"

Sally looks at the clock. I'm nearing her five-minute hard stop, but she's intrigued. "People used to go missing there a lot," she says. "Re-emerging days, even weeks later, with no memory of why they were there in the first place . . . but that was many years ago. Before the internet and Facebook. Now, someone goes missing for twelve hours, and people are already posting about it."

"How long has this been going on?"

"Heard about it first in the late nineties. A young girl—a Black female in her teens—was hiking or camping with her little brother. I can't remember the specifics, but they both disappeared. The Sheriff's Department called them runaways. Claimed they wanted to escape life at home with their foster parents. After the community pressured the department to take action, deputies launched a search effort with help from a nonprofit for missing and abducted children run by your late employer."

"David Bergman had a nonprofit?"

"You didn't know? I remember his face being on TV every night, talking about those missing kids. He even threatened to sue the Sheriff's Department if they didn't take the missing kid's case more seriously."

"How do you remember all this?"

"They were from South Gate. We lived four blocks from their foster parents' house. Posters of the girl and her brother hung everywhere—near parks, the mall, and schools. They were part of the community. It could've happened to any of us. The entire ordeal hit close to home."

"Did they find them?"

"A month later, the girl was found wandering on a beach. No recollection of where or what she'd been doing." Sally sighs, kneading her temple. "God, what was her name?"

"And the boy?"

"Discovered by hikers floating in a ravine. He'd been beaten and shot in the head. Someone killed him and stuffed him in a plastic drum like the ones on the freeways that collect rainwater."

"Damn . . . how do I not remember this?"

"Slipped under most people's radars," she says. "Back then, news like that didn't make headlines. No one reported on Black and brown victims unless their killings were gang-related."

"But a little boy . . ."

"In a way, the case made me want to be a cop. Seeing how nobody gave a damn about them. They deserved better." Sally gazes at the ceiling. "What was her name?" She drums a pattern on the table. "That's it . . . Sharice Murphy. No, not Murphy—Mitchell. Her last name was Mitchell."

"Visiting ends in five minutes," the guard shouts. "Got it? Five minutes! Not a second after."

"Shame about your brother," she says. "And about Bergman. I heard what Boston did to him. It was all over the news. An absolute shitty way to go."

"Still can't believe he's gone," I say. "We had our differences, but David was family."

"I get that," she says. "And you don't want to lose another family member."

"It's not only about me, but it's Pop, too," I say, feeling the weight of Avery's predicament on my shoulders. "He refuses to believe Avery would kill his girlfriend, and so far, there's no explanation as to why he was beaten when I found him."

"OK, but what if you find out otherwise? Say he had a role in it. Maybe they got mixed up with the wrong people. He got away, and she didn't."

"Everyone keeps asking me that."

"Well?"

"I'm prepared. Whatever the outcome, I'll deal with it."

"You've got the head for it," she says. "Stay objective and stick with it until you get your answers."

"It's all I know how to do," I say. "I appreciate your help, Sally."

"Anything to keep my mind off the shit going on in this place."

"Have you found a new attorney yet?"

"No one that'll work for what I can pay, but the public defender isn't a complete gilipollas. I mostly tell him what to do, and he listens. No different than being married, I guess." She simpers like she's been waiting to tell the joke for ages.

I can't recall the last time I saw Sally smile; she's still hoping for an appeal, and hope is gold behind bars. "Things must be going all right, then? Considering . . ."

"I can finally see it, Finn. Like it's clear to me."

"What's that?"

"A way out—a way back to my kids," she whispers. "Remember the deal I told you about?"

"Turning over evidence to the State on Cassandra?"

"They want it all, Finn. Everything I've got, and I'm going to give it to them."

"But Sally—"

"I'm not the only one. Others are cooperating."

"Who?"

"You didn't hear it from me, but whoever they are, they know the inner workings of her operations. I'm talking about details, the odds and ends. Cassandra's made enemies, Finn, and now it's all coming back to bite her in the ass."

"But how, Sally? The woman has been untouchable for decades."

"Which is why I'm convinced the informants are in tight with her—close associates, people who've worked with her for years. Family, maybe . . ."

"Family?"

"Time's up," the guard says. "Let's get back to our cells, ladies! No lollygagging, either. Line up and file out."

Guards shackle the women. Sally knows the drill; she's conditioned. She stands, holding out her arms. The guard clicks the bracelets around her wrists and nudges her forward.

"You should get that looked at," she says, pointing at my gash. "Might get infected."

"Yeah," I say, my fingers poking the swollen tissue.

Sally drifts into the line of inmates and doesn't look back.

Before leaving the prison, I collect my firearm, stun gun, switchblade, and hard drive from the guard's station and order an Uber back to Cassandra's place. I stand in front of the large concrete wall that circles the institution—a brutalist fortress in the middle of cow country. The app's GPS estimates the driver will take twenty minutes to arrive and over two hours to drop me in Malibu. I welcome the long ride. I haven't slept well in days and plan to nap. But Tori's text is nagging at me. I skim it again, searching for mention of Simone, relieved when there's none.

Tori asserts the same concerns as her last text—no job, worried about the future, feeling overwhelmed. I want to be supportive, but I fear she needs more from me than I can give. I don't know what governs our relationship. Are we friends outside of being parents? How much of her struggles should she be unloading to me? We share a child, and Simone's well-being is my foremost concern, but Tori's needs could affect how she cares for Simone, and I want nothing more than for my child to be safe.

I dial Tori. On the fourth ring, she answers. "Trevor?"

"Tori."

"It's nice to hear your voice."

"Is everything all right? How's Simone?"

"She's good . . . Perfect, as always."

"OK."

"She's such a blessing—you know that?"

"I do."

"Not sure how I got so lucky. I mean, I treated my parents horribly. Even though they deserved it, I still could've been better."

"Simone still has time," I joke. "We haven't even gotten to the teenage years yet."

Tori sucks her teeth. "You would say that." She's terse, annoyed. "I don't need that right now."

"I didn't mean for it to come off insensitive."

"I know how you meant it."

"You want to tell me what's going on, Tori? You seem—"

"Frustrated? Because I am. I made a mistake coming back here." She sounds more distant than ever. "Things were better in Vancouver."

"Better? Are you sure of that?"

"OK. Maybe not better, but I was happier."

"So you want to go back to Canada? That's what this is about?"

"I don't know . . . Maybe . . . I think, yeah, maybe I do."

"What about Simone?"

"I had a village in Vancouver. People looked after her."

"But they weren't family—they weren't me."

She sniffs, and I expect tears. "No, but I could count on them."

"You're saying I'm unreliable?"

She doesn't respond. Perhaps her silence is her answer.

"I wouldn't be able to see her very often," I say, warming with emotions. "I need to be in her life. That's the reason you came back to LA, right?"

"I'm losing it here, Trevor. Don't you understand that? I'm not like you. I can't just go on like that madman in the White House isn't going to destroy this country."

"You think I'm not worried?"

"Everyone is acting like it's normal. Even my mother refuses to acknowledge what it means to give a man like that power. This country just handed him the keys to the goddamn nuclear arsenal."

"I know . . . but what can we do about it? The country elected him, and honestly, they'll probably do it again."

"And that sits right with you?"

"Of course not, but I've been living in this country as a Black man my entire life, and nothing shocks me anymore."

"I'm sorry, Trevor. I can't raise Simone here—I won't."

"Can we discuss this in person? Let's meet tomorrow."

"Tomorrow? Aren't you still in France?"

"Never made it," I say, knowingly lighting a fuse. "It's complicated, but I got stuck working a case."

"You've been here the entire time, *working*?"

"Yes, but—"

"And you didn't bother to tell me or see Simone?" Her voice breaks with tears. "I can't believe you."

"I'm sorry. I wanted to tell you, but this case is—"

"Goodbye, Trevor."

"Hold on, Tori. Just give me a second. Please?"

"I don't know why I thought us coming back to LA would make you change. You've always put your work first. When we were together, I knew where I fell on your list of priorities, but Simone deserves better. She deserves a father who will be present . . . a father who won't hide from her."

"I wasn't hiding . . ." The Uber driver arrives. "Ah, shit. I have to go."

"What else is new?"

"Please give me a chance to explain. I'll meet you tonight. Anywhere you'd like."

"You're always begging for second chances, Trevor. When will it end?"

"Just this once," I say. "For Simone."

"Fine."

"Tell me when and where, and I'll be there."

"Tomorrow night at seven," she says, sucking in tears. "My place."

"OK, and Tori, I'm sorry—"

The call ends abruptly.

The Uber driver honks twice and waves his hand out the window. He's lost patience, and I worry the drive won't be pleasant, but I can't wait another twenty minutes for a driver willing to make the trip to Malibu.

I get in the back of the compact SUV. The burly driver in the striped beanie says nothing. Once I close the door, he presses the gas, and I struggle to put my seat belt on. The smell of marijuana overpowers the honeydew air freshener shaped like a tree dangling from the rearview mirror. When our eyes meet in the mirror, his disposition beckons a quarrel. Given my hostile mood, I want to oblige him, but arguing all the way to Malibu with a stranger won't help my cause. Besides, I can't risk him putting me out on the freeway.

After ten minutes of driving, it becomes apparent the driver is adept at the silent game. There's no pointless chit-chat or an attempt to alleviate the tension, which suits me fine. My thoughts are on Simone. Was it foolish to believe I'd watch her grow up? Walk her to class on her first day of school, sit on the sideline at soccer games, shower her with flowers after a dance recital . . . maybe comfort her after her first heartbreak? I've indulged in a dream, knowing I'd never escape the curse that plagues my family. Pop was right when he said, "Finnegans court disaster"; it overshadows any good that comes our way, and I pray Simone can evade its hold.

I search for the name Sharice Mitchell on my phone's browser. Multiple articles appear. The *LA Times* and *Los Angeles Sentinel* covered her and her brother's story. The articles describe her as a runaway with a history of drug and larceny charges, and her brother, a supposed gang member at age thirteen. Sally was correct—the Sheriff's Department asserted the two had escaped their foster home, and the department refused search efforts for a week. When Bergman's organization pushed for action, deputies searched the canyons for ten days before suspending their efforts, citing cost and limited resources as factors.

Sharice was the victim, but every mention of her background seems to eclipse what she went through. She said she was abducted but couldn't remember much about the culprits, and that was met with scrutiny—a deputy suggested she had lied; other deputies, some higher ranked, parroted the same.

The *LA Times* article ends with Sharice surmising: "I guess it could've happened to anybody. I'm just happy to be alive." But it couldn't have happened to *just* anybody. It happened to Sharice and victims like her and her brother—young, Black, poor—people overlooked every day because their peril measures as minuscule in the eyes of most. It fails to motivate law enforcement and doesn't demand coverage on the evening news.

I've known it for a long time, but when I joined the LAPD, it became clearer to me. Some people are disposable and devalued. Maybe that's what Tori senses? She wants to protect Simone from the cruelty of living in a place like this, where a young Black girl can be abducted and harmed, and no one believes her story.

Is it possible to shield Simone from the horrors that happen to children and women every day in this country? Is raising Simone in Canada the answer? Thinking about the homicide victims of the past—the bodies I've stood over—there's an undeniable truth: from their first breath, women are prey for all things wicked, but Black women suffer at a tremendous rate, and their suffering is routinely met with staggering apathy.

It's early evening when the Uber driver parks in Cassandra's driveway, and I exit the car. A barefoot Nigel is still repairing the Falcon in the garage, and from his sweaty tunic, it looks like he's been at it for hours.

"How was your trip?" he asks, chewing on licorice root. "Beneficial, I hope?"

"Hard to say, but I could use your help with something."

"What's that you've got?" He looks at the dusty hard drive in my hand. "Haven't seen that model in a while."

I give him the hard drive for inspection. "I need to know what's on it."

"It's certainly seen better days," he says, dusting it off with the palm of his hand.

"And I've got a name for you: Sharice Mitchell. I'm hoping she's still a resident of LA County, but I can't be sure. You think you could find her address?"

"If she's alive, I'll find her."

"Thanks, Nigel."

"What happened?" he asks, noticing the crusted wound above my eye.

"A couple of guys roughed me up . . . it finally stopped hurting an hour ago."

"You'll find an assortment of bandages in the medicine cabinet in the guest bathroom."

"You're a lifesaver," I say. "Is Cassandra around?"

"She's meditating in the greenhouse."

"Mind if I make myself a sandwich? I'm starving."

"I'd be happy to make it for you if you give me a moment."

"I'm not used to the full service around here," I say. "You've done enough. As a matter of fact, do you need something? Bottled water . . . lotus flower kombucha?"

"No need, Mr. Finnegan. I'm fine."

"OK, then."

I enter the kitchen from the garage, wash my hands in the sink, and dig in the refrigerator until I find deli-sliced turkey, pickles, Swiss cheese, and sourdough bread. I slather the bread with organic honey mustard and hastily arrange the sandwich before stuffing it into my mouth. I wrap the food in a paper towel, carry it upstairs into the bedroom, and set it on the dresser. I reload my pistol with the extra magazine in my duffle and curse the Russians for taking my bullets in Vegas.

Looking through the bathroom's medicine cabinet, I find antibiotic ointment and a butterfly bandage. I wash the wound with soapy water, dry it well, and apply the ointment and bandage. It stings like hell and will likely scar.

My cell phone rings. I hesitate to answer, dreading it might be Tori. She might've changed her mind about seeing me. I read the Caller ID, but it's unknown. "Hello?"

"Mr. Finnegan, it's Deputy Cohen."

"Deputy? I wasn't expecting to hear from you."

"The analysis on the victim's clothing came back, and I think we should meet."

"You sure? I wouldn't want you catching flack for being seen with me."

"I know a place," he says. "It's discreet and we can wait until dusk."

"Address?"

"I'll text it to you."

I receive the text: coordinates off Highway 1. "See you around seven," I say.

I end the call and finish my sandwich before taking a shower. After getting cleaned up, I set the alarm on my cell phone for six o'clock and lay down on the bed to rest.

*

The alarm sounds, and I wake from my three-hour nap rejuvenated. As I go downstairs, the sun is just beginning to set, and there's no sign of Cassandra.

I step outside. In the driveway, Nigel is taking a break, observing a butterfly that has landed on the Falcon's hood. I watch as he coaxes the insect into his palm, brings it inches from his nose, and strokes its wings with his finger. "Leaving again?" he asks.

"Got a meeting."

"You're a man in perpetual motion, Mr. Finnegan."

"Is that a nice way of saying I don't know how to sit my ass down?"

"Just remember, rest isn't solely for the body, but the mind as well."

"Yeah, well, I got a little bit of that today. Pretty sure if I hadn't slept, I'd be fighting off a migraine right about now," I say. "How's the Falcon's repairs coming?"

"Give me another couple of days," he says. "I'll have it in proper working order."

Nigel deserves a tip—one hundred bones might cover it, but I know he won't take it, no matter how much I insist.

"As for the hard drive and searching the name, I'll get started after dinner," he says, releasing the butterfly and watching it ascend into the trees. "I should have information for you this evening."

"I owe you, Nigel."

"Not at all," he says. "Ms. Cassandra is very fond of you. Her help comes without expectancies."

I've been alive long enough to know people rarely do things without expecting something in return. I don't know Cassandra's angle yet, but I'm certain she has one.

I get into the Beemer, start it, and ease down the driveway headed to Cohen's clandestine meeting spot.

The coordinates direct me to a secondary road. Signs designate it as an evacuation route. In the aftermath of an earthquake, catastrophic flooding, or wildfires, Highway 1 might be impassable. The route offers a safer alternative, and today, it's picturesque—a view I'd expect to see on a postcard. Deputy Cohen's cruiser is parked in a turn-out, an inlet overlooking the ocean. He's leaning against the SUV, staring at the endless blue reflecting the setting sun becoming an inflamed dot on the horizon. I park and join him in tranquility.

"It's quiet here," I say, noting the scarcity of traffic passing by. "Peaceful."

"That's never been this town's problem. One thing it's got an abundance of is quiet."

A few vehicles carrying surfboards and bicycles on roof racks pass by. I watch for sheriff cruisers or any vehicle that slows down long enough to notice us.

"Reminds me of a painting," I say, taking in the ocean's splendor. "Ever hear of the artist Katsushika Hokusai?"

"Can't say I have."

"He painted waves," I say. "Looked very much like those." I point toward the breaking waves near the headland.

"So you're an art guy?"

"I paint a bit. Attended an arts high school as a kid. Thought it'd be a profession, but life put me on a different path."

Cohen taps his phone's screen. "Hokusai, you say?"

"That's right. H-o-k-u-s-a-i."

"Here he is," Cohen says. "Not bad. A few of these pieces would look nice in my apartment. I could use something to look at besides white walls."

"I used to know that feeling . . ."

"Storm's rolling in," he says.

"But there's not a cloud in the sky."

"Look that way." He points miles out where the sky begins to darken. "It should make landfall in a few days."

"A deputy and a meteorologist?"

"Nah, nothing that scientific," he says. "I used to be something of a surfer. You learn to spot those things. Coming storms meant good waves. Have you ever been surfing?"

"My father hates the beach. I never went as a kid, which has to be a crime living in Southern California. The closest thing to surfing for me was skateboarding empty swimming pools."

"Something tells me you would've liked growing up here," Cohen says. "Good surf. Plenty of wicked places to skate."

"I'm not so sure people around here would've felt the same way."

"Can't argue there," he says. "People like to think they're welcoming, you know? Well-meaning and all that, but there's a reason you move to places like Malibu, and it isn't to join in a melting pot. It feels far away from the rest of the world."

A chill sets in; I pocket my hands to combat goose flesh. "All this beauty in someone's backyard? It's like hitting the lottery or something. I get why people would gatekeep this place."

"Well, with the eroding cliffside and rising sea level, it's more glitter than gold these days. Still, plenty of folks around here will die before they move anywhere else. It's more than their home; it's a haven."

"From what?"

"I'd say anything that doesn't look, smell, or feel like everything else in this town."

"Sounds pretty elitist, don't you think?"

"More than a little," he says. "Where is it you live?"

"Sierra Madre."

"It's nice there," Cohen says. "Did some hiking in that area years back."

"It's an acquired taste . . . can't say I'd choose to die over moving if I had to, but it also doesn't have these ocean views." The brisk ocean air causes my eyes to water. I dab away the tears and remember why I've come. "So, what's this about Keisha and Avery's clothes you couldn't tell me over the phone?"

Cohen reaches into the cruiser's passenger-side window and removes a brown folder from the seat. "You were right," he says. "The clothing was hand-made." He opens the folder; inside are photos of the patchwork threads Keisha and Avery wore the night they were found. "They're reproductions."

"Of what?"

"Period pieces from the 1800s. There's a product number on each item." A close-up photo reveals a cloth label, numbered and sewn onto the garment. "I searched the number online and found the trousers Avery wore listed for sale on a website."

"The company?"

"American Heritage Supply Company, based in Kansas City, Missouri, specializes in attire for historical reenactments. Civil War stuff, mostly. Uniforms for battles and ceremonies, even suits and bridal wear for plantation-themed weddings. Avery's and Keisha's garments were categorized under 'Antebellum.'"

"Someone dressed them as enslaved people?"

He nods. "Stuff isn't cheap, either. Each piece runs over a thousand dollars."

"So racist cosplay takes serious cash flow," I say. "Has anyone been staging Civil War battles up here?"

"It's not really the vibe in Malibu, but ten years ago, St. Catherine's showcased items like these as part of an early American history exhibit."

"Don't tell me they dressed people as slaves."

"God, no. The history department displayed period-correct outfits like these as part of the exhibit . . . *The Malibu Times* even reviewed it. Called it a 'visceral experience.'"

"How do you know all this?"

"I was a student then—a history major. I helped out with curation. It was the brainchild of our department chair."

"This chair got a name?"

"Alastair Webb," he says. "The exhibit was such a success that the university made him the chancellor the following year."

"And you became a cop?"

"You know how it is," Cohen says. "I thought about becoming a history teacher. Getting high schoolers to love this stuff as much as I do, but we cops' kids don't have much choice, do we? The damn siren call is too loud."

"No argument there. What else can you tell me about the supply company?"

"I'm afraid it's selling more than clothing." He looks uneasy, like his stomach has turned to jelly. "Their website advertises working chains modeled after ones used to bind enslaved people during transport and on the auction block."

"You showed this to Brennan?"

"I put it on her desk myself. But look, Detective—"

"Trevor is fine."

"I prefer Detective if it's all the same to you . . ."

"All right."

"Nobody can know you've seen this. Word gets out that I'm leaking information, and I'm washed."

A tractor-trailer approaches, stirring sand and debris. Cohen squints and puts his back to the road, shielding himself from blowing sand. I do the same until the truck passes.

Cohen fans the lingering dust and continues, "If Brennan realizes it's me, she'll have me removed from the investigation and maybe the station."

"It stays in the vault," I say, snapping photos of the file's pages with my phone.

"You're riding alone today?"

"My father's ill."

"I hope it isn't serious."

"Pop will be fine. He's not the lie-down-and-die type."

"My father was the same way until he wasn't," Cohen says. "If I'm being honest, Detective, this case makes me nervous. I've got a feeling things are going to end badly."

"With my track record, the odds are high."

"Just be careful," he says. "You could be kicking a hornet's nest."

"That's the thing, Deputy—I'm counting on it."

NINE

The following morning, I head to St. Catherine University. I spend twenty minutes strolling the campus before locating the chancellor's office situated in an administration building. Outside the office, a wild-haired girl is seated at a desk beside a door displaying a brass plate with the name Alastair Webb. She wears a heather gray collegiate hoodie featuring the school's peace dove mascot on the front, cleverly altered by replacing the dove's head with that of an ape, showcasing her sewing talent.

The space can best be described as a lobby, but it seems more like an afterthought: a lone potted plant is pushed into the corner, a few chairs, and a coffee table with magazines confined by mahogany paneled walls. Framed oil paintings of white men in paisley suits tell of the school's history—past chancellors and presidents. The portraits are from an era when posing with a pipe or at a desk with a smoldering cigar in an ashtray was meant to exude nobility and dignity, despite many colleges and universities being founded with money made from African enslavement.

"May I help you?" the girl asks, looking up from a textbook. Her hair is blonde with pink streaks and seems to be teased into a style that I can only describe as a bird's nest. She has a lip ring and ear piercings along her cartilage to her lobes: rainbow-colored hoops of varying sizes. She reminds me of the grunge and punk-loving kids I went to high school with.

"Nice sweatshirt," I say. "You got a thing for apes?"

"Not really," she says. "But it fits this place more than a dove."

"Not sure I follow . . ."

"Greed, man. That's what apes represent, dating back to the thirteenth century."

"So, it's a protest thing?"

"Call it what you want—it's fashion."

"I respect that."

"Is there something I can help you with besides fashion tips?"

"I'd like to speak to Chancellor Webb."

"Appointment?"

"Afraid not. Is he in?"

"Unavailable."

"That doesn't exactly answer my question." I point toward the door. "Is he in the office?"

"I'm sorry, maybe I wasn't clear." She rolls her eyes. "He's out for the day."

"Might've been easier telling me that up front."

"Everyone knows you won't find the chancellor on campus," she says. "Which means you're not a student, and you definitely don't work here, so what is it you need Chancellor Webb for?"

"Are you paid enough to ask these kinds of questions?"

"Dude, I'm on a work-study."

"So, that's a *no*," I say. "When will the esteemed chancellor return?"

"How about you leave your name and number? I'll be sure he calls you when he gets in." She sets her book aside, picks up a pen, and snatches a sticky note from a pad. "Name?"

"On second thought, I'll come back later."

"It doesn't matter how many times you come back. He won't be here."

"And why's that?"

"Because he's rarely here."

"You mean in his office?"

"No, on campus," she says. "He's always traveling or off fundraising for the school."

"So why bother with the sticky note?"

"Dude, I'm just being courteous, and I kinda want you to leave. I have exams to study for."

"Answer my questions, and you get back to your"—I crane my neck to see the textbook's spine—"Applied Physics."

"OK . . . so, what's your question?"

"Is the chancellor fundraising today?"

"Nope," she says, tossing the pen and sticky note aside. "He's busy preparing for his favorite night of the year."

"Favorite night?"

"Uh-huh."

"Can you elaborate?"

Her tongue tickles her lip ring as she eases back in her chair. "First, tell me why you're here."

"I'm selling life insurance. Ten percent off for St. Catherine's staff."

"An insurance salesman? You'll have to do better than that."

"Don't knock it," I say. "Going on my twelfth year. It's my passion."

"You want information from me, then give me the truth."

"OK—I'm an investigator." I show her my PI badge. "She looks away when she's satisfied. "I'm working a case."

"Shit . . . you're investigating Chancellor Webb, aren't you? What'd the old man do?"

"What makes you think I'm investigating Webb?"

The chair squeals as she leans forward. I've got her full attention now. "You'll understand when you meet him," she says. "Guy's perfected making the hair on my neck stand to attention."

"Then, why work for him?"

"Pays the most out of all the work-studies," she says. "And free pizza on Thursdays."

"Sound reasoning, I guess."

"I'm a broke student, and as long as he doesn't hit on me or touch me, I'm good," she says. "Not that I'm his type anyway . . ."

"How about we forego the innuendo?"

"All right," she says. "Let's just say I think the chancellor would do well if he were to live his truth."

"What the hell does that mean?"

It means he's jolliest when the football players come around."

"Aren't college athletes basically celebrities on campuses these days?"

"Maybe when they're on a winning team," she says. "Have you seen our record?"

"I don't get it. Are you saying Chancellor Webb is or isn't a football fan?"

"Oh, he's a fan, just not of the game. The players are another story, especially ones that look like you."

"So, he's got a thing for the Black players?"

"Probably," she says. "But it's hard to know where his interest lies. He's got one of those dead-fish faces. Expressionless. You never know if it's admiration or contempt."

"I take it that he's not your favorite person? Is that why you're telling me all this?"

"Webb's a neocon who's invested the school's pension in military weapons manufacturing and questionable tech stocks. He's the worst thing that ever happened to St. Catherine's, and the founders of this school literally enslaved people, so it's saying a lot. But as long as he brings in the big bucks from donors, the board of regents turn a blind eye to his agenda."

"What agenda would that be?"

"World domination—what else?"

"So, he's Lex Luthor?"

"Let's just say, if you are investigating him, I'm not surprised, and you shouldn't be surprised by anything you uncover. The man's got secrets."

"And you got all this dirt from doing a work-study job outside his office?"

"You'd be shocked by what people openly discuss when they think you're invisible."

"So, where can I find him?"

"It's no big revelation," she says. "He's at his beach house getting ready for the annual St. Catherine's Holiday Party that happens in a couple of days. The whole school knows it's like *his* thing. You probably could've asked the janitor, and they would've told you."

"A holiday party . . . people still have those? I thought they were considered high-risk situations for employees. Nightmares for HR."

"Not at St. Catherine's, apparently. I heard the chancellor goes all out. Unlimited food, cocktails, and champagne. And that means plenty of drunk professors, so yeah, 'high-risk' is a good word for it."

"Since you know so much, do you have an address for this party?"

"Dude, even if I did, I wouldn't tell you. I'm not an idiot. Besides, it's Malibu, and if you are a real investigator, you won't have trouble finding it," she says. "Rich people like to show off, and Webb shits money. Just look for the biggest mansion in Malibu Estates. That's where a lot of the wealthy people live around here."

"Is that supposed to be a luxury housing community?"

"More like a town within a town," she says. "There are acres of beachfront properties and like ten golf courses. There's even a supermarket, school, and post office—it'll make you choke."

"Why am I not shocked that you didn't get an invite?"

"Fuck that party, bro," she says. "But if you are planning to crash it, watch yourself. Security is armed, from what I hear."

"I appreciate the heads up."

"Sure, and I hope whatever you find on Webb sticks. People like him always get away with shit."

"People like Webb?"

"Yeah," she says. "The rich, immoral cretins of the world. If they had their way, they'd privatize everything essential and replace half of us with AI robots."

"Oh, boy," I say. "Maybe you ought to lay off the sci-fi."

"I read speculative fiction, and trust me, it's closer to reality than you think. You just wait and see."

TEN

Nigel calls as I'm driving back to Cassandra's place. He's out of breath, and I can hear him slurping down a refreshment as though he's finished a hot yoga session. I imagine it to be water with mint, lemon, and sea salt . . . maybe cucumber.

"Everything all right, Nigel?"

"Apologies," he says. "I was rearranging some things in the garage. I took a break to update you."

"Man, these days, it seems like you're living in that garage. Not that I'm unappreciative, but I hope there's a vacation in your future."

"As Ms. Cassandra likes to say, living in Malibu means we're on permanent *vacay*."

"Not really how that's supposed to work," I say. "What's up?"

"I have an address for Sharice Mitchell."

"Can you text it to my phone? I'm driving."

"Sure, but that's not all," he says. "I cracked the encryption on the hard drive rather easily."

"Let's hear it . . ."

"There were images . . . lots of images." He clears his throat. "Some were . . . disturbing."

I round the bluffs and turn into a small parking lot for a lookout point so I can give Nigel my full attention. "How disturbing are we talking here?" I ask, cutting the engine.

"The pictures are arranged in folders labeled by month and publication. Some are standard-looking submissions for websites and risqué magazines like *Black Tail*, *Ebony Bottoms*, *Pretty Brown Round* . . ."

"I get the idea, Nigel."

"One folder is labeled 'X' and contains what some might say borders on debased artistry. The woman—"

"Keisha?"

"I believe so. She's bound with ropes. Sometimes chains. In one photo, she's screaming . . . Tears are in her eyes . . . I don't understand how people find this material erotic."

"Kinks," I say. "Pain and violence can be arousing for some. I want to know whether Keisha took those photos by choice or if someone forced her to do so."

"I'm far too prudish for that world. I had a strong urge to shower afterward."

"You shouldn't have the stomach for it, and that's a good thing. People who do are wired differently."

"I'm sure it's staged, right? It has to be." Nigel wants to debunk the images as shock fare, but it's impossible to know if Keisha's suffering is authentic or a morbid performance.

It doesn't hurt to lie if it makes Nigel feel better. "Hard to tell, but yeah," I say, "they're probably staged."

It isn't the first time I've come across salacious material of a sexual nature. Three years out of the academy, I caught a vice case. A pimp had branched out into child pornography and sold pictures of minors to the highest bidders online. My soul burned to look at those images. I tried to convince myself they weren't real—image augmentation and age-reducing software had hit the market, but the images opened a pathway that spoke to me like a demon in my ear, telling me all the horrible things that happened in the darkest recesses of humanity—hellish and unnatural things. That day, I faced a world built upon depravity and suffering, separated from goodness and decency, and I mourned the victimized children that I couldn't save.

"Email me the folder," I say. "And Nigel, it's probably best Cassandra doesn't see the pictures. It could be triggering after what her daughters have gone through."

"I'll take proper care. Sending you the folders now."

"Thank you."

"Goodbye, Mr. Finnegan."

My phone chimes. Nigel has forwarded the folders to my inbox. I open the one labeled "X." It's as he described—the images deviate from the "sex-positive" distinction I've heard used in mental health circles regarding sexual exploration and embrace the grotesque. Were Keisha and Avery submitting this kind of "work"? And what type of publication would accept images like these?

Looking at the pictures gives me the same queasy feeling I had as a kid finding Pop's stash of skin mags under his mattress. I saw the lurid covers but never looked at the pages. I was afraid seeing a woman spread-eagled and nude would change how I thought about all women . . . and that meant my mother and aunts and Sarada. I was a sensitive romantic who saw women in verse, graceful couplets, and as mysterious keepers of secrets that I longed to know one day, but the pictures in the skin mags weren't any of that. They were something else in which love and adoration factored little; instead, what excreted from the pages was cheap and adulterated.

I enter Sharice's address into my phone's mapping app. It'll take me forty-five minutes to arrive at her residence in Downey. I tune the radio to smooth jazz, something I rarely do. Alternative and old-school hip-hop compose the soundtrack to my life, but 94.7 FM, *The Wave*, keeps my mind off undesirable things like Keisha's photos and her being found dead in slave cosplay attire.

I start the engine, turn up the volume, and endeavor to think only about the coastal drive ahead.

The address Nigel texted to me wasn't for a residence at all. It was for the Eternal Light Church on Paramount Boulevard. It's almost one p.m. when I park in the large lot enclosed by rod iron fencing. It isn't Sunday, but music plays from inside. Not wanting to disturb the service, I sit in the car for ten minutes until the music ends.

As I walk toward the door, music starts up again, and I recognize that I haven't attended a church service in a very long time. Not only are services held late afternoons midweek, but I've forgotten the order of events. *How many songs are sung before the sermon?*

I enter through a large wooden door. A stuffy odor greets me. Faded red carpeting, painted stained glass, and wood paneling are the earmarks of a church that looks to have been built in the 1960s or 1970s.

I sit in the pew along the back wall. A three-person band plays acoustic guitars and a piano for a congregation of ten. Song lyrics show on a projector screen as people sing. I presume a strawberry-blonde man, slight in stature, swaying and strumming his guitar with his eyes closed, is the minister of music. He's wearing a wrinkled flannel shirt, jeans, and Converse sneakers—as Pop would say, "It's one of those 'come as you are' churches." The man breaks from his spiritual trance, opens his eyes, and encourages members to "clap along" to a song with the composition of a nursery rhyme. I'm not religious anymore, but I appreciate traditional gospel hymns like "In the Upper Room" and recognize the value of a drummer and bassist, which are absent from the trio.

The piano player may be the best musician on stage and resembles a younger Sharice Mitchell. She pounds the keys, periodically turning her sheet music. I open my phone's browser, find one of the few photos of her taken after her abduction, and conduct a comparison. Naturally, she's older—her drooping face with weight gain around her neck, broader shoulders, and shorter hair, but it's indeed her in a snug-fitting Christmas sweater and matching tree-shaped earrings.

The music ends, and everyone is seated. A woman appears from the rear of the stage, passes an excessively decorated Christmas tree, and stands at the pulpit wearing a plus-size gold-trimmed white robe. With her arms outstretched, she greets her flock. "Good afternoon. I'm Pastor Karen Acevedo. I'd like to welcome our first-time visitors. Will you please stand and introduce yourselves?"

I stand and project my voice enough for Sharice to hear. "I'm Trevor," I say. "Happy to be here. I'm hoping to speak to Sharice."

Sharice rises from the bench, anxiously looking at Pastor Karen, whose gleaming smile emanates with love and compassion despite the potentially embarrassing moment I've caused. "It's OK," she says. "We'll have plenty of time for fellowship after the service. If she'd like, Sharice can speak to you then."

"I didn't mean to put you on the spot, Sharice, but your story—what you've overcome—it's changed my life." It's a ruse, but not completely untrue. I had no intention of lying in the Lord's house or conning the congregation, but my late God-fearing mother would have a fit if I didn't ask the Lord for forgiveness. My faith may have waned over the years, but if it weren't for God's grace, I would've died with David Bergman or maybe even at the hands of Joey Garcia. God has kept me alive through harrowing ordeals, and I have to believe it's for a purpose.

Pastor Karen hasn't stopped looking at me with unwavering joy. "Welcome to our midweek service, Trevor. We are pleased to have you with us," she says, then begins her sermon.

The sermon lasts twenty minutes without a reprise, which I've experienced at historically Black churches. It's similar to James Brown's charade of hobbling off stage, seemingly drained from his performance, only to return a sweaty mess, rejuvenated for an encore.

Pastor Karen walks slowly toward me with her arm around Sharice. "Greetings . . ." she says, then pauses to recollect my name. "Trevor, is it?"

"Yes, that's right."

"We're so happy you joined us today."

"It was a lovely service, Pastor."

"Sharice is always open to sharing the uplifting aspects of her story. She was cast in darkness but never stopped looking for the light. Isn't that right, Sharice?"

Sharice appears bashful, scrunches her shoulders, and speaks softly: "Yes, Pastor."

"Survival makes for a powerful testimony," I say, speaking like an earnest parishioner. I slide down the pew, leaving room for Sharice to sit.

"I'll give you two some time to talk," Pastor Karen says, leaning in to hug Sharice. "I'll be prepping in the kitchen if you need me."

Sharice nods, and Pastor Karen returns to the pulpit to gather her things.

"Thank you for speaking with me," I say.

"I believe it's my responsibility to share my story if it helps someone with their healing," she says, sitting beside me.

"It's courageous of you. Not sure I'd be here if I would've endured what you did."

"Here? You mean in church?"

"No," I say. "In the land of the living."

She's empathetic to my fragility, squeezing her knees as though she's bracing for an emotionally taxing conversation, which I imagine is always the case when she discusses her abduction.

"People always talk about *my* courage," she says, "but I didn't get here alone. I found strength in the divine, and I was delivered."

"You had your faith to lean on. I'm afraid that isn't the case for others who've been in your situation."

"God doesn't need people to believe in him to be spared, but in those moments when I thought I would surely die, I felt his presence. I knew he was there with me—with *us*."

"I'm sorry about your brother."

"Gabriel made the ultimate sacrifice for me. I honor him with my work."

"His sacrifice was helping you escape?"

"He saved my life by surrendering his own," she says. "Gabriel freed me from the men who abducted us."

"Can you tell me about these men?"

"I know why you've come, Mr. Trevor."

"You do?"

"Others have found me, too—reporters, writers, moviemakers who all wanted to make money off my story."

"I'm afraid I've come for other reasons."

"You're police?"

"A private investigator."

"So, it's happened again, hasn't it?"

"Yes," I say. "I believe it has."

She sighs, and her shoulders slump. "I'm sorry . . . I tried my best to warn the police and anyone who would listen, but no one believed me."

"The news articles said you remembered nothing about the abduction, and that's what you'd told the police?"

"I remembered nothing at first," she says. "I'd blocked

everything out, but things started coming back—little by little. And after a while, I recalled each detail as if it were a movie I could playback in my mind."

"Will you tell me everything you remember?"

"I'll walk you through it," she says, "but that's all I can offer. I'll never get on a witness stand or anything like that. I've managed to have a normal life despite what happened to me, and I won't give that up."

"I understand."

"OK," she says, biting her bottom lip before soldiering into the past. "Gabriel and I had left our foster home. We'd done it plenty of times before, but this time we wanted to go somewhere no one could find us . . . We thought we'd live like adventurers in the forest and lie on the beach all day. We'd make a shelter, gather food, and hunt little animals, but disappearing that way isn't easy. They came and took us from the campgrounds as we slept."

"Did you see their faces?"

"They wore hoods."

"Where did they take you?"

"Somewhere dark," she says. "It was damp and cold and smelly."

"Can you describe the smell?"

"It smelled of rainwater. Puddles after a fresh storm. Then came a sweetness in the air like communion wine, but the more time I spent in the dark, all I smelled was death—an old death," she says, clasping her hands together and bringing them to her lips.

"How long did they keep you from the light? Hours? Days?"

"We never saw daylight. Only bright lamps that made our eyes sore. It's how they took our pictures."

"What kinds of pictures?"

"Oh, I can't talk about that. Not here." She looks at the large wooden figure of a crucified Jesus above the pulpit. "I know the Lord loves me, but the shame I feel is always there." She touches the center of her chest, places four fingers over her heart. "Shame is an ugly thing."

"Why do you feel ashamed? What happened to you and Gabriel wasn't your fault."

"I don't tell many people this, but there was a moment I almost accepted my circumstances," she says. "I thought they would turn me out. Sell me for sex. It had happened to girls I'd gone to school with. They'd met some man at the mall who'd buy them whatever they wanted, and next thing you know, he'd have them selling their bodies in sleazy motel rooms. I knew I'd have to do things—horrible things—but at least I'd be living. Some girls in my neighborhood who worked the corners at night had pimps that put them through cosmetology school. I thought there had to be worst things in life than whoring."

"Tell me, did they keep chains on you when you took the pictures?"

"Usually," she says. "At first, I didn't understand it. Then it all made sense. They wanted us to look like we were . . ."

"Enslaved?"

She nods. "They fed and treated us like animals. Cold oatmeal and water. Everything they gave us tasted funny."

"Funny in what way?"

"Tainted," she says. "And it made us sleepy, even when we might've already slept for hours."

"All you ate was oatmeal?"

"Yes—till this day, I can't stand the sight or smell of it," she says. "Those men were the cruelest people I've ever met in my life. They talked to us like we were nothing—less than nothing. Slurs. Terrible names. One man spat on us and peed, too. He frequently kicked and slapped us. Anytime Gabriel tried to fight back, he'd beat him with what I think was a belt or leather strap. Our clothes stayed soiled, and when my time of the month came, they wouldn't even let me clean myself up. It was like they preferred me that way—filthy and helpless. It didn't matter how much I begged for a tampon, a rag, anything—they refused. One man said if I didn't like it, I could just be naked . . . and the more I cried, the more photos they took."

"They were taking pictures of you during all this abuse?"

"Yes," she says. "One man took pictures while the other

hurt us. The man behind the camera gave the orders—how hard we got hit, where we got hit. The more pain he could see in our faces, the more pictures he took. He was after something, and once he got what he wanted, he'd stop and stare at us like he couldn't believe we were all his. Then he'd leave, and we'd return to the dark."

"I don't know what to say . . . everything that you went through—"

"There isn't much to say. Only that I'm still here by the grace of God."

"Can you tell me how Gabriel got you out?"

"My brother was always good with details. Far better than me. I used to tell him he'd make a good detective someday. He was like a little private eye, and it made me laugh. When we were young, he'd notice the smallest things like a sauce stain on my shirt, or if I wasn't wearing my watch or necklace, he'd ask if I'd misplaced it. So, one time, when the men came to take photos, he whispered that he didn't hear the door close."

"What door?"

"They'd come through a door and walk downstairs to where we were kept. The door sounded heavy, and when it closed, it'd echo. On this day, Gabriel noticed there was no echo. He whispered that they'd forgotten to close the door. So, when they unchained us, and were getting ready to take more of our photos, Gabriel got free and cut one of them here," she says, dragging her finger across her cheek.

"He cut your abductor's face?"

"Yes," she says. "With a piece of glass."

"Where'd he get the glass?"

"He'd dug it out of the ground."

"It was a dirt floor?"

"That's right. Old, hard dirt. Gabriel dug until his fingers bled, trying to find something that would help us escape."

"Then what happened?"

"He told me to run, so I did. I ran upstairs and out the door. The men chased me, but I didn't stop. I ran right out of the house and onto a beach. I didn't see anyone around, but I kept running until I finally saw families and surfers. I screamed

'Help' so loud that the next thing I knew, I was face down in the sand. I'd tripped on a rock. The last thing I remember about that day was looking up at the sun—it was so bright and warm. I hadn't seen light, real natural light, for what felt like forever. It was like God himself had wrapped me in his arms, and I never wanted him to let me go."

"You say you ran out of a house?"

She nods. "Unlocked the front door and bolted out of there."

"Do you remember anything about the home? Wall color or furniture? Odors besides the sweetness in the dark?"

"Didn't look at anything except the front door. It was like running down a tunnel. All I saw was a door at the end. The only thing on my mind was getting free and getting help."

"How did they keep you from escaping before?"

"Always chains," she says. "We were chained to a wall by our wrists and ankles, sometimes our necks."

I access the internet app on my phone, return to the American Heritage Supply Company's website, and show Sharice the available chains. "Did the chains look like this?"

She nods, tugging at her Christmas sweater until a brown thread unravels part of the reindeer's hooves. "They said if we didn't do what they wanted, they'd kill us. I know that's why Gabriel did what he did, and every day, I thank him up in heaven for giving me a chance at life."

"And you told the sheriff all of this?"

"Yes," she says. "It's like I said, no one believed me. Not my foster parents and not the police. They wanted me to forget the whole thing, and I grew tired of being called a liar. I've never lied in my life, Mr. Trevor. Not even a *white lie*. The Bible says it's a sin. I believed that even before the sweet blood of Jesus saved me."

"I don't doubt you, Sharice . . ."

"I tried hard to get the sheriff to go back and at least look for the house, but they refused."

"Do you remember anything about the neighborhood? Maybe a street or landmark of some kind?"

"Oh, it's been too long. I wouldn't trust my memories when it came to things like that. Everything I told you is what's been burned into my mind, but I do remember one other thing about the house: the front door."

"What about it?"

"It was like a castle door. Wooden and heavy, and it looked like this," she says, arching her fingers into the shape of a steeple. "When I pulled it open, it felt like something from medieval times, you know? Maybe I should've tried to find it when it was still fresh in my mind, but I couldn't bring myself to go back to Malibu."

"That's understandable, Sharice. You were a child and did what you could."

"It all angers me so much. Not just what happened to me, but what probably happened to other people like me. They did that to us, and we were children . . ."

"I'm starting to think anger is all I've got."

"It's all right to be angry, Mr. Trevor, but you can't stay in that place. When I get to feeling like it's burning me up inside, I remind myself of the good things I've got. People I love and who love me."

"I'm not always sure that's enough," I say. "My anger's a strong current. It sweeps away everything in its path."

"I don't believe that." She pats my shoulder. "Love surrounds you—I can sense it. And you've got to remember that. Find some way to remind yourself every single day that you're loved—it's our strength and protection, the sword and staff—and it's what separates us from the monsters."

"How is it, after everything that happened, you're so—"

"At peace?"

"I was going to say forgiving, but yes, peace comes to mind."

"I forgave those men long ago, but peace is something I've worked at. It may not look like it, but what happened to *us* was supposed to happen."

"Supposed to?"

"Gabriel is in heaven now, away from gangs and violence. In life, all he knew was pain and suffering, and now he's at peace in the presence of the Lord. And me, I'm a miracle," she says. "Pastor Karen says my story gives hope to the families of those with missing loved ones that, one day, they'll be found, too."

"It's good you have Pastor Karen in your life. I can see that she cares about you a great deal."

"She gave me a job as a church custodian and allowed me to live in the cottage for free."

"There's a cottage here?"

"The little house behind the church. It isn't much, but it's home." Her pink Timex with purple flowers plays a kitschy tune at the start of the hour. It reminds me of the Teenage Mutant Ninja Turtle-themed watch I had as a kid, with a neon green glow-in-the-dark spandex band. She notices me looking at it. "I was wearing this watch when they took me," she says. "My brother gave it to me on my eleventh birthday. I couldn't part with it. It's how I keep him close. I better go help Pastor prepare for the community feast. We're serving spaghetti in the great hall . . . you should join us."

"I wish I could, but . . ."

"You're a man on a mission," she says. "Can I pray with you before you go?"

"OK," I say, figuring I need all the prayers I can get.

Sharice closes her eyes, and we hold hands. "Father God, we are all your children, and we come to you humbly asking for your grace. We ask that you deliver Trevor from his anger and bring peace and joy into his heart so he may one day know forgiveness, and we ask that you bring justice to all of us who have suffered at the hands of wickedness. Keep Trevor safe as he walks through darkness, and may he never forsake your will."

She finishes the prayer and opens her eyes, moist with tears. "How do you feel?" she asks.

"Better," I say, a little choked up. "Thank you."

"You're welcome."

"Be well, Trevor."

"You too, Sharice."

Sharice's prayer reminded me of one my mother would murmur in the dark, sitting at my father's bedside while he slept. He had finished his shift, working out of Newton Division, and as she often did, she thanked God for bringing him home safely, prayed for his continued protection, and bound her prayer with a tender kiss on his forehead. Though their relationship was imperfect, she loved my father despite the damage he did to our family and their marriage, and I know if she were alive today, she'd want me to forgive him, but he doesn't make it easy.

ELEVEN

I check my watch before getting into the Beemer. In a few short hours, I'll meet Tori for a tough discussion, which may be the most consequential in the canon of our relationship, and I'm unprepared. I want to be in Simone's life, but pleading with Tori to stay seems wrong. Her life is her own, and if she did stay, she'd only resent me in the long run. Still, there has to be room for compromise, a way to make it work.

It's 4:30 p.m. Depending on traffic, it'll take an hour or more to get to North Hollywood. I should arrive by six o'clock, which is enough time to get dinner and manage my nerves before seeing Tori. I start the engine and pull out of the parking lot. I have less than a quarter of fuel and will need to fill the tank before driving to the Valley.

I drive down Paramount Boulevard and pull into a gas station. I get out and pump, noticing a pickup truck parked two pumps over. The driver is a big man. His reddish knuckles grip the steering wheel, and a long-brimmed trucker hat obscures his face so I can't see his eyes, but I sense he's watching me intently; he either knows me or wants to.

I finish fueling, get back inside the car, and pretend to look for something in the passenger seat while stealing glances at the truck. If my instincts are correct, I've had a run-in with the truck before. It followed Pop and me through the canyon, nearly running us off the road. The driver might've also been responsible for tampering with the Falcon's suspension. I had wondered if the truck would make another appearance. I'm far from Malibu, which means the driver followed me, or someone tipped him off to my location. I'm leaning toward the latter. The Beemer isn't slow; it hauls, and a tail would've stuck out on the canyon roads and in lean traffic. The truck's presence suggests that Sharice's hellish ordeal and Keisha's murder are somehow connected, which means the driver might have the answers I need.

I rack a round in my Glock's chamber, tuck the weapon in my waistband, and get out of the car. I walk toward the truck, staunch stride, eyes focused on the driver. I bang on the window. "Who are you?" I ask.

The driver attempts to exit the truck, opening the driver's side door. I press against the door with my shoulder and hips, pinning him inside. He's plenty heavy, but his clothing is restricting, cumbersome: a bulking bubble vest over a flannel shirt. He's a balloon squeezed into a glass jar. The contest of will and strength leaves him winded. Without room to negotiate, he concedes. Preparing to flee, he yells and curses at me, shifting from park to reverse.

I bang on the window again. "Tell me who you are, dammit! Why are you following me?"

The deep bellow under the hood hints that the truck's engine is a V8 or larger. The truck slings backward. I dart out of the way and avoid the tire rolling over my foot. The driver tugs at his hat, pulling it down to hide his face and jerks the steering wheel. With all the movement, his hat shifts, becoming askew. Our eyes meet—his piercing blue, cold stare gives me pause, and then I see the long, deep, angled scar down his cheek, noticeable through spotty gray scruff. He floors the truck forward, barely evading a collision with a minivan pulling up to a pump.

I run to the Beemer, start her up, and follow in pursuit. We travel eastbound on Paramount, crossing Imperial Highway. The truck is gathering speed, switching lanes, and cutting off drivers. I keep up with little effort, but traveling at high speeds on a major street is sure to get the attention of law enforcement. If he intends to shake me, he'll need to use the secondary roads.

We're nearing the City of Industry—a decaying manufacturing hub where lingering factories pump poison into an exceedingly polluted sky. The truck makes a hard left onto a service road parallel to the 105 freeway and speeds toward an industrial park. It's a maze of warehouses and office buildings. He turns hard, cuts down a narrow alley, and accelerates toward a dirt lot filled with tractor-trailers and abandoned train cars. He won't outrun me—he can't—but one thing is working in his favor: the pickup is jacked high on fat off-roading tires, and the Beemer is low, which limits my field of vision. The truck driver can see miles ahead of him, while my view is of the truck's tailgate.

Once in the open lot, I floor the Beemer, getting around the truck to trap him between two railway cars. He reacts with menace, threatening to sideswipe me. I brake hard, shifting back into his wake. He makes a sharp turn, spawning a cyclone of dirt that momentarily impedes my vision. The truck idles before me as the dust clears, the engine revving loudly—a bull sizing up a matador. The truck lurches forward—it's a warning: stay put and be shredded to death, or flee and live. I hold steady as the truck gains speed. Tires bounce over the dirt. I shift into second gear, bolting forward. The Goliath isn't backing off. Smoke spews from the truck's rear; diesel hangs in the air. We're close now, mere feet from a head-on collision.

I cut the wheel hard, narrowly escaping the truck's fender. The Beemer fishtails, I pull the emergency brake and come to a stop. I'm rattled but uninjured. Dirt covers the windshield; the wipers swat it away, and I see what remains of the truck: a smoldering heap of metal smashed into a boxcar.

Shit.

I climb out of the car, a little dizzy, and run toward the truck. Fuel drips from the undercarriage. I move around to the driver's side door, crouching low and watching for any sudden movements by the driver. Through the window, I see the man hunched over the steering wheel, bleeding from his head—the truck is a late-model, too old for an airbag. I step onto the running board and try to open the door. It doesn't budge; it's locked from the inside. I reach through the broken window, trying not to cut myself on the remaining glass shards, and pull the door's lock. When I do, the driver awakens, snatches my arm, and rakes it across the glass fragments embedded in the window's rubber seal.

I scream out, as the glass digs into my forearm. "Get your fucking hands off me," I say.

"You're going to ruin it," he says, his teeth broken and lip bloodied. "I won't let you ruin it."

"I'm trying to help your ass." I slip my arm free. "The truck is leaking fuel, you idiot. We have to get clear of it."

"Leave me!"

"There's nothing I want more, but I need your ass alive." I open the door, yank the man from the driver's seat, and drag him across dirt and gravel to safety. As I near the Beemer, I look over my shoulder as a flickering wire dangles under the truck. I prop the man's back against the Beemer's rear tire. There's a cacophony as the truck's dripping fuel ignites into flames, engulfing the cabin, exploding the hood and sending the metal sailing through the sky.

"My truck," the man says, his words wispy from missing teeth. "Look what you've done to my truck."

"Fuck your truck."

"You're an animal. A goddamn animal."

"Watch your mouth, or I'll break whatever teeth you've got left."

"You're fucking darkness, an absolute pit of it," he says. "And we're going to purge you from this earth. Erasing every last one of you."

"Big talk for a man bleeding to death." I press my fingers into his chest, and he coughs more blood. "You've got internal bleeding."

"Go to hell," he says. "It doesn't matter what happens to me. I've fulfilled my purpose."

"You're not getting off that easy. Tell me who you are and why you were following me." I pull my Glock and aim it at his blubbery gut. "Play games and get bullets."

"This ain't no game, you spook. Not anymore," he says. "It's the beginning of the end for your kind, and I promise you and your people will have nothing to celebrate."

The man braces his palm between his shoulder and chest, slightly above his armpit. I push his vest back until I'm able to see his wound. A long, thick piece of windshield is lodged between his shoulder and fatty pectoral.

"Would you look at that," I say. "You've got to be losing a pint a minute. You start talking, and I'll put some pressure on it for you. Slow the bleeding."

I can feel the searing heat radiating from the burning truck. Emergency responders will arrive soon, and I'll have much to answer for, but none of this will be worth it if I can't get this man to talk.

"I don't have time for this. You're going to talk, dammit!" I tighten my hand around the Glock's barrel, raise the gun's butt over my head, and hammer the glass deeper into his shoulder.

His howl is deafening. Seconds of agony turn into minutes, and then I no longer hear his bloodcurdling screams. The crackling blaze is all I hear—it's all I want to hear.

He regains enough strength to speak: "Fuck you, nigg—"

I hammer the glass further into his shoulder. This time, tears accompany his howling. "I can keep at it, or you can tell me what I want to know."

"You mutherfucker."

"Tell me!" Again, I raise the gun's butt. "Tell me, and this ends."

"It'll only end one way, and you won't like it."

I prepare to hit him again. "Any last words?"

"All right . . . all right," he says, blood and mucus drooling down his chin. "My wallet—it's in my vest pocket."

I remove a worn-out billfold from the man's vest pocket.

Inside is his driver's license—Jack Baskin, fifty-six years of age and a resident of Signal Hill—and a laminated employee identification card for St. Catherine University. I take pictures with my cell phone of the license's front and back, along with his ID.

"How long have you worked at St. Catherine's?" I ask, noting the card's yellowish tint and pealing lamination.

The color is gone from his lips; he can hardly keep his eyes open. "For over twenty fucking years," he says.

"Doing what?"

"Maintenance."

"You're building facilities?"

"That's my job, but my purpose is to be a servant to a righteous cause . . . I'm a soldier in this holy war."

"You tampered with my car at the hospital, didn't you? Chased us down the hill and nearly killed us."

"If I wanted to kill you, I would have. My orders were to run you out of town."

"Ordered by whom?"

"You're going to have to kill me."

"The way you killed Keisha Landry?"

"That was her name? Hell, I can't even remember faces."

"How many were there?"

"Not enough, I'll tell you that." He coughs up more blood; his skin is bone white. "Not nearly enough . . ."

Everything about this man is revolting. He's vermin, having emerged from a bottomless cesspool—a Hellmouth.

How long has he been at it? People believed to be missing, *his* victims all along, a serial killer in Malibu. But he didn't act alone. He speaks of someone else—someone giving orders. How many others are involved? It could be vast, a cabal of killers.

"Go ahead, pull the trigger, *boy*. See the hell you unleash."

A quick death is far too good for him. No need to hasten his departure, but every word he mutters is begging me to kill him. I press the gun flush against his temple. My finger rests on the trigger. Damnation awaits this man . . . this much I know. A simple squeeze. Four pounds of pressure, that's all it takes . . .

"Fucking pussy," he says, fighting to breathe. "Do it, boy! Grow a pair and pull the trigger!"

I want to kill him more than I've wanted anything in a long time. I'd be doing the world a favor. Cutting out cancer . . . one less devil living among us.

But I can't . . .

Sharice wouldn't want this.

Her prayer for peace and healing beats in my head. She sees hope for me, a path to salvation, and slaughtering Baskin is not the way.

I pound the glass shard into his shoulder for the final time. The shard's tip meets resistance, an almost undetectable vibration. I've struck bone—it feels like jamming a twig into concrete.

Baskin is too exhausted to scream, or he's lost feeling. Maybe the glass has severed nerves, numbing the pain? Lumps of blood flow darker and heavier now, seeping profusely.

"You're going to die," I say.

His rebuttal is a gaping smile. "God's glory awaits me," he says. "A new day is rising. Soon, you bottom-feeders will no longer suck the heart and soul out of this great country. My only regret is I don't get to watch you and all you love burn to ash."

"So, you're just a good old boy on a Nazi kick?"

"I'm a patriot."

"You were targeting victims by skin color. That was your criterion for killing?"

"*Victims?* Never. They were parasites and I was a small piece of the cure." Blood covers his chin and oozes down onto his chest. "*We* are the final solution."

His chin drops to his chest as his last breaths turn shallow. The reflection of his burning truck dances in his pupils. Baskin's dead. Once a predator that evaded detection, he's no longer stalking and ravaging innocent lives, and I take solace in that.

Yet his death comes with little satisfaction, knowing he didn't act alone. A loathsome disciple of this country's abhorrent past, he hid in plain sight behind gawks and frowns, unable to reveal himself because conventions wouldn't allow it, but as Tori once said with looming fright, "Things are changing." Hate is becoming emboldened by those who have revered it in the dark. It no longer resides in pockets of society; it's mainstream, and Baskin may be right—*a new day is rising*—and if what he's done is an intimation, it's far uglier than I've imagined.

I dial 911 and tell the dispatcher to send help: "Send the sheriff and the fire department," I say. "A man is dead."

"Do you know how he died?"

"Car accident."

"Make yourself safe and stay at the location until officers and paramedics arrive."

"I'm not going anywhere," I say, then end the call.

I dig into Baskin's pockets, finding his phone and loose dollar bills. The phone is locked and soaked with blood. It prompts me to enter a passcode or open the phone using facial ID. I force Baskin's eyelids up, but they fall to half-mast. The phone refuses to unlock, and I don't have time to keep at it.

The sirens sound like they're a few blocks away and closing in quickly. When the deputies arrive, they'll want to confiscate Baskin's phone. I can't allow that—the phone may hold evidence vital to my investigation, and with Baskin dead, it's the only lead I've got. I open the Beemer's glove box, toss the phone in, and lock it.

Once my nerves are calm, I rehearse my statement for the authorities. It'll need to sound natural, so I should keep to the truth, barring some obligatory omissions. The shorter the statement, the better. Elaborated statements are often difficult to recall under stress and can indicate that a person is being deceptive. As a police detective, I exploited those tells every chance I got, usually resulting in a suspect's confession.

But in the interview room, I won't make those mistakes.

TWELVE

The City of Industry Sheriff's Station is one of the oldest stations I've ever seen—its condition is an embarrassment. It would've been demolished and rebuilt decades ago if the city had the funding. The exterior is painted white and green, but not the dark green found on older deputy uniforms, which might've been the intent forty years ago.

The interview room is warmer than I expected, but the scuffed white walls are no surprise. LAPD's divisions are far from immaculate, but this station hasn't been properly maintained for years.

The investigator enters and introduces himself as Hector Navarro. He's a thin man with a handlebar mustache and thick head of hair, which is uncommon for most veterans. Between sleep deprivation, poor diet, and stress, balding deputies are run-of-the-mill, and so are their sagging bellies and bad backs.

Navarro offers me water instead of soda or coffee. Typically, stimulants are reserved for suspects, which means right now he doesn't know which category to place me in. I try to get comfortable in a wooden chair, which might be as old as the building. I anticipate it'll take an hour for Navarro to take my statement. I'll miss seeing Tori and Simone at seven, as promised—another failure in Tori's book.

"Any chance you can talk to Detective Brennan out of the Malibu Station?" I ask. "She might be able to clear this up."

"She a friend of yours?" he asks, brushing his tie down before sipping water from a paper cup.

"I don't have any friends in the Sheriff's Department."

"Sorry to hear that," he says. "Although we hope LA County citizens like yourself see us all as friends."

"Hate to break it to you, but they don't. Could be the business with the Banditos, the Regulators, the Spartans, the Gladiators, and the—"

"You made your point, wise guy, though you're not in much of a position to talk. You're no Serpico, Finnegan."

"Congratulations, you know how to Google."

"Wow—you're ramping up already. Great way to start this."

"And what exactly is *this*? How about we make this time productive and get Brennan down here?"

"Sure, I'll work on that . . ."

"Let's skip the warm-up, shall we? Get on with it and ask me what you want to know."

"OK," he says. "No time like the present. So, tell me, how did Jack Baskin end up dead and his truck on fire?"

"He crashed."

"Did you know Mr. Baskin prior to the accident?"

"I knew of him," I say, keeping my answers vague. "He was a suspect in a homicide investigation."

"The same investigation this Detective Brennan is working on?"

"That'd be the one," I say. "I followed Baskin to the lot, and he lost control and crashed. I managed to pull him to safety, but he sustained an injury that ultimately took his life."

"What kind of injury?"

"A piece of windshield lodged in his chest. Before he bled to death, he confessed that he committed a series of homicides."

"A voluntary confession?"

"There's no other kind as far as I'm concerned."

Navarro smiles. "OK, we'll get to all that," he says. "How long after the accident did you call nine-one-one?"

"Couple minutes, maybe. I was busy rendering aid."

"Did you see anyone nearby and call out for help?"

"You saw that place. There wasn't a person in sight."

"It was pretty desolate, and you say you pursued Baskin?"

"I followed him," I say. "My goal was to talk to him. That's it."

Navarro coughs and takes a long sip of water. He's stalling—a hackneyed tactic to assert power dominance once an investigator feels they've lost control, and what better way to show power than to waste someone's time, something they can't get back?

I look at my watch. I'm supposed to meet Tori in thirty minutes. I need to let her know I'll be late. "Mind if I send a text?"

"How about you finish answering my questions, and you can be on your way."

"What else do you want to know?"

"You say Baskin is a murder suspect, correct? So, if I can talk to this Detective Brennan, she'll corroborate that he was being investigated."

"Not exactly," I say. "She has a suspect, but he's innocent. Baskin is the guy; she just doesn't know it."

"Is that right? A case of the wrong man?"

Ordinarily, I'd be more forthcoming: my investigation led me to Baskin, a white supremacist serial killer who confessed to multiple homicides with an unknown accomplice, but I'd only be wasting my breath. Even if Navarro did believe me, he'd murk things up by sharing my conjecture with Brennan, which is worthless without evidence.

"There's no point in me talking to you about this," I say. "If you're not going to get Brennan here, stop wasting my time."

"I'm not so sure this is a waste of time. I'm learning a lot. So, let me get this straight—Baskin confessed that he was a serial murderer to you before he died?"

"Yes."

"And why you? Why not go to his grave with his secret?"

"He was proud of it, wanted me to know."

There's a knock at the door. "Come in," Navarro says.

A female deputy enters, sizes me up, and passes Navarro a note on a three-by-five card. She stands a moment as he reads. I try to determine how long people have been on the job based on how they stand. I've done it so long that it's involuntary, more like a nervous tick. There's rounding in the deputy's shoulders, and they jut forward. Her holstered firearm is on her right hip, which is slightly cocked. She's been standing this way so long that it's second nature. I'd venture that she hasn't spent twenty years on the job but more than ten, long enough to develop poor posture because carrying thirty pounds of gear takes its toll.

Navarro returns the note to the deputy, and she leaves. There's no telling what the note says, but maybe someone with more sense than Navarro knows there's no point in keeping me here. No one wants the ex-cop who successfully sued the LAPD for over a million dollars around longer than necessary. Any flagrant disregard of my rights could mean Navarro and others having to go to court in a civil trial, and cops hate civil trials.

"Are you going to call Detective Brennan or not?" I ask.

"No," he says. "I'm not."

"Then our business is done here unless you intend to arrest me."

"And what would I arrest you for? Theft?"

"What?"

"Just got confirmation that Baskin didn't have a mobile phone on him. No device whatsoever."

"So?"

"Who doesn't carry a phone these days?"

"Probably burned up in the fire," I say. "All I know is that when I pulled him to safety, he didn't have shit on him except his wallet."

"You were in law enforcement long enough. Doesn't it strike you as odd for a person not to have a phone?"

"Everything strikes me as odd these days, but a man like Baskin might've wanted to avoid leaving a digital fingerprint. Could've been one of those off-the-grid types."

"I guess we'll never know, will we?"

As Sarada instructs in our yoga sessions, I stand, stretch my back, and exhale deeply to combat stress and tension. It's a temporary fix, but it beats taking up smoking. "I'll be leaving now."

"You think you're so smart."

"Not this shit . . ."

"Yeah, you've got a real chip on your shoulder."

"*Me*? Navarro, I don't even know you, but I can tell you're probably the most hated guy in this station."

"Feeling's mutual, asshole."

"OK, let's hear it . . ."

"You haven't been a LEO for a good while," Navarro says, "so let me remind you that you've got no jurisdiction and no protections. You fuck up out there, and it's your ass. Don't think we're idiots because you're walking out of here. I know what you're doing, and murderer or not, if I find out you removed property or evidence from Baskin's car, person, or residence, I'll arrest you myself."

"I get it, Navarro. You've got big balls," I say. "Now imagine if you had the balls to disband the Banditos and the rest of those deputy gangs. Maybe then you'd earn a little trust back from citizens and make a few, as you say, *friends* in the community."

"I'd much rather imagine locking you up when you get caught operating outside legal bounds," he says.

"Spoken like a true servant of the people."

"See you around, Finnegan."

"Let's hope you don't, for both our sakes."

I leave the station after eight o'clock. The travel app tells me I'll get to Tori's place around 9:45 a.m. I text her, letting her know I was stuck at the Sheriff's Station and on my way. She replies quickly: **Don't bother. Simone is asleep. I need to be up early.**

Fucked by Navarro . . . If I had texted her earlier, it might've made a difference. Still, I can't let Tori disappear without telling her where I stand. Simone is my daughter, too, and I've missed out on so much already that the thought of not seeing her drives a pin through my heart.

Before going to Tori's apartment, I stop at a nearby taco stand, get a plate of twelve pollo and carne tacos with extra limes, and eat them in the car.

Afterward, I go to Tori's place and park in front of her building. The neighborhood is decent. Mostly entertainment types: actors, dancers, and screenwriters . . . It reminds me of my old loft downtown in the Arts District.

I clean the blood off Baskin's phone with a rag from the trunk and antibacterial hand wipes. I spend an hour attempting to unlock it, trying dates like Baskin's birthday, which I crib from the picture I took of his license, along with the day he started his employment at St. Catherine's. Nothing works, and shortly after the last attempt, I fall asleep with my jacket over my chest, concealing my gun in my lap.

THIRTEEN

Morning comes, ending a restless night. The Beemer's seats reclined flat, helping me avoid leg cramps and a sore back, but I couldn't stay warm. The overnight temps dipped into the low 40s, chilling the leather. I turned on the heater at three a.m. but feared falling asleep with it running. Driving the Beemer is like getting acquainted with a stranger. I'm cautiously feeling the car out. While it performs as expected, there is still plenty unknown. Sometimes, older cars can seep fumes from the heater's blower that can be toxic and deadly.

I'm awake now, and my toes are ice cubes that need to thaw. I turn on the car, blast the heater, and watch commuters heading to work. I don't miss the nine-to-five, the daily grind. It would take something compelling to make me return to wearing a badge and working sixteen-hour shifts for shitty pay. I told the Russian bookie most of my settlement money was gone, but it was a lie. I've squirreled away plenty and have no intention of using it—not even to pay off Avery's debt. I earned that money in blood, almost dying from a stab wound, and the city wanted to erase me as if I had never worn the badge. I sued them for wrongful termination, back wages, and the medical care they denied me, and every cent they gave me sent a message to the department that officers are more than numbers, more than workhorses who risk their lives every day and get little in return. After the job breaks us, and it surely breaks all of us, the most the city can do is make us whole.

My phone needs to charge; it shows a ten percent battery life. There's a text from Sarada that reads: **I love you and hope you're being safe. I believe in you.** Her words always come at the right time; she has a gift for knowing when they're needed most. I text her that I love and miss her, and exit the car.

It's 7:30, so Tori should be up soon. Simone is an early riser and likes to eat shortly after waking up. I walk the sidewalk to the stairs leading to her apartment. I was wrong about my back not being sore. There's a prickly pain above my tailbone and a knot in my left butt cheek. It throbs with each step, but the pain subsides when I reach the security door. I press the button for Tori's unit and wait.

The intercom pops, followed by a sustained crackle. "Who is it?" Tori asks.

"It's Trevor."

The metal gate buzzes. "It's open."

"I'll be right up."

I climb the stairs to the second floor. Tori must recognize my hard walk because she peeks through the blinds, then opens her door, popping her head out. "Hi," she says, in full makeup and styled hair, wearing a beige turtleneck sweater, black denim, and matching riding boots.

"Good morning," I say.

"Simone just got up . . . come on in."

I enter the apartment. Simone is sitting on a playmat in the living room, holding the stuffed dolphin I bought her from a hotel gift shop last month. I begin walking toward her when Tori takes my arm. "Hold on," she says. "Is that blood on your jacket?"

I look at my arm, and there are blood stains on the sleeve.

"You should take that off," Tori says.

I remove the jacket, and she gasps, looking at my bandaged arm where more blood has accumulated on my shirt. "It's not as bad as it looks."

"Really? Because it looks awful."

"You should see the other guy . . ."

Tori cuts a look. She isn't amused.

"Actually, you shouldn't," I say. "See the other guy, I mean."

"Is that supposed to be funny?"

"Not really."

"And where is this *other* guy?"

"You don't want to know."

"Maybe I do, Trevor. It seems to be worth joking about and I can use some humor this morning."

"I take it back. It isn't funny, not even a little."

"Too late," she says. "Tell me."

"He shuffled off this mortal coil."

"And you had a hand in that shuffling?"

"Fortunately, yes. No one is going to miss him, I assure you."

"Is that why you were in the Sheriff's Station?"

"It was routine questioning."

"Is anything ever really routine with you?"

"I'm here now, Tori—that's what matters."

"And you show up like this?"

"Sometimes things don't go as planned."

"How many times have I heard that?"

"I really can do without the third degree."

She nudges me into the kitchen, where she's preparing Simone's rice cereal. "You're telling me that you killed some guy. How else should I react?"

"I didn't kill him. He died on his own in my presence. That's a big difference."

"I don't get you," she says. "How can you be so nonchalant about this?"

"How would you rather I behave? This is the job."

"When was the last time you showered? You smell like a campfire."

"Not since yesterday morning. I slept in my car."

"This whole cowboy act is not a good look. I don't care what you do on your time, but have the decency to show up halfway presentable when you're coming to see our daughter."

"All right. I'm sorry," I say, recalling the sinking feeling I had once when Pop came home from a shift with his knuckles split and bleeding. I had never seen the aftermath of physical violence, and it frightened me.

"You can get cleaned up in the bathroom. A bag of my dad's clothes is at the bottom of my closet. You might find something in there that'll fit you."

"Your deceased father?"

"I only had one, Trevor," she says, spooning cereal into a bowl. "So, yes, the clothes belong to a dead man."

"OK. No problem."

Tori's room is cluttered with moving boxes and suitcases. She hasn't gotten around to unpacking or decided not to bother since she plans to leave LA. The room leads into the adjoining bathroom. I've been needing to piss all night, and it smells sourer than usual. I'm probably dehydrated. I wash my hands, rinse my face, and clean the dried blood from around my bandages.

Inside Tori's closet is the plastic bag filled with her father's golf polos, a *Make America Great Again* mesh cap, a red, white, and blue sweatsuit designed to resemble the American flag, khaki pants, argyle socks, and a collection of tacky Hawaiian shirts. I dig at the bottom of the bag for something suitable, find a solid black long-sleeve Henley, and put it on. The shirt fits baggy and is long past my waist. My shoulders are broader than her father's, and he carried more weight in the midsection. It's strange wearing the clothes of a man who despised me. Tori has only told me a few of the more mildly disagreeable comments he made in the past about me, and I can only infer he spoke more disparagingly, but she's too kind to tell me. What is certain is that he never wanted a biracial grandchild. It's something he and Pop could've agreed on. While Pop says his reasons aren't bigoted, Tori's father proudly expounded on his belief that people should "stick with their own."

Pop spent his childhood tormented by his father. An immigrant from Ireland, he married my grandmother and planted roots in North Carolina. When he faced the social, economic, and political ramifications of marrying and siring children with a Black woman, he blamed her for his failings. Turning to whiskey, he became an abusive drunk, and one night, he nearly beat Pop to death. Pop's never given me a rationale for why Simone is a blight on our family outside of pro-black rhetoric and his disregard for Tori, but I surmise Simone's presence reminds him of the terror that was his father.

While I know Pop's pain and trauma can be blinding, it angers me that he rejects his granddaughter. Simone is family, whether he accepts her or not, and if he's open to loving Avery, why can't he be open to loving my daughter?

Back in the living room, Tori feeds Simone breakfast. I join them on the floor and kiss Simone's cheek. She coos, exploring my stubbled jawline. She's not a fan of spikey, coarse hair; it must feel like a scouring pad.

"Daddy needs to shave," I say.

"Daddy needs a whole lot more than that," Tori mumbles.

"So, have you decided on your next move?"

"Not yet."

"Well, I didn't come here to change your mind. I've come to tell you that you're right. Things in this country may never improve. Lately, it seems to be getting worse. But I have to hold on to hope, Tori. It's what gets me out of bed in the morning."

"The hope this country is getting better?" she asks.

"No," I say, "believing this country is *trying* to get better. It's all anyone can hope for."

"God . . . doesn't that depress you?"

"My scar tissue is thick, Tori, and I've got years of it, but it doesn't mean Simone has to endure what I've had to."

"I just want to protect her as long as I can."

"I want the same, and if there's someplace better out there for her, she deserves it."

"Canada has its problems," she says. "It won't be perfect, but it's far better than life here."

"No place is perfect, but if it means her going to school without active shooter drills, isn't it worth it?"

"Yes," Tori says. "I believe it is."

"I'll see her as much as I can. Fly up a couple of weekends a month."

"You promise?"

"You know I'm terrible with promises, but nothing short of death will keep me from being in Simone's life."

I check my watch. It's after eight thirty. "Sorry, I need to go, and I'm stinking up your place."

"It's fine," Tori says. "We're meeting my mother for brunch in Irvine and need to beat the traffic."

"Have you told her you're moving back to Vancouver?"

"I'll break the news to her today," she says. "It'll be another disappointment. She's convinced herself we're going to move to Orange County to be nearer to her, and she keeps suggesting I change Simone's last name to Krause. I told her that'll never happen. She doesn't think Finnegan suits her."

"Her malice knows no bounds."

"She thinks if Simone's last name is Finnegan, she'll inherit . . ." She pauses, looking into Simone's brown eyes—*my eyes*, Finnegans' eyes.

"What, Tori? Say it."

"Nothing."

"Tell me."

"I shouldn't. It's vicious."

"I'd expect nothing less from her, and I'm sure it isn't the worst thing I'm thinking of."

"*Cursed* is the word she used—she thinks your name is cursed."

"Trust me, it isn't the name that's cursed."

"She's old and cooky, Trevor. Most of what she says is either conservative talking points or religious mumbo jumbo."

I lie for my sake: "It's fine . . ."

"I shouldn't have told you that," she says. "It was stupid of me."

"I said it's fine, Tori. Her opinion isn't my reality, and it won't be Simone's either. What about the lease on this place?"

"Talked to the landlord. I can move out free and clear if I pay for three months in advance. It'll give him enough time to find a renter. He doesn't think renting it will be difficult in this market."

"That's a chunk of change, Tori. Where are you getting the money?"

"Drawing from my life insurance policy."

"You sure you want to do that?"

"Well, I'm definitely not taking any money from my mother, and you've helped us enough, so yes, I'm sure."

"Let me talk to your landlord. I might be able to get him to reduce it."

"No, Trevor. I prefer you don't get involved. I'll pay the money and vacate."

"But you could use that money for movers."

"It's taken care of," she says. "Please, leave it alone. OK?"

"All right."

"I know I shouldn't ask, but this investigation you're working on . . . I won't see you on the news or anything, right?"

"I don't know—it feels big. I'm not sure I've even scratched the surface."

"Bigger than tussling with the LAPD?"

"In a way, yes. My brother is involved."

"Brother? What brother?"

"Half-brother. I just met the guy for the first time in the hospital."

"Simone has an uncle?"

"Yeah, I guess she does."

"Your dad kept that from you this entire time?"

"Decades."

"Wow—that's some high-level family secrets."

"There's more to it, but I don't want to spoil your day." I moan as I rise from the mat, arching my back until it cracks, relieving a ball of pressure from my spine.

"How's it feeling?" she asks.

"It's holding together."

"Probably shouldn't make a habit of sleeping in your car," she says, dabbing cereal from Simone's chin.

"Desperate times and all that . . . Besides, I treated it like a stakeout, minus junk food and caffeine. Speaking of which, any coffee?"

"There should be some left, and ibuprofen is on the counter."

"Thanks," I say, walking into the kitchen. I open the medicine bottle, drop two pills in my mouth, and wash them down with a cup of lukewarm coffee.

I place the mug on the counter and turn to see Tori putting on a wool car coat and Simone bundled in a quilted onesie. "We'll walk you out," she says, grabbing her purse and keys from a wooden hook on the wall, the only thing she managed to hang during her short stay in the apartment. "Can you hold her for a second?" she asks, passing me Simone.

I tuck my jacket under my arm and carry the baby outside.

Tori locks the door, and I follow her downstairs to her Volkswagen Beetle parked in a numbered stall.

"You'll keep me in the loop on things?" I ask.

"Of course. I'm not going to slip away in the night."

The notion hadn't entered my mind, but Tori's turn of phrase is unsettling. Could Pop be right? Is she hiding something . . . another reason she's so eager to return to Vancouver? I should probe deeper and see what she might be keeping from me, but I don't have the time. Avery's situation is as much as I can handle right now, and I'm making it a priority to see Simone once they're settled up north.

I kiss my daughter, then give her to Tori, who works to put her in the car seat. Nothing about the Beetle makes traveling with Simone easy. Tori needs a larger vehicle, but she's made it clear she doesn't want any more of my financial help. Still, knowing she's driving around in a half-mooned clown car gives me a complex. I try to ignore the impending feelings of doom. If I allowed every terrible thought to preside over me, Simone would never leave my sight.

"See you soon," Tori says, moving in for a hug.

Our embrace is longer than I expected, not because of harbored romantic feelings but because I worry about how they'll get by. Tori usually lands on her feet, but sooner or later, everybody's luck runs out, and this time, goodbye feels different . . . it feels like forever.

"You OK?" she asks, releasing her arms from around me.

I give a subtle nod; it isn't the time for honesty. "If you need anything, call me," I say, trying not to show my trepidation.

"You know I will."

"Promise."

"Really?"

"Just promise me."

She sighs, and I wait until I hear the words. "OK—I promise," she says. "Please, don't worry about us, Trevor. We're good. It'll all work out. Just take care of yourself. Simone needs her father."

I wave goodbye to Simone, whose car seat is wedged in the backseat, and return to the Beemer. I access the LA County inmate online locator from my phone and search for Avery. My speculation was wrong. He hasn't been transferred from the Twin Towers. A change in the presiding judge caused the delay. Sharice said her recollection of her abduction came back a little at a time. Maybe Avery's starting to remember details that might help shed light on Baskin's accomplice. It's time I visit him and get some much-needed answers.

FOURTEEN

I've been sitting in a cracked plastic chair for eight minutes, and there's still no Avery. Maybe he's shaken and doesn't want to see me. I still give off cop vibes, and if other inmates suspect he's conversing with law enforcement, it could make him a bigger target than he already is.

I decide to hang around for another ten minutes, and then Avery arrives in a blue jumpsuit and white lace-less sneakers. The guard uncuffs him, and he sits in a plastic chair shabby like mine and puts the visitation phone to his ear. "I knew you'd come," he says, glaring at me through the glass partition.

"It's time we talked."

"Where's Shaun?"

"Rehab."

"Is he getting me a real lawyer?"

"Afraid not, but I'm working on it. I have an associate who's putting feelers out for a lawyer who will take your case."

"Good, because my public defender ain't shit. The fool probably rode the short bus to school."

"You want out of here, then you're going to need to answer my questions."

"What kinda questions?"

"I saw Keisha's photos."

"So?"

"You took them?"

"Mostly."

"And the BDSM stuff? Was that your idea?"

"It's not like I forced her to do it," he says. "We were trying to get her portfolio strong and show range."

"I accessed your hard drive, too. Those photos were taken last month. Before that, it was bikini thongs and pasties. Risqué, but nothing that would get you fired if caught peeping on the job."

"Depends on the job."

"That isn't the point."

"Yeah, well, vanilla doesn't sell. Twenty years ago, Keisha would've been *Jet* magazine's beauty of the week. But no one's checking for pretty brown girls with nice smiles anymore. Pictures have to tell a story, hint at something that'll give a man pause. Make 'em think something nasty for a second."

"Some men can't leave it there," I say. "Thoughts become actions. Those photos might've gotten her killed."

"You think some perve hard up for Keisha did this to us?"

"I don't know," I say. "What about the money you owe? You were looking for a payday. Tell me, Avery, did you pimp her to the highest bidder, and shit went south?"

"Man, you're way off."

"Then tell me what happened. What can you remember?"

"What good is telling you anything? Sure, we're blood, but you're not police anymore. How are you gonna help me?"

"Start talking, and you'll see. Or don't and rot in here."

"I'm not about to die in here over some shit I didn't even do."

"I came thinking you'd spill the moment you saw me," I say. "That you'd be chomping at the bit to walk me through that night, but so far, you haven't offered one solid defense."

"There's nothing to defend. I didn't kill Keisha. I loved her. Period."

"Don't you want to know who did this to you two? Don't you want justice?"

"I already know who did it, but there's not a jury that will believe it. Not my attorney and damn sure not a judge."

"Then who did it? You can't just let them get away with it."

"They already have. Can't you see that? And this whole mess is my fault. Yeah, I pushed Keisha into this shit, but only because we had to. A few girls she knew had made an easy deuce taking photos for websites and magazines. They kept it light—leather, chains, showing off their piercings. Nothing crazy."

"Dog collars?"

"You a Mormon? A Jesus freak or something? Yeah, man, studded fucking collars. So what?"

"Who were you sending the photos to?"

"Some of Keisha's model friends told us about a website. Only BDSM-type stuff was allowed, and people on there were looking to work with dark-skinned girls. We posted a few pictures and threw up a profile saying Keisha was open for work. By the next day, her inbox was full."

"Job offers?"

"Mostly for sex work," he says. "Dudes were claiming she could make serious money doing videos."

"Porn."

"Yeah, man, but she wasn't about to do that shit. We deleted all those messages. But one guy's offer seemed legit: ten thousand in cash for two days of work. Not Bitcoin or that NFT bullshit, either. I'm talking real cash. All Keisha had to do was dress in some funny clothes, and I'd be on set the entire time."

"What'd he want her to wear?"

"Rags, man. Shit somebody on the street would wear, but it was more like costumes. He said it was a niche market. People would pay top dollar for what he called *antebellum chic.*"

"Slave attire."

"Call it what you want. It was good money."

"You took the job?"

"He agreed to get us a hotel room near the beach, so we left for LA the next day."

"To meet him in Malibu?"

"I know this shit sounds sketchy, but it's the truth. You have to understand that we needed that money. I asked Shaun for a loan, but he wouldn't give it to me. My entire life, I never asked him for shit. I didn't even want to meet him for the longest. I wondered what was the point. He clearly didn't give a damn about me. The one time I need a favor, he says he can't raise the cash."

"He wasn't lying."

"Bullshit! My mother told me he was selling his condo and would pocket over a million."

"He needed it for rehab."

"No way rehab is that expensive."

"Or he smelled your lie a mile away . . ."

"What the hell are you talking about?"

"He wouldn't have given you the money if he suspected you were a gambling addict. Pop likes sports—it's probably the only thing you and him have in common—but gamblers have a way of talking about sports, unlike casual fans. Sounds more like a man lusting over a woman he can never have, the pretty stripper who just talked him into a twenty-dollar lap dance, and he's got empty pockets, just lint and chewing gum."

"We talked about other shit besides sports . . . Even talked about you and how you got yourself this nice place in a white part of town and some model chick that bakes."

"Just tell me, where in Malibu were you supposed to meet this guy?"

"Some lame-ass pub, but he never showed. We ate, had a few beers, and got ready to leave. Then Keisha got a message on her phone. The dude said he'd meet us in the parking lot. We went outside, where a man stood by a big-ass pickup truck. He said he worked for the guy who hired Keisha and wanted us to follow him to a hotel he had already booked for us. I'm thinking, cool—it's Malibu, right? Probably some swanky three- or four-star hotel with a jacuzzi tub and king-size bed."

"What time was this?"

"Hell if I know. You think I remember those kinds of details?"

"So you followed him to a hotel?"

"Nope. We barely made it a mile before Keisha's car stalled. Then, as if that fat mutherfucker was heaven-sent, he tells us he's got a hitch and can tow the car. We just needed to ride with him in the truck. He must've knocked us out with something because the next thing I knew, we were chained up in what looked like a cave, and someone was taking pictures of Keisha."

"Someone?"

"I first thought it was the bastard that kidnapped us, but this fool was skinnier."

"And the man with the truck? Did you see him?"

"Did I see him?" he repeats. "That mutherfucker beat me so bad I thought I was bleeding on the insides."

"And he did the same to Keisha?"

"We both caught hell, but Keisha was as small as a minute. He was beating her with something long and metal, just wailing on her like no tomorrow. Seemed like the more she cried, the more he hit her, and that skinny mutherfucker was taking pictures the whole time—it was like he was getting off on it."

"How'd you escape?"

"It took a while. Days maybe," he says. "They had my ankle chained pretty good, but I was able to loosen the anchor. I found some glass and picked the lock until it snapped off. Got that shit off of Keisha and waited in the dark until that fat bastard came to beat on us some more. So, I whooped his ass, cleared out, and took the stairs to what ended up being the kitchen."

"Tell me about the kitchen. Anything stand out?"

"White walls. Tiled floor. Big bulky fridge and big-ass stove—all stainless-steel shit, professional-looking. Not the type of stuff you see in everyday kitchens, know what I mean?"

"Anything else?"

"Nah. I thought about taking a butcher's knife to old Jelly Roll, but Keisha said to run."

"And the skinny man? Any idea where he was?"

"House was massive," he says. "I wasn't about to look for him. We wanted out. After running all night, we came across a big glass dome. It was like a greenhouse or something, and stayed inside until someone showed up and chased us off."

"You couldn't have gone to a house? Rang the doorbell?"

"Are you crazy? For all we knew, the whole town was in on that bullshit. And what do you think they'd say, seeing two bleeding people at their doorstep . . . Black people in that town? They might've shot our asses right then . . . Nah, bruh, we ran."

"What about Keisha's car? Your phones? What happened to them?"

"The fat bastard was the one who probably tampered with Keisha's ride while we were in the diner. I bet they made her car disappear that night, the same as our phones."

"The autopsy said Keisha suffered blunt force trauma to the

head. They found blood and hair on a rock near her body and under *your* fingernails, which is why you're in that jumpsuit. Can you explain that?"

"No, I can't," he says. "But I've been piecing shit together in my head. The only thing they fed us was oatmeal in the morning and, I'm guessing, at night, too. Since we couldn't see outside, we never were sure of the time of day. I think something in that oatmeal made us confused and forgetful."

"The toxicology report didn't find anything in Keisha's system, but it may have dissipated."

"Fuck, man, these synthetic drugs nowadays can trick all them blood tests," he says. "But it had to be odorless and tasteless. They made sure the helpings were small. That way, we stayed hungry and ate every bite."

"But the tissue under your nails . . . it's what they'll use against you in court. You need to be straight with me."

"Look at me, man. See my face? If I killed Keisha, who the hell did this to me?"

His face still shows the violence he endured: cuts, swelling, and purple bruising. Not the types of injuries a man could self-inflict, but I've seen prosecutors suggest far greater implausibilities a jury ultimately believed. Narcotics are a kind of alchemy in the minds of most people. It's feasible that a man under the influence of psychotropic drugs could mutilate himself and bash his girlfriend's skull, but it is highly unlikely.

"And that's what you're going with? That you've got no idea how your girlfriend's head got bashed in?"

Avery pounds the phone against the table. He makes such a racket the guard looks over and glares, but he's deep in it, reliving that night, a scene playing behind his eyes. He puts the phone back to his ear. "All right, man," he says, needled for the truth. "She slipped . . . we were running, and her foot caught something, and she smacked her head on that rock. It was dark. I couldn't see well. I thought maybe she was knocked out, so I touched her. You know? Just seeing if she was breathing."

"Was she?"

"Barely," he says. "Her pulse was real faint. I didn't know

what to do, so I ran through the woods, up a hill, and toward the headlights. Thought that if I could wave someone down, it'd be over, and we'd be saved. I've never been lucky, but it was like hitting the jackpot when you found me. I mean, what were the odds?"

"That you'd survive, and she wouldn't?"

"Man, I went for help. I did what I could."

"You left her behind, and she bled to death," I say. "She had a cracked skull, Avery. How could you not have seen that?"

"I told you, it was dark."

"And what about the website where you posted her pictures? You have a name or an IP address?"

"We tried to pull up the site on our phones in the diner," he says. "We both figured we'd been hustled or something because that shit had been removed. The entire website was shut down."

"All you've got is reasons but not any real answers."

"Fuck you know about it? You weren't there," he says. "I loved that girl, would've died for her."

"Maybe you should've." I signal the guard so he knows our visit is over.

"You're leaving already?"

"Someone has to get justice for Keisha."

"What about me?"

"It was never about you meeting our father. You needed an excuse to come here so your mother wouldn't worry. Let me guess, she funded your little road trip?"

"I didn't have a choice," he says. "It was the only way she'd give up some cash. I told her Keisha and I were getting engaged and wanted to meet the old man. She was geeked, fucking over the moon that Keisha and I were going to tie the knot. She gave me the money and didn't ask questions, but I didn't give two shits about meeting *your* father. Because that's all he is—your father and my sperm donor."

"Pop was looking forward to seeing you."

Avery's grip is tight around the phone's handle, squeezing it like he's about to snap it in two. "Yeah, well, he owes me," he says, pulling away from the guard. "All those years and not once did he come to see me. Not fucking once. He abandoned me and he's doing it all over again!"

"Good luck with the public defender."

"That's how it's going to be, huh? You ain't shit, and neither is Shaun." He tries slipping his arm from the guard's hold, but the guard wields his considerable size and yanks Avery from the seat. "I hate you mutherfuckers," he screams. "Shaun owes me, dammit. He can't leave me in here! I didn't fucking do it. You hear me? I'm innocent of this shit."

I hang up the phone as the guard drags Avery away, spitting muffled curses behind the thick glass. Like Pop said after I told him about Simone: "Blood doesn't make family." It was heartless, and I've never forgiven him, but the saying is true of Avery. Despite sharing DNA, we aren't brothers. He gambled away his future, then exploited a woman he claimed to love for easy money. The medical examiner said she had old wounds, which means Avery might've been abusing her, and for that, he can sit in lockup for a few more days.

FIFTEEN

Aside from the massive Blue Lives Matter flag hanging in their lobby, the Malibu/Lost Hills Sheriff's Station isn't at all what I expected. It's modernized: newer flooring and furnishings, unlike the City of Industry's Station with Cold War-era bunker aesthetics and uncomfortable chairs.

A bulletin board hangs in the lobby with pictures of missing people. Out of the twelve, eight are young, Black, and female. The dates they were reported missing range from 1999 to 2014.

The deputies give me the stink eye as I wave to Brennan. She wants to shine me on, but the longer I'm in the station, the more her colleagues talk, and she doesn't need any more of the wrong kind of attention.

I wave and annoyingly call her name, until she has an attending deputy walk me to her desk. "You have five minutes," she says, plucking away on her keyboard. "After that, I'm throwing you out, and if you come back, I'm arresting you."

Files clutter her desk; her computer monitor is layered with dust, packed in grooves and at the base. She hasn't cleaned it in years, if ever. Untidy cops bother me; it means they're comfortable with leaving things in disarray.

"I don't believe Avery is a murderer," I say. "Two men abducted him and Keisha. At least one is local and may be using his home to commit these crimes."

She scoffs. "Someone's home? This isn't LA, Finnegan. Around here, sounds of murder and carnage don't go unnoticed."

"Most homes in the area were built without basements or panic rooms, which means the space would've been added later, but wine cellars are common around here and date back decades."

"You think a Malibu resident is abducting people and keeping them in a wine cellar?"

"It's possible . . ."

"I deal in evidence rather than hang my badge on possibilities." Brennan chews the end of her pen. "I take it you've been talking to Avery?"

"I saw him this morning. He remembers everything."

"Or he's had plenty of time to concoct a wild tale, which you ate right up . . ."

"The abductors drugged him and Keisha. That's why he couldn't remember much. I suspect they were micro-dosed over a few days. Now that the drug is out of his system, he has near total recall."

"Convenient."

"You mean inconvenient. I know you've put the wheels in motion so that he ends up on Death Row, but you've got the wrong man. There's something afoot here, and burying Avery isn't going to make your superiors forget they've seen you in a thong."

"You're a total fucking asshole—you know that?"

"Doesn't mean I'm wrong."

"Really? How much do you know about your brother?"

"Learning more every day, and I'll be the first to say I don't like him. But it doesn't make him a killer."

She pulls a file from her desk drawer and drops it on top of her keyboard. "It's his Nevada rap sheet. Three DUIs in four years. One arrest for aggravated assault. Another for domestic violence . . ."

"What was the charge?"

"Assault with a deadly weapon," she says, skimming the report. "He threatened his girlfriend, identified as Keisha Landry, with a golf club. Later, the club was determined stolen from the trunk of a neighbor's car."

There's nothing I can say that'll make Avery's past not sound as horrible as it does. His behavior is indefensible, but it doesn't mean he committed homicide.

Brennan returns to chewing the pen. "What? Nothing to say?"

"Nothing you'll want to hear."

"Then your disruption is over. I've got work to do."

"One more thing," I say. "You'd be wise to look into something."

"What is it now?"

"An address . . ."

"Yeah, whose?"

"The man from yesterday who died in the car crash."

"Oh, the victim in your road-rage incident?"

"You talked to Navarro?"

"Briefly."

"It wasn't road rage."

"He said you suspected the man to be involved in *something* but didn't say what, and you chased this man like a maniac through the streets."

"That's not what happened. He tried to ram me with his truck and ended up wrecking."

"Well, Navarro thought my coming down would be a waste of time. I agreed."

"You chose wrong, Brennan. The man, Jack Baskin, confessed to killing multiple people in this area and suggested he didn't act alone. I believe he's one of the men responsible for what happened to Avery and Keisha—their abduction, torture, and Keisha's murder. And they weren't the first. Over twenty years ago, Sharice Mitchell escaped with similar injuries and recounted the same experience. She and her brother, Gabriel, might've been the earliest known victims. He was found dead from a gunshot wound, floating in a ravine. They were just kids. Evidence of these crimes and others might be at Baskin's address."

"So, you want me to go poking around this guy's house on a hunch?"

"Whatever happened to dotting every 'i' and crossing every 't'?"

"We've got our suspect sitting in the county lockup."

"And if you're wrong, then what?"

Brennan's eyes drift across the room to the captain's office, where her superior, a puffy-chested white man in uniform, watches our interaction through mini blinds. Deputies walk past, looking busy, and stay within earshot of our conversation. The entire station is concentrated on us. "You really shouldn't be here," she says. "What you're doing could be considered tampering."

"What's the worst that'll happen, Brennan? Maybe you'll find out the real reason those people on that 'missing wall' in your lobby have never been found."

Brennan stops chewing the pen and sets it on her desk. Then she asks, "You said his first name is Jack?"

"Jack Baskin . . . I'd go myself, but anything I'd find would be inadmissible."

She hands me what's left of the chewed pen and a sticky note. "Write down the address."

I copy the address from the picture of Baskin's license on my phone and give her back the lime-green sticky note and mangled pen.

"On second thought," she says, "you're coming with me."

"Me? But why?"

"Because I need you to see how misguided this quest of yours is, and I want to witness the moment you realize you've been chasing your tail."

"What reason do you have not to believe me?"

"And what reason do you have not to believe the evidence?"

"A man tramples through the woods after beating himself to a pulp and killing his girlfriend?"

"Bath salts, meth—who knows what he was on?"

"Traces would've shown up in his blood samples. The pieces don't fit, Brennan. You know it, and so does that prosecutor. That's why he's fishing for a judge who won't see through the bullshit."

"You have been poking around . . ."

"Face it: no judge is going to risk their career overseeing a trial when the state's case is riddled with holes and unanswered questions."

"Look, you can spin this all you want, but Avery is guilty—he killed Keisha Landry, and if going to this Baskin guy's residence is the only way to get you to see that, fine. But when nothing checks out, I want your guarantee that you'll drop it. Then you can go back to ruining cops' lives and whatever the hell else you do."

"That isn't what I do—"

"Well, the only person who believes that is Cohen. For some reason, he thinks the world of you. Sees you as some shining knight."

Rumors that I've been exposing corrupt cops have grown in the last month. Since the discovery and subsequent death of Amanda "Boston" Walsh, I've gone from an inconvenient boogeyman to a full-blown enemy of the *blue*. Every police officer that David Bergman and I exposed was found guilty and terminated, yet no one wants to acknowledge that. We did important work—necessary work—and put citizens first when officers and departments failed to uphold their mandates. The work must continue, but I'm unsure how I'll manage without David.

"What are you standing around for?" Brennan claps me out of my stupor. "Let's get this over with."

"Fine. Lead the way."

SIXTEEN

Baskin's house is an old tract home across the street from drill rigs that are still in operation. There are at least a dozen throughout Signal Hill and Long Beach; this one is loud, and I can smell the crude through the cruiser's vents.

The house may be the last post-war designed home remaining in the vacated neighborhood. Decades ago, it might've attracted photographers from *Architectural Digest* who were keen on showcasing what suburban life was like after World War II. Nowadays, people keep clear of homes near the drills, which explains Baskin's lack of neighbors and the decaying bungalows needing to be torn down.

"You think this is it?" Brennan asks, parking the cruiser in front of Baskin's mailbox. Far-right political signs cover a fence that surrounds the home: *Don't Tread On Me, Blue Lives Matter, End White Genocide,* and *Anudda Shoah.*

"Looks that way."

"Are you sure about this address?"

"It's what was on his driver's license," I say. "Fits the profile, too."

"Did he mention if he lived with anyone?"

"We didn't exactly have a polite conversation. Although you two might've hit it off. Wouldn't be surprised if he was a fan of yours . . . an appreciator of *patriotic swimwear and machine guns.*"

"I'm doing you a favor, Finnegan. I didn't have to come out here. Don't forget that."

"But you did, which means part of you knows I might be right."

"A bigger part wants you out of my life. I figure this is the easiest way to make that happen. Remember, if I don't find shit, I never have to see or hear from you again."

"Yeah, I got it," I say, unbuckling my seat belt.

"Nope. Your ass stays here."

"What?"

"You heard me. I'll check it out. If there is evidence in there, I don't want you mucking it up."

"I should be watching your back. You didn't interact with this guy. He was dangerous."

"And he's dead, right?"

"Yes, but it's like I told you: he was working with someone. Maybe more than one person, and you can't be certain they aren't in that house."

"I'll take my chances."

"How about I stand outside? At least that way—"

"No," she says. "You leave this vehicle, and our deal is off."

"Ah, hell, Brennan."

"I'm not some wet-behind-the-ears rookie," she says. "I know what I'm doing."

Brennan gets out of the car, scans the neighborhood, and walks to the gate. She inspects the latch and pops it. The lawn is overgrown, and there's a rusted washing machine on the porch, along with two folding chairs. She knocks on the door and waits; there's no answer.

I call her cell. She stands clear of the door to take the call. "What now?"

"You won't get through that door," I say. "The front of the house looks undisturbed."

"How can you tell? The place is a shithole."

"All the flags and posters are like a message board. Baskin wouldn't want to detract from that," I say. "Trust me. He likely parked in the driveway and entered through a rear door. Go around back and see."

"You're giving me orders now? Don't forget who has the badge."

"I'm trying to help."

"All right," she says. "I'm going." Brennan steps off the porch and moves around to the rear of the house. I watch her until she vanishes behind an overgrown bush that obscures my view.

"I lost your visual. Can you stay on the line?"

"What are you, my babysitter?"

"Just tell me what you see."

She sighs. "Fucking ridiculous . . . OK, I see a lawn in need of mowing. Tons of weeds. Maybe a few marijuana plants growing with the dandelions."

"And the door? What about the door?"

"Pretty basic. Thin with a deadbolt . . . I'm giving it a try now." I listen as she jiggles the handle. "Anything?"

"Locked," she says. "But wait, I think I got something . . ."

"What is it?"

"Might be old blood on the doorpost. A couple of drops . . . there's more leading under the door."

"You have to go in."

"Breaching now," she says, kicking the door in. "Fuck!"

"What is it?"

"Reeks."

"Decomp?"

"No, more like a porta-potty," she says, coughing. "Lots of flies in here."

"You see a computer? A laptop?"

"Yeah, he's got it on his table."

"Good. You're going to need that."

"I'm doing a sweep now," she says. "I think I know where the smell is coming from. Approaching the rear of the house."

"What do you see?"

"I'm in the rear bedroom. This guy has jars shelved in here. Rows of them on the walls."

"What's in them?"

"Ah, fucking sick," she says. "This can't be for real . . ."

"Tell me what you see."

"Jars, man—fingers and toes and tongues are soaking in piss, I think. Ah, Jesus . . . it's definitely piss."

"Remains from his victims. Trophies."

"That's not the worst of it."

"What else you got?"

"Genitals," she says, her voice dampened like she's talking through her palm. "Baskin was preserving genitals belonging to males . . . Black men, from the looks of it. There has to be more than one hundred jars here."

"I'm coming in."

"We need locals down here," she says. "Maybe even the FBI."

"OK, don't touch any—"

It's a sudden eruption, ear-piercing like fireworks exploding, followed by ivory smoke and flames and screams. I get out of the car and sprint toward the house. Smoke pours from the blown-out windows; it smells acrid and garlicky.

My nose burns; the searing pain rears high in the nasal cavity and puts knives in my eyes. I hold my breath and keep running toward the rear of the house. As I approach, Brennan bursts through the door, her face and body covered in what looks to be white phosphorus. She's coughing hard in agony, drenched in the sticky white powder.

The gas continues to pour from the house, and there's a loud *clicking*.

"Hold on, Brennan. I'm going to get you out of here."

The clicking grows louder . . .

"It burns, dammit," she says. "It burns!"

I tuck my hands under her arms, pull her up to my chest, and start dragging her away from the house. "We have to get out of here," I say. "There's not much time."

"What the hell did he do to me?" she asks between coughs. "I can't fucking see anything."

"We have to keep moving."

The gas was the first stage of the attack; the clicking foretells the second. I drag Brennan to the front of the house, careful to avoid breathing in the toxic air. I open the gate and pull, but something is holding us back. Her pant leg is snagged on a piece of fence, twisted in the cuff. I pull, but her leg isn't budging.

"Shit," I say, trying to work the metal barb free from the denim.

"What is it? What's wrong!?"

"I have to cut it." I take out my switchblade and slice the denim from around her ankle, freeing her leg. I collapse the knife, put it in my pocket, and continue to drag Brennan toward the car. We're feet from safety when another explosion rocks the house, igniting the smoke and hurling flames into the sky.

"Call it in," she says, gasping for air. "Before it all burns."

"It might be too late," I say, dialing 911 as fire engulfs the house. "Baskin planned for this. No one was ever supposed to get this far . . ."

"Who the hell are these people, Finnegan?"

"I don't know, but easy now," I say. "Focus on breathing."

The emergency responder comes on the line. "Nine-one-one. What's your emergency?"

"Officer down, Code Three. Seven-one-one East Burnett Street. Signal Hill. Requesting an ambulance and fire; there's a house burning with hazardous materials inside. Responders will need to exercise extreme caution."

It's after five o'clock when I ring Cassandra's doorbell. Nigel answers in his usual frock, holding a bamboo cup and slurping green liquid through a paper straw. "Good evening, Mr. Finnegan."

I enter the house, which smells of basil and garlic. "We need to talk."

"Is everything all right? You've been gone so long that Ms. Cassandra was about to organize a search."

"That Downey address you gave me for Sharice Mitchell. Did you tell anyone else I was going there?"

"No one," he says. "Did the address check out? Did you find Ms. Mitchell?"

"I found her," I say, "but you're telling me you didn't even tell Cassandra?"

"I didn't see any need—"

"Then how'd someone who previously tried to run me and Pop off a canyon road know my precise location? And before you suggest it, I've ruled out being followed."

"I assure you, I told no one."

"Well, someone knew I was going to see Sharice."

"I wish I could be of more help, sir."

I work the crick in my neck. I'm beginning to feel the effects of sleeping in the car, or maybe it's from having to drag Baskin and then Brennan out of harm's way. "There's something I'm not seeing," I say, digging deeper into the muscle.

"Are you OK?" Nigel asks. "I'm a certified massage therapist, and I know a muscle sprain when I see one."

"It'll be fine. My only concern is knowing how someone could've found me in Downey."

"Have you considered you're being tracked, sir? I'd be happy to scan your clothing for any bugs or transmitters."

"You can do that?"

"Given the nature of Ms. Cassandra's work . . . yes."

"I'm not sure how someone could have bugged me," I say, "but I'll check my own clothes."

"I'm very sorry for your trouble, Mr. Finnegan."

Nigel doesn't comment on my odor, but it's strong, and I'm beginning to offend myself. "I need a shower."

"Should I prepare the massage table for afterward? Really, it's no trouble at all."

"That won't be necessary."

"If you're not interested in a massage, is there anything else I can help you with?"

"Actually . . ." I pull Baskin's cell phone from my pocket. "I need to know what's stored on this phone."

"Is that blood, sir?" Nigel asks, noticing the remaining red dots on the device I wasn't able to clean.

"Is that going to be a problem?"

"Not at all."

"Thanks, Nigel."

"Will you be joining us for dinner?"

"What's on the menu?"

"Black truffle pasta in pomodoro sauce."

"Not sure what pomodoro sauce is, but I don't make a habit of turning down meals you cook."

"Excellent—I'll prepare your setting."

Upstairs, I search my smoke-filled clothes for any tracking devices and find nothing. The idea of someone bugging me seemed far-fetched, but stranger things have happened.

After a shower, I dress in my last pair of clean clothes—jeans and a sweater—and go downstairs. Nigel isn't present, but he's set a place for me at the table: pasta, garden salad, and breadsticks brushed with herb butter. Cassandra is seated, drinking red wine and nibbling on a breadstick.

"Nigel thinks eating these things is lowbrow, but it's a guilty pleasure."

"Bread is your guilty pleasure? Seems a little repressive."

"I prefer a disciplined life, and there are worse vices than carbs."

"I highly doubt on your deathbed you'll be rejoicing over all the bread you didn't eat."

"Well, like most people, I fold on occasion," she says. "Nigel has caught me gorging on these things more times than I'd care to admit." She wipes the waxy butter from her lips. "I told myself I'd never set foot in a national chain restaurant, but then I had one of these things . . ."

"Hard to imagine you feasting on unlimited breadsticks," I say, sitting across from her.

"Unlimited? No, no," she says. "That much gluten would kill me. I'd ordered six to go, but after a while, Nigel refused to pick them up. Instead, he discovered the official recipe online and made me a healthier version, minus the GMOs, preservatives, and who the hell knows what else."

"He offered to massage me earlier."

"And you didn't take him up on it? He's got good hands. Massages that are transformational."

"Between fixing the Falcon, being a tech wizard, and massages, it made me wonder if there is anything that man can't do. I mean, besides have intercourse in your home."

"You think I was upset about him having a romp?"

"Seemed that way."

"Despite what you may think, Nigel and I have always maintained a platonic relationship. He works for me—that's it. Who he sleeps with is his business."

"I wasn't suggesting you two had a thing."

"Good," she says. "Because it never happened and never will."

"But you must wonder if he's happy here."

"I never wonder that."

"Content, then . . . Do you wonder that?"

"He's taken care of financially, and if he wants to enjoy himself with a co-ed twit, who am I to stand in his way? I only object when it has the potential to jeopardize my business. The presence of outsiders undoubtedly leads to excessive risks."

"What am I, if not an outsider?"

"You're different . . ." She continues to eat her breadstick, considering how to classify me. "What I'm trying to say is, you're Trevor. I mean, you're a . . . friend."

"Friends tell each other the truth, right?"

"Good friends do."

"OK, then, did you know I was in Downey yesterday?"

"Downey? I presume that's a city?"

"Yes, where a man tried to kill me, or I thought so at the time."

"A *random* man?"

"Not exactly."

"And what became of him?"

"What's it matter?"

"Is he dead?"

"Yes, but I didn't kill him."

"Did you want to?"

"I don't see how that pertains to this . . ."

"Professional curiosity."

"Yes," I say. "I wanted to."

"Interesting."

"But he didn't kill me, even though he could've, and it got me wondering about this thing you've got with looking out for me."

"You're talking about Vegas?"

"Yes, Vegas, where your driver asked if I wanted someone shot because I got roughed up a little."

"And what did you say?"

"I told him it wouldn't be necessary."

"Well, just so you know, had you agreed, you would've been free from implication."

"*Free* is a stretch, and I'm no killer."

"You just keep company with them, is that it?"

"I don't know what you mean."

"Yes, you do," she says, dropping the half-eaten breadstick onto her plate. "Why are you here, staying in my house?"

"You offered."

"Because you were too noble to ask . . . but nobility is an act, Trevor. It's a game we play, but it doesn't explain why you're having dinner with me now."

"Hunger."

"Maybe, but not for bowtie pasta. I fascinate you, don't I? I'm a puzzle you haven't solved."

"Don't give yourself so much credit. I solved a Rubik's cube at seven."

Cassandra takes my hand and toys with a scab on my thumb from an injury, probably when I pulled Baskin from his wrecked truck. "You risk so much for these people . . . so much sacrifice and pain, but who looks after you?"

I slip my hand from her grasp. "Is that why you instructed your driver to keep me from being harmed? You were looking out for me?"

"Consider it a friendly gesture from a woman with very few friends."

"You're keeping things from me, Cassandra, and you know good and well where Downey is."

"Why would I lie about something so trivial? You think I'm involved in whatever this case is?"

"All I know is that you're hiding something, and I want to know why."

"Please, Trevor. This is silly," she says. "Let's just enjoy the delicious meal Nigel prepared."

"Not much of an appetite." I get up from the table. "When you're ready to tell me your angle in all this, we'll talk . . . OK, *friend*?"

"No matter what you think of me, I'd never do anything to put you in danger."

I push the chair under the table and head toward the stairs. "Even if I posed a threat to your precious business?"

"Trevor, come back and sit down. Please?"

"We'll talk tomorrow," I say. "Unless you prefer I leave."

"I'm not petty like the many women I'm sure you've dated. You know you're welcome to stay as long as you need."

"All right, then . . . Goodnight."

I leave Cassandra drinking wine, which has become a common occurrence, and go upstairs to the guest room. I change out of my pants and get in bed. I have two missed text messages, one from Sarada and another from Tori.

Sarada's message is encouraging, and attached is a picture of her smiling next to her latest creation, captioned: **Meringues.** The dumpling-like cookies look delicious.

I text back: **Can't wait to try them. Miss you.**

Tori's message feels compulsory. She apologizes for being rude to me at her place and blames her poor attitude on stress. She's decided to leave LA at the end of the month, as I expected, and wants me to spend more time with Simone before they go.

I'm too tired to respond thoughtfully, so I defer texting her until the morning. The phone rings as I'm about to silence it for the night—it's Cohen.

"Cohen? How's Brennan?"

"She's hanging in there," he says. "She has some pretty extensive burns, but the doctors at Long Beach Memorial are optimistic she'll make a full recovery."

"Good."

"You want to tell me what happened? Who's this Baskin guy she's going on about?"

"Probably best we speak about that in person," I say. "What about Baskin's house? Anything salvaged?"

"Unfortunately, no. The computer was destroyed, along with most of the evidence Brennan had found in the room. A treasure trove of DNA gone . . . Long Beach PD has been asking about you."

"What did Brennan tell them?"

"Nothing . . . from what I can tell."

"Can't believe all that evidence is gone," I say, realizing Baskin's jar collection was the only evidence I had connecting him to the crimes. "I have to keep digging."

"Be nice to know what you two were digging for. Brennan's on morphine and can't stay coherent long enough to give me the rundown."

"I'll explain it all tomorrow."

"OK. Goodnight, Detective."

There's a shallow knock at the door. I anticipate Cassandra coming to make amends, or, if there's one honest bone in her body, coming to discuss the secret she's keeping.

"Come in," I say.

Nigel opens the door, holding Baskin's phone and sheets of printed paper. "I heard you didn't eat. Was the food not to your liking?"

"Lost my appetite," I say. "What's that you've got?"

"The phone had a burn bag program."

"What the hell is that?"

"Two layers of encryption," he says. "The first I managed to bypass, but the second required me to use facial ID or enter a thirteen-digit passcode within five minutes before it purged all data from the phone."

"So it was wiped clean?"

"Yes, but not before I downloaded these chat logs."

"You're shitting me? You got something?"

"It was challenging, not impossible." Nigel hands me the pages. "There are about sixty exchanges with one number."

"Just one?"

"It appears the user only communicated with one person over the last one month."

"You get a hit on the number?"

"Nothing . . . likely it's spoofed."

"Why only a month of messages? I have texts going back years."

"Scrubbed on a cadence," he says. "Probably by a cleaning program that wipes the phone every thirty days."

"That asshole was really covering his tracks."

"Appears that way."

"Thanks, Nigel."

"Of course, sir." He turns to leave but lingers a moment. "I heard you and Ms. Cassandra earlier. It's not my place, but you should know that having you here has brought her much joy. I haven't seen her remotely cheerful since her daughters filled the house with laughter . . . and twerking. I know she doesn't show it, or perhaps she isn't able to, but she respects you greatly and considers you a friend. I just thought you should know that."

"I hear you, Nigel, but there's no delusions between us. Cassandra is who she is, and I am who I am."

"I understand, sir."

"How's Cree?" I ask.

"Busy with finals," he says. "We haven't had a moment to talk—not even about what happened the other night. I fear she's angry or *freaked out*, as she'd say."

"I'm sure she'll come around."

"You've likely suspected I haven't had much experience with dating. Females tend to find me eccentric. However, Cree looked past my idiosyncrasies. I think she found my quirky nature endearing."

"My mother used to say there's someone for everyone. If you two are meant for each other, it'll work out. Have a little faith."

"Faith, yes, I'll work on that. Pleasant night, Mr. Finnegan." He leaves the room.

I'm exhausted but compelled to review the chat logs. The first exchange references something called "Bone Machine." The only things that come to mind are Tom Waits' album and the Pixies' song, which both share the title. Numbers are next to the term, written as "Bone Machine #2" and "Bone Machine #4." The subsequent chats are more cryptic. There's mention of a location called "Haus des Sonnenscheins." An online translator reveals it's German for "House of Sunshine"; is this their murder site? Avery and Sharice both noted the lack of sunlight where they were chained, but could Baskin and his accomplice be referring to their murder dungeon as the House of Sunshine, which would be demented irony . . .

My eyes are dry and twitchy, with pressure building in the sockets. I need to sleep. I'll tackle more of the logs in the morning before I see Brennan at the hospital.

SEVENTEEN

I'm up before sunrise. Turning in early did me good. My back was able to recover on the thousand-coil spring mattress. One good thing about Cassandra is that she only buys the best, even if it is with money from her criminal enterprises. I shower, get dressed, and review the chat logs until daybreak, going downstairs when my stomach growls.

In the kitchen, Nigel hasn't made breakfast yet. I take a banana and a bran muffin from a bowl on the counter, put them in my pocket, and head toward the front door. When I open it, the alarm goes off—an incessant chirping. Nigel stomps upstairs from his quarters, brandishing a shotgun in boxers and slippers.

"It's just me," I say, with my hands up.

"Oh, Mr. Finnegan. I wasn't expecting you'd be up this early."

"Thought I'd get a jump on the day."

Nigel silences the alarm by entering a passcode into the keypad. "I can make you breakfast if you'd like."

"That's all right. Grabbed a little something from the counter."

"Big day?"

"Feels like it."

"How's the E28 treating you?"

"Purrs like a dream. I couldn't ask for a better ride."

"Excellent."

"And not a scratch on her, in case you were worried."

"Not for a second," he says, looking relieved. "Your Falcon should be ready this evening."

"I appreciate it. Check you later, Nigel."

Outside, I get into the Beemer and enter the address for Long Beach Memorial Hospital, where Brennan is receiving care. It's early. Traffic is light; it should take me an hour, but given the streak I'm on, I'll allow additional time for calamity.

A collision on the 405 delayed my arrival at the hospital by fifteen minutes; otherwise, the commute was uneventful. I wait in the lobby, trying to ascertain who Brennan's attending nurse is. I identify her as a petite Asian woman with a tattooed heart on her wrist and a nose ring. We exchange smiles. Hers is brilliant white and unconvincingly perfect like veneers.

"Good morning," I say.

"Good morning."

"God, you must brighten these patients' days with that smile . . ."

"Oh, me? Like a ray of sunshine."

"Don't doubt it for a bit," I say.

"Is that right, charmer?"

"Sure, a smile like that is a work of art—"

"A little early for pickup lines, don't you think?"

"Early? Nah, I appreciate a pretty smile anytime."

"Corny but cute." She blushes, pushing bangs from her eyes. I haven't seen a woman with bangs as long and retro as hers since the early 2000s, and despite the style being dated, she makes it work. "Are you here to see a patient?" she asks. "Because you've got another hour until visiting is allowed."

"I was hoping you'd make an exception. I'd like to see Detective Brennan . . . I'm kind of the reason she's here."

"You're responsible?" She sounds horrified, eying the security guard standing near a door. "That poor woman came in with second-degree burns."

"It would've been worse if I hadn't dragged her out of the house." I show her my PI badge. "Name's Trevor Finnegan. I'm a private investigator."

"And you're the one who saved her?"

"She would've done the same for me."

"Didn't know I was talking to the *hero* of Signal Hill," she says, smirking.

"I'm detecting sarcasm."

"Well, you are a *detective*, right?"

"I was only trying to help."

"I respect that, but let's not clout-chase on heroics," she says. "Plenty of people save lives every day, and if you haven't noticed, a lot of them are in this very building."

"Understood," I say humbly.

"My cousin is Highway Patrol, so I get it," she says. "Once, he had to rescue a woman and her dog from a burning car. He was on the news and everything."

As a nurse, the likelihood of her knowing a law enforcement officer is above average. If they aren't related to a cop, maybe they dated a few. High stress and long hours might not kindle a romance between civilians, but it's foreplay for those with front-row seats to trauma and death.

"So, are you going to let the rules slide this once?" I ask.

She surveys the hallway, her neck whipping left, then right. When she doesn't see her supervisors, she says, "Just this time, but if you get caught, I don't know you."

"Fair enough."

"It's room eight."

"Thank you . . . and tell your cousin to stay safe out there."

She smiles and returns to her duties. I walk the hallway to room eight and enter when I hear the television. The drawn curtain dims the room; the TV's glow washes Brennan's gauzed face and neck in indigo.

"Finnegan," she says, oxygen tubes protruding from her nose. "I wondered if you'd come by."

"Wanted to see how you were doing."

"Shitty, but I'm alive."

I sit in a pink recliner, pushed into the corner next to the IV pump and pulsometer machine. It's hard to look at her. A wretched odor lingers in the room, reminiscent of charred chicken.

"Have you told your captain what you found in Baskin's home?"

"No," she says. "And no one's asking."

"I don't get it. I thought the sheriff would be all over this."

"Over what, exactly? Everything burned in the explosion."

"But you saw what was in there. We had him—we were close to finding the truth."

"We had piss-filled jars of what looked like body parts, Finnegan. There's no telling if they were real or not."

"Forensics could determine that . . ."

"As you can see, human tissue doesn't do very well when it comes in contact with phosphorus." She points to her bandaged face. "Add fire to that mix and there's probably not a damn thing left in that house of horrors that could be tested."

"They should try, at least."

"No one's going to investigate what happened in that house, Finnegan. Long Beach PD is talking about dropping the whole thing."

"They want to bury it?"

"And I'm not going to fight them," she says. "They're doing me a favor. Especially since I entered the home without a search warrant."

"You have to tell someone. Get your captain involved—"

"Forget my captain. I can't even explain this to my lieutenant. I can't justify going into that house."

"You were following a hunch . . ."

"Not my hunch," she says. "It was a disgraced ex-cop's hunch. A man I had no business putting in my cruiser."

"Disgraced? C'mon, Brennan."

"Listen to me, Finnegan. You've got no credibility, which means, by proxy, neither do I. Me being in the same vicinity as you marks me as damaged goods."

"I understand you're angry, but we were doing the right thing."

"You don't get it. My department doesn't have my back on this. Right now, they're probably brainstorming ways to boot me out. It could be the end of my career."

"They'd be jerking your chain," I say. "You were doing good cop work. Who could find fault with that?"

"Me," she says, "I'm the one in the fucking burn unit because I listened to you. Doctors say I'll need at least three skin grafts, and for what? I nearly get blown to hell over some sick fuck that's already dead."

"Baskin didn't work alone. We know that."

"Then prove it," she says. "Go out there and find whoever the hell was helping him and fucking . . ." She ices up, gripped by something unseen.

It must be the painkillers. Narcosis, maybe?

I follow her gaze to an empty corner of the room. "Brennan? Should I call someone?"

Silence . . .

"Brennan, can you hear me?"

"You shouldn't be here," she says, coming out of it. "Go, now."

"I'm sorry, Brennan. I didn't mean for you to get hurt."

"Leave, Finnegan."

"But just tell me one thing. A victim mentioned a house in Malibu with a front door like a castle's. Does that mean anything to you?"

"Oh, for God's sake. I said go, goddamn it!"

"Please think about it. Maybe you've seen the house on patrol."

"Go!"

"OK—I'm going . . . I'm going."

I step outside the room. Cohen approaches from the elevator. "Detective," he says. "Everything all right?"

"Not really the best time . . ."

"Is Brennan all right?"

"She'll need to rest."

"There's a lot of talk at the station about what you and Brennan were doing in that house."

"I know, and I owe you an explanation."

"Is it true? About what Brennan found inside that place. I was here when they brought her in. She was going on about jars filled with—"

"It's true," I say. "Jack Baskin admitted to me that he committed multiple homicides, which could tally in the hundreds. I'm certain he acted with accomplices, and together they tortured Avery and Keisha. Brennan and I were investigating a lead, which led us to Baskin's residence. He had booby-trapped the home to ignite phosphorus. I got Brennan out before everything went up in flames, but not before she was exposed to the chemical."

"Jesus . . ."

"I need to find whoever was helping Baskin, and I've got thin leads, at best."

"Like what? Maybe I could help."

"Avery's account of how he and Keisha escaped, mirrors that of an earlier survivor who said she fled a home near the beach."

"That'll be tough to narrow down. Hundreds of homes have beach access."

"The only distinguishing characteristic the prior victim could remember was the home's arched front door, something medieval-looking."

"Doesn't ring a bell, but there's miles of coastline. Figuring out which house could take days, and you won't have access to homes behind security gates. I'm sorry, Detective, but without a team to assist you, I don't see how it's possible . . ."

"Implausible, maybe, but not impossible," I say. "I'll focus on the beachfront homes I can get to, then figure out how to access others. The first survivor hadn't run a significant distance like Avery and Keisha when she came upon a beach with families and surfers."

"Sounds like Carbon or Latigo."

"Never heard of them."

"They're private beaches. Local spots. Luxury homes feet from the shore. People around here call them Billionaire's Beach."

"I'll start there," I say. "Could I trouble you for binoculars?"

"Sure thing. I have an extra pair in my trunk."

After driving for thirty minutes, I identify a road running through numerous neighborhoods along the coastline, some gated, others accessible but monitored by private security. A small sign advertises Carbon Beach, and there's a long, sandy staircase leading to the shore. I park on the side of the road and take in my surroundings.

People who look like me stand out in ethnically challenged

enclaves like Malibu, but in the Beemer, I draw less attention. The Falcon, on the other hand, with its primer gray, dented body, is neither high-end nor rare. If it were a restored 1967 Corvette or *Bullitt* Mustang, it'd be acceptable, but for residents around here, a Black man driving a hunk of pitted steel means reports of a "suspicious man" or "hot prowler" to the Sheriff's Station.

Even though Cohen knows I'm working the case, I don't want to make life harder for him as I did for Brennan.

It's already ten a.m. Sunset is around five o'clock, and I have six hours to identify the house with the castle door. Outside of a mental picture, I have no way of knowing what the door looks like. I can only visualize it as arched and possibly wooden.

An hour into canvassing, three motorists slow down to observe me. I wave, thinking it'll ease concern or, at best, call attention to their intrusive behavior. One person scowls, and two awkwardly wave with smiles that smack of artifice.

I'm about twenty yards from the Beemer when a hawk-eyed man in a late-model green Jag creeps behind me. He mean-mugs and drives past, returning five minutes later, and, through a cracked window, inquires if I'm lost. "No. I'm fine," I say, with a sweaty brow. He digs in his seat, comes up with a water bottle, and offers it to me. I force a smile. "No, thank you. I've got water in my car." I point to the Beemer. He looks at the car, and I swear he grunts, though I'm too far away to hear. His window rises, reinstating the barrier between us, and he drives away.

As much as I'd like to believe that his actions came from a place of kindness and concern, I know he was attempting to gauge my presence in the community. I'm an outsider here, and I stoke fears. In the hospital, Avery said there was something wrong with this place. I thought it was his shock talking, casting the town as an insidious player in his suffering, but what if there is more to it? Has the Sheriff's Department been investigating the missing persons over the years, or have they come to accept that the faces on the wall will never be found?

My cell phone rings, and I answer: "Hello?"
"So, how goes the search?" Cohen asks.
"Let me guess. You just received a call that a suspicious man is walking in a neighborhood?"
"Sorry, Detective."
"It's expected . . ."
"I'll note it as unsubstantiated."
"Thanks, Cohen."
"How much ground have you covered?"
"Very little."
"Wish I could help, but you know . . ."
"It's all good, Deputy. I'll give you a holler if something breaks."

I end the call, and once in the car, I mull over my next move. Attempting to find the *house of horrors* this way is futile. I could return to the Twin Towers and question Avery again. He might remember more details, something he overlooked. What appears trivial at the time can have consequential implications for the investigation. For instance, a distinctive tree in the front yard or an odd-shaped cliff obstructing the horizon that could be seen from the suspect's home. I welcome any lead that could shrink my search radius to a few square miles.

But Avery made it clear he didn't want to see me, and making another attempt could waste more valuable time. I have to keep going. Something will break—it has to.

I continue driving, hitting dead ends and doubting my resolve. When I encounter a gated neighborhood that I'm unable to access, I park on a hilltop or a lookout point and use Cohen's binoculars to gauge structural details. It all feels hopeless, and after another hour, I park at a seafood café, go inside where I garner a few stares, and order a lobster roll, fries seasoned with Old Bay, and a hoppy ale that takes the edge off.

What if I don't find the house, and these devils get away with murder?

It won't be the first time an investigation has faltered, but it will mean imprisonment for Avery and what I believe to be a band of murderers allowed to commit more killings. My investment in seeing the killers prosecuted means working until I find the truth, no matter how long it takes.

    The sun sinks lower to the horizon; dusk is near. Back in the car, I quickly respond to a text from Sarada asking me to wish her luck as she prepares for her final baking challenge—the Gâteau St. Honoré. I have no clue what it entails, but the prestigious name leads me to believe it's as challenging as she says. A presage comes over me that I may not see Sarada again. I've experienced the feeling before, many times, but never this dominant, and I dare not put credence behind it. Telling Sarada what I'm up against would do little good, and she knows better than to ask. I send a message wishing her all the success, telling her I miss and love her and always will.

EIGHTEEN

It's nightfall, a quarter past six o'clock. The temperature has dropped to fifty-five degrees, accompanied by briny gusts, which is balmy for Southern California. I've decided to return to Cassandra's place and resume my search first thing in the morning.

Descending a winding canyon road, I slow behind unexpected traffic. A convoy of luxury cars is turning into a gated community from the main road—a sign reads "Malibu Estates" in gold, spotlit by floodlights. I recall what the chancellor's work-study student said about the richest people in Malibu living in the estate community, but when I think of the one percent, a university department chair turned chancellor isn't the one who comes to mind. Perhaps he's a man with a varied or questionable revenue stream.

I notice small decals for St. Catherine University on vehicles' back windows—the white dove mascot and red numbers indicating the year. Looking closer, I see they're faculty and staff parking passes. I remember the chancellor's holiday party. It must be tonight, and judging by the number of vehicles, it's as momentous as the chancellor's work-study student suggested.

I opt to follow a luxury SUV and assume my place in a queue leading through the gated entrance. A security guard, a younger Black man, stands outside a guardhouse in a windbreaker, his breath steaming. He's talking fast and shining his flashlight into vehicles. Annoyed drivers shield their eyes from the blinding beam. After the third driver, a stately-looking white woman in a pearl-colored C-Class, sticks her head out of the window and berates him, he puts the flashlight away. By the time the fifth driver reaches the checkpoint, the browbeaten guard waves them forward with little scrutiny, and I figure my odds of not being turned away have improved.

When I reach the guardhouse, the young man looks as if

he's considering quitting. The weather's shitty, and he was just scolded for doing his job. I can't read lips, but I'm an expert at interpreting gestures and body language, and I'm certain the woman's berating was needlessly degrading.

"Good evening, sir. Are you here for the party?" he asks, braids tucked under his work cap. "I'll need to see your invitation."

"First day on the job?" I ask.

"No. What gives you that impression?" he asks. "I've been doing the night shift for two months now."

"Might be your last, though."

"What's that mean?" he asks. "Do you work for Allied Security? You checking up on me?"

"No, kid. I'm not here to fire you. It's just that I know the look. *Karen* back there rubbed you like a bad massage."

"Damn, you saw that?"

"Nothing I haven't dealt with before." I notice a small university mascot pinned on his jacket's collar. "You go to St. Catherine's?"

"Yeah."

"What do you study?"

"Sports Medicine . . ."

"So when injured football players hobble off the field, you're the guy they'll see?"

"Sorry, man. I'm not trying to be rude, but I don't have the time to chop it up with you. If you don't have an invitation or live here, I can't let you through."

I show him my PI badge. "I'm an investigator working a case."

"OK—you have a warrant or something?"

"Didn't say I was a cop."

"I need to see something official to let you in."

"Tell me about the event inside, and I'll disappear."

"Doesn't work that way. I need you to move along. You got a bunch of cars behind you, and people are about to start honking, and I don't need that tonight."

"You're not even curious about who I'm investigating?"

He looks at the string of cars: glowing headlights and clouds of exhaust as if they foretell his doom. "Unless you're investigating me, I really don't give a shit."

"It's a St. Catherine's event, right? Chancellor Webb's holiday party?"

"Ah, c'mon, man. Will you please just get out of here?"

"I give it two more minutes until the first honk. After that, it'll be a symphony of horns because impulsiveness and assholiness are contagious."

"You're really not leaving?"

"Not until you answer my question."

"Fuck it," he says. "Yes, it's Chancellor Webb's party. He throws it for faculty and staff every year. Now, can you leave so I can do my job?"

"I didn't think a chancellor's salary could afford someone a house in the Malibu Estates."

"What the hell do I know about the dude's finances?"

"Nothing I'd expect you to know."

"Whatever, man." He points to the roundabout; in its center, a colorful spectrum of perennials surrounds a fountain lit with holiday lights. "You can make a U-turn and exit the gate."

I roll up the window, come slowly off the clutch, and press the gas, steering the car around the stone fountain. As I come out of the turn, I jerk the wheel to the right and accelerate until I catch up with the other vehicles driving to the chancellor's mansion. It won't be long until the gate attendant mobilizes a response to the breach. I'm sure he's radioed the other guards on the grounds to converge on the chancellor's home and could've warned the chancellor of a potential intruder.

Security will have their eyes peeled for the Beemer. I may be better off avoiding detection on foot. It's dark, but the streets are generally well lit, and I can see plenty of front doors from the street's distance. I'll concentrate on the homes with rears that face the beach, starting with the chancellor's gaudy mansion. His property, like that of his next-door neighbors, has private beach access, which correlates with what Sharice told me about her escape.

After I inspect the chancellor's door, I'll walk the street. I should be able to inspect six or seven properties before security finds and detains me.

Scores of parked luxury cars pack the chancellor's driveway and line the street for blocks. I squeeze the Beemer between massive SUVs parked two blocks from the home, and hope their size will conceal the modest sedan.

People in tuxedos and cocktail dresses converge on the stately manor of stone and brick trimmed in blinking lights and garlands.

I dial Cohen. In case things go to shit, he'll need to know where to find me.

No answer, straight to voicemail: "Cohen, it's me. I might be on to something. I'm sending you my location. If you can't get hold of me in the next couple of hours, come immediately." I end the call, send him my coordinates via the GPS app, and continue watching the procession of guests as they approach the house. It's reminiscent of a high school prom—not that I ever attended mine or anyone else's—but the attendees are more debonair. Instead of worn-out rentals, they likely own their gowns and tuxedos.

I'm unquestionably underdressed for the chancellor's party. I've got no shot at blending in. It's wishful thinking, but maybe I'll go unnoticed among the drove of people preoccupied with joining the holiday festivities. I wait for a break in foot traffic as people pass, then exit the car.

Spending hours sitting in the driver's seat and walking in boots has caused pain and soreness in my knees, shins, and ankles. It's a nostalgic discomfort, like when I worked a foot beat for an entire summer in downtown LA. Aside from the constant walking during a record-setting heatwave, aggressive panhandlers, and drunks, it was cushy.

Exhaust puffs from a late-model Honda Civic, a standout among the fancier rides. It's missing hubcaps and chortles loudly through an after-market muffler. As I get closer, I notice a woman sitting inside vaping. She's dressed in a white collared shirt and dark tie, her hair pinned in a bun. She could be an attendee—a student or teaching assistant with an invite, but it's unlikely. The party feels overtly posh, has less to do with academia, and is more about flaunting wealth.

She hops out of the car, and I'm able to see her attire better: a banquet uniform and black sneakers. She hastily moves toward the rear of the house, where a familiar face waves her through the door—it's *Fife*, Deputy Ortiz, who hassled me and my father at Keisha's crime scene.

What are the chances? It's a good thing I don't believe in coincidences.

He looks perturbed as he bickers with the girl. It wouldn't be out of the norm for a cop to moonlight as security, but it does present me with a greater challenge: he may not be the only deputy at this event who could recognize me.

Fife hikes his poorly fitting suit pants over his belly. Once the girl is inside, he slams the door.

The girl was late, needing to get stoned before her shift. Not that I blame her. Serving the rich and entitled deviled eggs or bacon-wrapped dates seems an awful way to spend the evening, even for a paycheck, but I'm betting she isn't the only one tardy to the event. Fife will likely be monitoring the door for the next ten minutes, so stragglers can enter, which means I'll need to enter through the front.

I walk behind a man and a woman dressed as if they've come to sip from champagne flutes and toast Jay Gatsby. The front door opens as they approach, greeted by a young man, tall with a swimmer's build and long, sun-bleached hair. He's too young to be a deputy, and his hair doesn't meet the regulation standards for any law enforcement agency. He seems to know the couple; they exchange pleasantries, and he allows them to enter, closing the door in my face.

I didn't expect to waltz in, but the huffish boy didn't waste time entertaining me, leaving me to stare at the front door: wooden, arched, and archaic, reminiscent of the 1400s.

Damn—I supposed I've suspected it all along . . .

Unless the Middle Ages inspired the design of another garish mansion on the block, this is the door I've been searching for.

I knock hard, and the boy opens. He quickly inspects my clothing with a snootiness that makes me want to smack him. "Invitation?"

"I don't have one."

"Then, what do you want?"

"I'm an investigator," I say, showing my badge. "I need to speak to Chancellor Webb."

"You'll have to come back another time. As you can see, the chancellor is busy tonight."

"There won't be another time."

"Not my problem. Now, leave."

The boy looks past me, staring coldly in the distance. "They here for you?" he asks, smirking.

I turn around, and two security guards in golf carts approach. There's no use in arguing: the boy won't let me in, and the security guards won't hesitate to remove me by force.

I shove the boy aside. He stumbles, arms flailing. A woman moves clear of the danger, shrieking as the boy crashes into a standing vase, scattering porcelain pieces across the foyer. I dart toward the kitchen; people splinter in multiple directions, tripping and knocking into each other.

A menacing Fife looms on my right, bumping guests from his path to get to me. I've made a mess of things tonight—a tactical failure, sloppy and impetuous. Cohen won't be able to dig me out of this hole . . .

I see the kitchen ahead: a galley layout, as Avery described.

Three men block my path; one looks afraid, holding his champagne flute. I commend their determination, but there's no defying physics. The speed at which I'm moving and the fact they're standing still results in me striking two of them while the other man dodges my blow and miraculously doesn't shatter his flute.

Avery said the door he escaped through led into the kitchen, but I can only see a pantry.

A security guard grabs my jacket and jerks me back hard. I slip away but lose my footing and roll my ankle. I'd forgotten about Fife. His slug to my gut reminds me. I drop to my knees; the wind's knocked out of me, and I'm seething on glazed tile. Keeping my guard up, I deflect a few strikes, but there's no staving off the clobbering—first fists and kicks, then someone slips an arm around my neck, attempting a sleeper hold. I work my way free after gouging the man's eyes, stopping short of blinding him when I feel warm, oily fluid coat my fingertips.

"Enough!" a man says, quieting the room.

The men release me, and I'm allowed to stand. Fife disarms me of my Glock, knife, Taser, and PI badge.

"He's got himself a little arsenal," Fife says, releasing the pistol's magazine. It's the second time someone's removed bullets from my gun. First, the Russians and now Fife—it's becoming an unwelcome trend.

A slim white man parts the crowd—he's well groomed, with tapered gray hair and a mustache. His tuxedo is undoubtedly bespoke, featuring a frilled lapel with a poinsettia pin. "Who are you?" he asks. "Why are you here?"

"You're Chancellor Webb . . ." I say.

"Do I know you?"

"This man breached the gate tonight," the guard says, dabbing his leaking eye with a napkin.

"Care to explain yourself?" the chancellor asks. "Or should I turn you over to Deputy Ortiz?"

"Oh, Fife? I'm not going anywhere with him."

"I'd be happy to take him in," Fife says—the slavering ape.

"Fuck off—call Deputy Cohen. Tell him it's Finnegan."

"Too bad Cohen's not available. He has the night off." Fife hands my ID badge to the chancellor.

"Trevor Finnegan?" he asks, reading the ID's details. "Is that name supposed to mean something?"

"Maybe not now, but it will."

"How ominous . . ."

"You have no fucking idea."

"You're a vulgar little man, aren't you?"

"Guess you bring it out in me."

"Ruining our annual holiday party like this. Such a shame."

"Get used to it. Where you're going, there won't be many parties. Not the kinds you'll enjoy, anyway."

"I simply want to know why you've come here. Is that so difficult to answer? What are your intentions? Otherwise, I'm handing you over to the deputy."

"My intentions? Where do I start . . . ?"

"Don't bother, Chancellor. He's a nobody," Fife says. "Some private investigator digging his nose in the local homicide case. I'll haul his ass into the station and get answers out of him."

"Answers would be nice," I say. "But I've got a question for you, Chancellor. Where's Jack Baskin tonight? Longtime university staff like him. I figured he'd be front and center at this get-together. Although he didn't seem the type to own a tux."

Then I see it—an unmistakable twitch on the chancellor's face, the middle-aged male equivalent of pissing one's pants. "How do you know Mr. Baskin?"

"I didn't know him," I say. "Not well, not like you. But we had a little chat near a fire once."

"What do you mean, you *didn't* know him? Did something happen to Mr. Baskin?"

"Oh, you don't know? Well, don't shoot the messenger, but Baskin is dead."

Chancellor Webb looks to Fife and swallows hard. "Please inform our guests that, regretfully, the night must end. Clear everyone out."

Fife and the security guards begin ushering people out the front door. Disgruntled guests snatch hors d'oeuvres, including tiger prawns and cucumbers wrapped in deli meat, from the trays. They pinch bottles of unopened champagne before leaving, muttering among themselves. My mother always said, "Even the rich can't buy class," and the chancellor's sycophants are no exception.

Fife clears the room of guests, then orders the wait staff and security out as well. Chancellor Webb reaches into his tuxedo pocket, takes out his cell phone, and dials.

My jacket pocket vibrates, followed by the ringtone of the *Dukes of Hazzard* theme. No surprise that Baskin was a fan of a show that featured a 1969 Dodge Charger named the "General Lee," with a Confederate flag painted on its roof.

"It's like I told you," I say. "Jack's dead. All that's left of him is the phone in my pocket."

"I thought you searched him?" Chancellor Webb asks.

"My mistake, boss. I didn't see it." Fife removes Jack's phone from my jacket pocket and hands it to the chancellor.

"Did you kill him?" the chancellor asks.

"Didn't have the pleasure, but Fife here should've told you about Jack's parting gift."

"What's he talking about, Deputy?"

"Asshole rigged his house to explode," I say. "Destroying all that evidence and nearly killing Ortiz's colleague, Sheriff Brennan."

"Brennan is involved now?"

"She doesn't know anything," Fife says. "Baskin made sure nothing was left behind."

"Almost nothing. I managed to get the texts off his phone before it wiped itself clean. It won't be hard figuring out who he was communicating with and what 'Bone Machine' means."

"He's bluffing," Fife says.

"Time will tell," I say. "So, are you some kind of limp-dick murder club? I'm guessing the chancellor here is the one getting off on taking pictures. Am I right? You look like the type."

"Get him downstairs," the chancellor says. "I'll join you soon enough."

Fife opens the pantry door. Boxed foods and canned goods line shelves. He slides a jar of pickles over, reaches in, finds a recessed latch, and pulls it, retracting the door to reveal a staircase leading into darkness.

"Start walking," he says, pressing my Glock into my ribs and pushing me forward. "Try anything, and I'll shoot you on the spot."

I walk down wooden stairs and instantly catch a whiff of the ambrosial sweetness of Pinot Noir and Merlot that's been stored for decades. It's a wine cellar, as I predicted: cold, damp, and dark. Aromas of wine permeate the deep cavern, but just as Sharice found, there's an undercurrent of death. The walls are likely stone or concrete, and the floor is sand, fossilized and compacted over time. It couldn't have been easy to dig for glass, but Sharice's brother Gabriel was determined to set himself free and save his sister. This is where so many lives ended, and others were changed forever.

Glass shards crunch under my heels, likely from broken bottles. Fife turns on a flashlight; the walls are splattered red in every direction, either wine, blood, or both.

Gathered along the wall is camera equipment—light boxes and stands, tripods, and white sheets—and positioned in the cellar's center is a wooden chair and desk with a lamp, computer monitor, and tower. He walks to a wall and shackles my ankles with iron chains, then turns on the desk lamp; like a candle burning in a cave, the glow radiates a few feet. He places my Glock, switchblade, Taser, and badge on the desk.

"What's your stake in all this, Fife?"

"Stop calling me Fife—it's Deputy Ortiz."

"Here's what I think . . ."

"Like it matters what you think—"

"Indulge me."

"Fine, asshole. Probably your last words anyway," he says, squeezing his fat hands into leather gloves. "Go ahead, talk."

"Your trifecta has been at this for decades now. It began in the nineties, but since then, you've refined the operation. Sharice and her brother, Gabriel, were your first victims, but she escaped, and you or Baskin put the bullet in the boy. Mistakes were made, but you learned from them and continued to kill for the next two decades. But something happened with Avery and Keisha. Someone got sloppy and let their guard down, but it wasn't you. No, I'm thinking Baskin slipped up."

Fife interlocks his fingers, flexes them outward until they pop, and rolls his neck in a circle . . . it's a ritual. He's loosening up. I know what comes next . . .

I focus on his massive hands, mentally preparing myself for how he may use them. "You were the scout, am I right?" I ask. "Driving around in your sheriff cruiser looking for people you didn't think belonged—usually Black people, I presume. Outsiders who wandered into your prized community. You're all sadists, in case you didn't know that term, but Baskin was something else. He took souvenirs, and as a cop, that made you nervous, didn't it?"

"Baskin was a freak," Fife says. "Goddamn hillbilly without a modicum of sense. Small gene pool, those people . . ."

"But you didn't disagree with him," I say. "Same mission, a different approach, but you all made a mistake taking Avery and Keisha."

"You know nothing about that little whore, do you?"

"Besides the fact you fuckers tortured and killed her?"

"Here's the Cliffs Notes since you're such a shitty detective. She was arrested for prostitution and solicitation twice in Michigan at the age of sixteen. By the age of eighteen, she'd been arrested once for drug possession: opioids and meth. Then she moved to Nevada, a state far more relaxed about whoring, and continued her stint on the streets. She was a prime candidate," he says, looking prideful. "And that brother of yours—a gambling degenerate and thief. You know as well as I do how they would've ended up. In prison or likely dead. Another case of NHI: *No Humans Involved*."

"But you lured them here, made them think it was a modeling job. They wouldn't have been in Malibu if not for that posting online."

"The chancellor's idea . . . We'd gone months without a kill," he says. "He was getting antsy, starting to look in the wrong places. See, no one misses the people we take, but taking vacationers or beachgoers looking to spend the day up here is risky. Who knows what they mean to the rest of the world? We mess up and snag someone important, and now reporters and people who want to organize search parties are camped out in front of the station and City Hall—all the brouhaha, even for *you people*, is too much attention."

"You actually thought no one would look for Avery and Keisha? That no one would notice?"

"No one worth listening to," he says. "I suppose we didn't count on him being family with the Finnegans. Otherwise, both of them would've been nothing more than pictures on that wall in the sheriff station. Imagine it: for twenty-five years, I've stared into the brown faces of all those now dead, knowing exactly how they ended. I can't tell you the last time my department mobilized for one of you *bone machines*. If you knew the numbers of people who have been right where you are, chained, pissing themselves, pleading for mercy—"

"Oh, I'm not pleading."

"And why's that?"

"Because I know how this ends. With you either in cuffs or dead."

"Look around you." He draws his fist back, lines it up with my face, and delivers a right cross to my jaw. My neck snaps and recoils like a Jack-in-the-box. I spit blood, and my face starts to swell. "No one's coming, Finnegan. It's just *us*."

"Settle down, Deputy Ortiz. He's our guest," the chancellor says, stepping into the light. He's wearing a red velvet smoking jacket, an ascot, and black leather gloves. It's more than regalia. It's his uniform for pogrom.

"We were just discussing how detestable you all are," I say, tonguing a loosened tooth. "But I've got questions for you, Chancellor Webb . . ."

"You're wasting your time, Finnegan," Fife says. "You'll never understand what we're accomplishing here. You're too damn simple. It's how you were bred."

"Fife, you incel, your antebellum fantasy isn't complicated. There's nothing complex about you, but the chancellor taking pictures of people chained and dressed in rags? That's a kink I've never heard of."

"A kink? What I do is no kink." The chancellor smooths and tucks his ascot. "Drug dealers, whores, gangbangers . . ."

"Human beings."

"By your definition. Not mine. What do you think it takes to keep this community looking as it does—"

"You mean white?"

"Pure . . ."

"C'mon, the purity argument? You know there's no such thing—never was. When will you *all* give it up? This pining for the good ole days."

"Most are afraid to admit it, but things were simpler then," he says. "We were honest about who we were, and you people were better off under our thumbs, not just in this country but around the world. Africans can't govern themselves, and the Middle East serves no value but to provide crude oil—soon, they'll be obsolete. Our only competition is China, which I pray a virus wipes out soon enough."

"You can't believe this bullshit, Fife. Have you looked in the mirror?"

He looks eager to slug me again. "The chancellor knows what he's talking about, and I'll have you know, Spaniard blood runs through my veins. The blood of conquistadors! I was birthed to have dominion over this earth."

"Dominion," I say. "Well, shit, Chancellor Webb, you've done a bang-up job on him. But that's what years of brainwashing will do, am I right?"

"I only revealed the truth to him, and the truth speaks volumes," the chancellor says. "There was a time when everyone knew their place. Now, we've gone from one to seven rappers who have bought mansions on *our* beaches, and I have to pretend they belong here. Well, I'm tired of pretending. I'm tired of smiling and acting as if everything that's happening around me is OK. It's not OK, dammit. But if I speak out, I'm a bigot . . . a racist . . . canceled out of a job."

"And your solution was to become a torturing murderer?"

"Trivialities," he says. "Down here, in this place, we're discovering our purpose. Our manhood . . ." He stretches his arms wide, marveling at the hell he's created. "We're kings—tamers of beasts. What we do down here, these moments matter: immortalized to remind *all* of us of our inherent greatness."

"All of you?"

"An entire network of people, Mr. Finnegan, who share our beliefs . . ."

"So that's who buys the pictures?"

"Auctioned to the highest bidder because what good is a Black body that can't be sold?" He turns to Fife, "This one has heart. Try not to kill him too quickly . . . I want to see him break."

Fife drags the wooden chair toward me. He lifts and drops me onto the seat. "I'm going to enjoy this," he says, squaring up and raising his fists. "How long do I keep at it, boss?"

"Until that look in his eyes fades," he says.

"What look?"

"The prideful one."

"Um, OK," Fife says, looking perplexed.

"Go easy on the face. He still needs to photograph well. People will pay handsomely to see such a spirited subject broken."

I shut my eyes.

Fife drives his knuckles into my stomach and ribs over and over again. The wind escapes my body, and I stave off passing out, fearing if I do, I won't wake again.

He pounds away; he's no Golden Gloves contender, but he doesn't have to be to deliver sharp, concentrated blasts along my chest, stomach, and flank . . .

Upper torso.

Right rib.

Lower abdomen.

Left rib.

Below the navel.

Is this what it all led up to, dying in a wine cellar?

I think about Sarada and Pop and Simone and Tori . . . I think about what Sharice said—how I'm loved—and the speeches they'll give at my funeral. I could see Pop telling funny stories, and Sarada—well, I don't know what she'd say . . . maybe she'd lament that I was a good man at heart, or at least I tried to be, and I didn't deserve my fate. And there'd be others, people from my past—LAPD officers and personnel, Kimber from the law firm, maybe Cassandra and Nigel, and names and faces I can't recall.

Thoughts drift to my mother—my sweet, loving, dead mother. I swear I smell her perfume, hear her melodious voice drifting from the netherworld, and wonder if, this time, we'll be reunited.

NINETEEN

"Wake up," a voice says. "Mr. Finnegan, we need to go."

"Cohen? Is that you?" I ask, prying my eyes open.

"Sir, we need to leave now."

But it isn't Cohen. "Nigel?"

"It's me, sir. We must go."

He's already removed the shackles from my ankles, and he's helping me to my feet. "But how did you find me?"

"I can explain later. The authorities will arrive soon."

"That's good," I say, my voice strained and cracking. "So they can arrest these bastards."

Nigel helps me up the stairs. I stop midway when I remember—"My things are on the desk, and we need that computer."

"Your personal effects, certainly, but a computer?"

"I'll carry it."

"You can barely walk, sir."

"Then you have to do it, Nigel. We can't go without it—it's evidence."

Nigel leaves me holding on to the handrail, gathers my belongings from the desk, rips the peripherals from the computer tower, and tucks it under his arm.

"I've got it," he says. "Now, quickly, sir. We don't have much time."

I use his shoulder to steady myself, slowly climbing the staircase. Each step is excruciating, and I can feel knots of fluid and tender tissue all over my body from where Fife pounded me.

We enter the kitchen, now free from the wine cellar turned torture chamber. Barely conscious, I heard the cries of all their victims rising from the darkness, their agony bound in the pits and recesses—but what about the bodies? Buried? Burned? What had the chancellor done with their remains?

"This way," Nigel says, crossing the kitchen.

"What about the chancellor and Ortiz?"

"They no longer pose a danger."

"What the hell do you mean they aren't dangerous?"

Entering the living room, I understand what Nigel refuses to say—they're dead. Chancellor Webb and Ortiz are lying on the floor, victims of gunshot wounds. Both receiving two shots to the head with a small-caliber pistol.

"They were supposed to be arrested. I told Deputy Cohen to come here if he hadn't heard from me. It's been hours, hasn't it?"

"He did, sir . . ."

"What?"

Nigel points to Cohen's lifeless body: he's in civilian clothes, which means Ortiz was right: he wasn't on duty, but he came anyway. He's still holding his gun, bleeding from his gut where a large knife is protruding through his flannel shirt. "He was dead when I arrived," Nigel says.

The shock compounds. "No, no . . . Cohen," I say. "Look what they've done to him. We can't leave him like this."

"Mr. Finnegan, under no circumstances can Ms. Cassandra or I be connected to this. I came for you, and I'm leaving with you. Do you understand that?"

"But he . . . he didn't deserve this. He tried to help me."

"I'm sorry, but we're leaving now."

I don't protest and follow Nigel out the front door, where Cassandra's white Tesla waits. It smells like rain; cold dollops begin to fall.

A Ford Ranger—I believe it's Cohen's—is parked on the front lawn.

"Get in the Tesla," Nigel says, putting the computer tower and my things in the trunk.

"What about the Beemer?"

"It's of little concern." Realizing I'm unable to get in on my own, he leaves the rear of the Tesla to aid me on the passenger side. "I'll collect the BMW at a more opportune time."

"I don't understand. Where are the first responders? Someone had to have heard the gunshots."

"Cohen didn't kill those men. He was stabbed by one of them before ever firing his gun," Nigel says. "I killed them, and I took precautions."

"You killed them?"

"A suppressor . . . it was quiet and efficient."

"But how'd you know to come here? I don't understand."

"There'll be plenty of time for explanations, but right now, please get in the car."

The rain picks up, along with wind gusts. Nigel opens the door and lowers me onto the passenger seat. I'm bleeding on the white upholstery. He hops in the driver's seat, keeps the headlights off, and begins driving away from the chancellor's home. The near-silent hum of the electric motor won't attract the interest of the neighbors, who are likely asleep at three a.m. and used to the late-night comings and goings of the annual holiday party.

"How'd you get past the gate attendant?" I ask.

Nigel looks at me, perplexed. "I–I acted like I belonged."

I snicker, "Right."

We exit through the gate, just as easily as Nigel entered, and drive in the direction of Cassandra's home. I look in the visor mirror and identify where the blood is coming from. There's a cut on my jaw from where Fife delivered the first blow—it's wide and deep—it'll need stitches. The rest of the damage is internal.

"I'm hurt bad," I say. "I need to see a doctor."

"Not a problem. I'll have Ms. Cassandra arrange it."

"And Nigel . . ."

"Yes, sir?"

"Thank you for coming tonight. You saved my life."

"You can thank Ms. Cassandra. She alerted me there might be a problem."

"So she tracked me?" I consider the ways Cassandra might've bugged me, but they all seem sloppy or overly complicated. "The Beemer . . . of course."

"LoJack, sir. Her ex-boyfriend had it installed. It merely needed reactivation."

"And when did she do that?"

"A few days ago, I think."

"Days ago?"

"Rest now," he says, his focus on the wet road. "We'll get you assessed soon."

"You're taking me to an emergency room?"

Nigel cuts his eyes.

"Oh, right, stupid question."

"Ms. Cassandra has a very accommodating physician who makes house calls."

"She thinks of everything, doesn't she?"

"Yes, Mr. Finnegan—she does."

TWENTY

The olive-skinned man with dark hair in the gray sharkskin suit introduces himself as Dr. Tony Britton. I've never seen a doctor dressed as if an algorithm curated his style with the prompt "Rich, unlicensed physician." I'd say he drives a Porsche 911 Carrera and hasn't paid income taxes in ten years.

"Doesn't feel like anything's broken. I don't think X-rays are needed." Britton probes my ribs and taps my abdomen while listening through a stethoscope. "You'll have some discomfort for a few days, but you should heal fine."

I adjust the pillow behind my back, trying to get comfortable. "What can you give me for the pain?"

"A mild opioid analgesic," he says, reaching into his medical bag and bringing out an orange bottle. "It's codeine, but if the pain persists or you start coughing up blood, get to the hospital, and I'd suggest keeping your hands off that facial laceration. You don't want it to get infected. The skin glue should keep the wound sealed until it heals."

"Hemorrhaging's bad. Got it."

"Thank you, Doctor," Nigel says, handing Britton an envelope of cash before he leaves the room.

"You hear anything about tonight?" I ask, swallowing a pill and washing it down with a glass of water.

"I've been monitoring the police scanner since we arrived. So far, nothing has come over the channel."

"We should've called it in."

"Not possible, Mr. Finnegan . . ."

"Yeah, yeah, I know. But still, there's a house full of dead bodies, and two are sheriff deputies, and there's bound to be evidence implicating the chancellor in what they were doing."

"And what exactly were they doing, sir?"

"When people go missing here, they aren't exactly *missing*."

"You're suggesting they were behind these disappearances?"

"Serial killers."

"I see," Nigel says. "My understanding is serial killers are quite rare."

"They are, but in places like this—homogenous, privileged, unquestionably vapid—it's the perfect cover."

"You have a very poor opinion of this town, don't you?"

"So far, I've been here for a week, and people keep trying to kill me. The only thing I haven't figured out is how those assholes disposed of the bodies. I mean, these people vanished without a trace. Not easy to pull off."

"Yes," he says. "Well, I'm sure you'll figure it out. I am sorry about Cohen. I know you'd grown fond of him."

"And I'm sorry you had to get involved, Nigel."

"As I said before, I look out for Ms. Cassandra's interests."

I take another sip of water when I feel the pill lodged in my throat. "You and Cree reconciled yet?"

"Afraid not," he says. "I suppose I've been *ghosted*."

"Bummer, Nigel—it's never easy."

"Such are matters of the heart." He sighs—the ripe ache of a burdened man. "Ms. Cassandra will be awake soon, and I'll need to prepare breakfast for after her yoga and meditation sessions. Sleep well, Mr. Finnegan." Nigel turns off the light and fades into the hallway.

"Wait—about the computer. Can you take a look?"

He returns to the doorway; his moonlit face floats in the darkness. "May I ask, why do you want it? Wouldn't it have been best to leave it for the authorities to find?"

"Those men have been killing for years. That doesn't happen without people looking the other way. Longtime enablers, and I'm not just talking about Deputy Ortiz, but others. Whatever is on that computer could reveal something bigger than even I can imagine . . ."

"A conspiracy?"

"If what Chancellor Webb said is true, these people are methodical and have taken precautions to remain in the shadows. It'll take work, but I intend to expose them."

"Understood. I'll see what I can find." Nigel shuts the door and leaves me to sulk, my eyes heavy as the codeine takes hold. I set my phone to vibrate and burrow under the covers.

Sunrise is in two hours, and by then, someone should notice Cohen's truck or his absence. Since he was off-duty, he wouldn't have radioed in his location to dispatch. He only mentioned having a dead father, but hopefully he has a friend—someone better than me—who'll be concerned and know something is amiss.

Rest now, Trevor . . . my mother's voice, a calming refrain *. . . Rest, Son—it will all be revealed in time . . .*

Just rest . . .

It's seven a.m. I've barely slept four hours because of the lingering pain, and I can't stop thinking about the victims who bled and died in the chancellor's wine cellar.

I cough hard, and the throbbing in my chest intensifies. Dr. Britton's pills are marginally effective. I could've used a heavier dose. All they've done is make me slightly dizzy and thirsty, and my water glass is empty.

I get out of bed. Everything hurts and probably will for months. I shuffle into the bathroom and look in the mirror—sutures and glue, purple and blue bruising, blood blisters, and welts—what will Sarada say? First shock, maybe, then anger and disappointment for not telling her everything about the case, but I needed to spare her from worry. What I'm into now, I've never faced such wickedness and death, and it doesn't feel over.

I put on my slippers and walk downstairs with my empty glass. The kitchen tile is cold under my feet as I press my glass into the fridge's water dispenser and watch it fill. After a few sips, I start to feel better.

Out the window, the rain has stopped, and a misty fog lingers in the backyard. I see Cassandra carrying black trash bags from the garage. She sweeps through the early-morning brume and enters the greenhouse wearing overalls and boots instead of her usual yoga or meditation attire. Her hair is in a ponytail, a departure from the voluminous way it typically flows down her back. I guess this is what Cassandra Boyle looks like when performing manual labor, something I've never known her to do—she doesn't even clear her plate after dinner.

I know Cassandra's been lying to me since I set foot in her home, and while deception is a requisite for how she thrives, whatever she's keeping from me must be far worse than trafficking narcotics or blackmailing corrupt cops. She's never hidden those elicit activities from me because she's proud of them, but whatever it is she's doing in the greenhouse feels unconventional for even her. She's a creature of habit, and waking before eight a.m., or what she calls an "ungodly hour," is odd. And why would she wake early to transport surreptitious trash bags into the greenhouse?

My intrigue gets the better of me, and I open the French doors leading from the dining room to the backyard patio. It's frigid, and I'm underdressed in a pair of lounge pants and a sweatshirt Nigel lent me. I walk the stepping stones through the flower garden, past the koi pond, and to the greenhouse door. I breathe the cold, wet air and wheeze from the exertion. Though the walk is short, every movement is arduous. Taking a beating might be more exhausting than running a marathon, and there's no upside like winning a medal or enjoying a cold beer afterward.

I catch my breath and then enter the twenty-foot-long greenhouse. Each step I take is soft, as if it were a sin to leave a deep impression on the soil. The greenhouse is a holy place—Cassandra's sanctum—though void of spirituality. Meditation for Cassandra isn't about mindfulness, gratitude, or communing with nature. There's nothing transcendental about her practice; rather, its purpose is to eliminate distractions. The greenhouse offers a utilitarian solution. The vegetation absorbs noise and produces oxygen-rich air that improves her cognitive ability, allowing her to be at her optimal best to scheme and chart her next nefarious moves.

She stands between three large, above-ground planters that are more like troughs, about eighteen inches deep, and filled with potting soil. The trash bags rest at her feet, and I'm able to glimpse an item inside—a sweater, seafoam green with hints of gold and brown.

I gather the strength to stand with command presence, and in my most authoritative voice, I ask, "What's in the bags, Cassandra?"

"You sound like a cop," she says, slowly turning around. "I hate it."

"Are you going to answer my question, or do I have to look for myself?"

"I heard you had a rough night. You should go lie down."

"Maybe I will after I take a look."

"Probably better if you didn't."

"And why's that?"

"You know why . . ."

"Whose clothes are they?"

"Don't make this into a thing, Trevor. Forget you ever saw me in here."

"I can't do that—"

"Why not?"

"Because . . ."

"Because you're *you*."

"There's only one reason you'd have clothes that don't belong to you in bags."

She moves closer, reaches for my chin, and kisses me. I'm too wounded to put up a fight, but after a second or so, I draw away, nearly falling backward. "What are you doing?" I ask.

"If you look in the bags, it'll be the end of everything—you and me."

"Cassandra, I already told you, there is no you and me . . ."

"Fine," she says. "If there's no changing your mind, go ahead. Look."

She tosses the bags at my feet. I immediately notice small red dots that look like old blood on the sweater. Then it's confirmed. I see it—Cree's butterfly pendant is tarnished with dried blood. "You said you wouldn't hurt her."

"It couldn't be helped," she says.

"People don't just disappear, Cassandra. And what about Nigel? He's been trying to reach her and thinks she's ignoring him."

"He'll get over it."

"Damn you . . ."

"Don't act so surprised."

"But you promised you wouldn't hurt her!"

"What did I tell you about outsiders? I can't afford to take a risk like that. Not for Nigel—not for anyone."

I study the planting troughs—long, wide, and able to accommodate bodies that aren't too large or tall . . . like very petite women that have been hacked into pieces. If one trough is for Cree, who are the other two for?

"You think Nigel won't realize what you've done? Burying Cree in an oversized planter."

"You don't know what you're talking about."

"She's in there, isn't she?" I say, pointing to the dry soil in the trough. "But those other planters, who are they reserved for?"

"The painkillers must be getting to you," Cassandra says. "You're not thinking straight."

"I'm thinking just fine."

"Go back inside, Trevor . . . forget about all this. You got Webb. Now, end this crusade."

"I visited Sally Munoz, and she told me the feds had multiple witnesses willing to testify against you—people close to you and who know the operation well. Nigel was my first thought, but he would never betray you. But your adopted daughters . . . where are they, Cassandra?"

"Boulder, like I told you."

"Prove it."

"You think I killed and buried my children in this planter?"

"Despite the many terrible offenses you've carried out in your life, I want to say killing your girls is unquestionably out of bounds, but I've been wrong before."

"You're being ridiculous. I'd never hurt my children."

"Call them—get them on the phone so I can hear their voices."

"Oh, go to hell, Trevor. I don't answer to you."

"Do it, Cassandra! Let me hear their voices."

"You really think I'm a monster, don't you? You've lived in the darkness so long you think everyone is capable of such horrible acts."

"Because everyone *is* capable, Cassandra. Even you . . ."

She takes her phone from her pocket and dials; the call rings loudly through the speaker. A young woman answers groggily. "Hello? Mom?"

"It's me, hunny . . ."

"What time is it?"

"Early," Cassandra says. "You and your sister all right?"

"A little hungover, but we're fine."

"Just what a mother wants to hear. Go on back to bed. I was only checking on you."

"OK, Mom. Talk later?"

"Sure, hunny," Cassandra says, then ends the call, eying Trevor with contempt. "Happy now?"

"So, you didn't kill them, but Cree . . . it doesn't change what you've done to Cree. She didn't deserve to die."

"Most people don't deserve to die, Trevor. It's the ugly side of my business."

"Nothing comes between you and your business, right?"

"My daughters are the reason I've kept at this for so long. It's all been for them. So they could have a better life."

"So, if it isn't your daughters who are cooperating with the feds, then who is it?"

"My girls know the game, Trevor. They're keeping the feds busy, feeding them information that amounts to nothing. They've been buying me time."

"Time for what?"

"So I can walk away for good," she says. "The girls don't know anything except what I tell them, and when the feds check out the information they've been given, they'll find nothing prosecutable."

"You're giving up the life?"

"If you mean my illegal activities, then yes, I am."

"Why the change of heart?"

"When you asked to stay here, I thought, this is it. My one chance to prove I'm more than the deeds I've done. I thought if you could see me—the *real* me—then, maybe you'd—"

"Love you?"

"Or at least try. I even put up with your father's chauvinism and crassness. I tried to conceive what it would be like to be part of your world. Maybe even your family someday."

"Cassandra, I never meant to give you that impression."

"You didn't have to," she says. "The mind imagines what it desires, and if it does it long enough, it convinces itself that what it desires is possible."

"You need help, Cassandra. A mental health intervention."

"What I need is for you to understand me. Am I not a person?" she asks without blinking. "Do I not deserve happiness?"

"This whole investment in keeping me alive was because of a fantasy that we'd run off together?"

"You make me sound like an imbecile," she says. "But I was weak and allowed myself to dream of a life I was never supposed to have."

"And tonight, you had Nigel save me by killing Chancellor Webb and Ortiz, knowing it could potentially bring heat on you. You may say you love me, but not nearly as much as you love your freedom. You would never have sent Nigel to that house unless you had a far more compelling reason than keeping them from killing me."

"I never said I love you. But I cared for you enough to intervene on your behalf."

"I don't accept that," I say, quelling the urge to vomit. I've been standing too long. My body is pleading for rest. "If they wanted me dead, they would've gotten it over with."

"No, you were just fortunate that Nigel got there in time."

"It's more than that. You wanted them dead for a reason."

"And what reason would that have been, besides the fact they were going to kill you?"

"They were acting on your orders."

"I don't know what you're talking about . . ."

"All these years, and you sat by as they carried out murder after murder. You could've dropped a dime, a goddamn anonymous tip, but you did nothing. What did the chancellor have on you?"

"Nothing," she says. "I figured out what they were doing, and I helped you stop it."

"You're lying."

"I'm not—"

"Bullshit. You knew what they were doing long before I set foot in Malibu. It's your business to know things. Serial killers or not, you've got tabs on everybody. They were using the campgrounds, beaches, and highways as a hunting ground, and that could've brought federal law enforcement—the FBI—and that's bad for your business."

"What Webb and those maniacs were doing was getting out of control, but I honestly didn't know they were going after—"

"People like me—Black folks. Would that have made a difference in your eyes?"

"I'm just saying, if I'd known, I would've done things differently."

"So that's it, you expect me to believe that's why you kept your mouth shut all these years while they slaughtered people—because you didn't want police snooping around?"

"Yes," she says. "But it's over now. Webb and his acolytes are dead. Nigel took care of that tonight. The town is free of it—we're free of it."

"No, there's something else," I say, staring into her eyes. "You're not telling me everything."

"This is paranoia, Trevor. You're conjuring these ideas, these thoughts that are just figments of your—"

"No! You stayed quiet for another reason."

"And what reason would that be? You think I was a member of their freaky murder fetish club?"

"It had to have been the bodies," I say. "You helped them dispose of the bodies, didn't you?"

"What?"

"How many bodies did you dump for them, Cassandra? Hundreds?"

"Do you even know what you're saying?"

"When they shot Sharice's brother, Gabriel, it was sloppy. They left him in a place where he was sure to be found. Sheriff deputies were crawling all over town, so I figure Webb got scared and came to you—the friendly neighborhood drug lord. How much did he offer? Millions to be sure the bodies were never found?"

"It wasn't like that," she says. "It's complicated."

"Tell me about the agreement you made with him!"

"It wasn't an agreement. He forced me to help him," she says. "Webb knew about my business, my real business. Decades before he worked at St. Catherine's, he'd managed my grandfather's estate. It's where he made most of his money. When my grandfather passed away, I took over, but Webb remained the accountant. I tried to hide my off-the-books revenue streams, but he found them. I was new to narcotic sales and money laundering, and I hadn't made it difficult for him. So we talked quid pro quo. He told me about his *needs*, as much as I could stomach. He said he'd pick people no one would miss—vagrants, hookers, and runaways that find their way into the canyons and onto the beaches. He never said anything about targeting people because of their race."

"Neither did Hitler."

"Then he said if I took care of the bodies, he'd keep my business from the prying eyes of the IRS and law enforcement. So I agreed, and he laundered my money through a series of shell corporations that made charitable donations to the university. He moved the money around so much, no one was the wiser."

"And what about the victims? Where are they buried?"

"I don't know," she says. "Nigel always took care of it."

"Nigel?"

"I never asked how he did it. I didn't want to know. It was just business, Trevor—that's all."

"Business? Do you know what they did to those people?"

"None of us are clean here," she says. "It's bigger than just Webb, and that's why Nigel can't tell you what's on that computer tower. Some very powerful individuals are involved in this."

"Avery was right. It's the whole damn town. Except poor Cohen—"

"It's not just the town, Trevor. Webb's operation touches every corner of this country, which was why I tried to keep it from you. You've never faced anything this dangerous."

"I've heard that before..."

"After Webb's redneck janitor tampered with your car, I thought you'd stop, back off."

"Baskin..."

"The dimwit was only supposed to scare you, not kill you."

"And you told him where to find me in Downey?"

"I warned him that you were no pushover, but he didn't believe me," she says. "He didn't understand that you never back down. And all in the name of Avery, an estranged brother? If not for biology, he'd be a total stranger to you, but you still risked everything for him."

"I didn't do it for him."

"Of course not; it's your brother's dead girlfriend who haunts you now—is that it? Same as Brandon Soledad, and how many others? Do you finally feel vindicated now?"

"Her name was Keisha."

"I'll always admire your willingness to be a champion for the dead, but it's also your weakness." She pulls a small-caliber pistol with a suppressor at the barrel's end from her coat pocket. I recognize it as the gun Nigel was carrying in the chancellor's home. "Are you armed?" she asks.

"Didn't think I needed a gun to visit a greenhouse."

"This isn't what I wanted, Trevor..."

"Yet here we are," I say. "So, what now, Cassandra? Are you going to disappear me, too, or use that gun to frame me for the murders in Webb's home?"

"You're too smart for your own good."

"So I've been told..."

"I don't want to hurt you, but I need to know if I can trust you."

"You expect me to keep quiet about all this?"

"I expect you to want to live," she says. "Think about Sarada and your daughter. You really want to leave them in this world alone?"

"So, those are my choices: shut up and keep breathing or—"

"I pull the trigger and spend the rest of my life mourning what could've been."

"Not sure either option works for me."

"Don't be a fool, Trevor. These people you surround yourself with lie and use you. You owe them nothing."

"You know nothing about my life."

"I know about Tori and why she left Vancouver. Did she tell you about her out-of-work actor ex-boyfriend and her restraining order against him?"

"What are you talking about?"

"He's been stalking her. That's why she came back to Los Angeles."

"You're keeping tabs on Tori?"

"For your sake, yes. A spyware program Nigel wrote and tucked in an email advertising discounted Manolo Blahnik pumps. It only took her clicking on the ad for us to access her inbox. We have pages of communications between them. The vicious things he said to her, yet, like a fool, she believes in giving second chances."

"She said she came back so that I could be a part of Simone's life."

"Well, Trevor, she lied, and now that she's rekindled her romance with the possessive lunk, it's clear she isn't putting your daughter's interests first."

"Why are you telling me this?"

"Because I only want to protect you. Don't you see that? We can take Simone and go. Never having to look back."

"And Sarada? Are you also tapping her phone? What about mine?"

"Only Tori's, for no other reason than curiosity. Sarada, on the other hand, leaves little to the imagination. I mean, how interesting could a baker be?"

"You're going to leave my family alone."

"I have no desire to hurt them," she says. "I know it would destroy you, and that's the last thing I want. I understand you, Trevor. Better than Sarada or Tori ever will."

"*You* understand me?"

"We're kindred spirits. Simpatico. If you give me a chance, I'll show you true happiness—I'll show you freedom."

"Says the woman holding me at gunpoint."

Cassandra doesn't lower the weapon and steps forward,

closing more distance. The pistol isn't powerful, but at this range and with half-decent aim, any shot could be fatal. "It's the only way you'd take me seriously," she says. "And I need you to believe me."

"I've never doubted your seriousness, Cassandra. I've always counted on it, which is why I'm leaving."

"To go where? You can barely stand."

"Far away from here." I turn around and begin the arduous walk out of the greenhouse and back to Cassandra's mansion. "And for the record, I gave up on freedom a long time ago."

"Don't turn your back on me, Trevor!"

With each painful step, I consider the revelations Cassandra has levied. Has Tori been keeping things from me as to her true motives for returning and now going back to Vancouver? Cassandra is many things—a sociopath, murderer, and drug trafficker—but would she lie about this?"

There's a whizzing, and then bits of dirt pop as if tiny landmines have detonated around my feet. I turn around to see Cassandra aiming the pistol at the ground, having fired warning shots into the moist dirt.

"If you go to the police, you'll force my hand," she says without deference.

"I know," I say, continuing to walk calmly with my head raised high.

"Then stop, Trevor . . . Stop or I'll . . ."

I continue, blearily eying the French doors in the distance. Another yard or so, and I'm clear. She won't shoot me inside the house.

Cassandra follows behind me. I listen closely to the sound of a bullet sliding into the chamber. She's breathing hard, panting almost. I imagine that inside of her exists an epic conflict. Not of right and wrong, but something far more entangled. If what she says is true, love is her weakness, while violence is her default action. Shooting me should be easy for a woman who has killed for less than heartbreak, or what she believes to be such. Cassandra may confess to love me, but I don't believe she's capable of loving anyone, not even her daughters—not really.

More deep breaths . . . "I want to hear you say it," she says. "Own it."

I turn and face her again. "Own what?"

"That you feel nothing for me . . . that it's all in my head, and I dreamt you up."

The next words I speak will either buy me time or place me in a category of traitor, turncoat, and worthy of death.

She readies the gun to fire, her finger snug on the trigger. "Answer me, dammit!"

"You've already made your decision, Cassandra. It doesn't matter what I feel. Even if there were a part of me that dared see you as more than what you are, I'd never act on it. So do whatever you have to. Just get it over with—"

"Thank you for your honesty," she says. "I could always count on you for that . . ."

Nigel appears, walking at a feverish pace. In the past, I've observed this look, if only for a second—an acute lividity in his sunken eyes, a simmering wrath. I saw it when Cassandra barged in on him and Cree, and he swallowed it back, returning to the persona of a mild-mannered, affable assistant. Yet that persona has sustained cracks, crucial damage like a tired vessel battered by choppy seas.

He looks past me, maybe through me, at Cassandra. Time slows, and a gun materializes in his hand—a long-barreled revolver. He raises it, aims, and fires.

Bang . . . a single bullet scores the mist and releases a miasma of cordite: sulfuric and earthy.

I dive to the ground, roll from Nigel's path, and assume the prone position.

Nigel fires again—*bang*. I watch as the bullet strikes Cassandra's thigh. Her gun falls to the ground. She wails in pain, limping back toward the greenhouse.

"Don't move," Nigel says, his pistol aimed at Cassandra's back. "I beg you not to take another step."

She holds still, struggling to remain upright as blood flows from her wound. "What the hell, Nigel? Do you know what you've done?"

"It isn't a fatal wound, Ms. Cassandra, but it is deserved."

"You pathetic fool. How can you be this fragile? Or maybe you are truly this obtuse. I should've seen it. All these years, how could I not have seen what you are? A sniveling, little—"

"Consider this my resignation," Nigel says. "It ends. No more killing. No more death."

"What are you going on about? You're making the rules now?" She presses her palm over the bullet hole. "I never thought I'd witness a grown man's tantrum."

"I can't take it any longer," he says. "Cree's gone because of you."

"Is that what this is about? The hairy-legged hippie."

"Don't talk about her that way."

"The girl was wrong for you."

"She didn't have to die."

"Nigel, you knew about Cree?" I ask.

"Ms. Cassandra convinced me it was the only way," he says. "She said we have to protect the empire at all costs."

"She was just a kid—she didn't know anything."

Nigel's breaking down, heaving as his tears fall. The gun appears to be slipping from his grasp. "I know . . . I know, but she got in my head. That's what she does—"

"You killed Cree?" I ask.

"It was painless," he says. "I made sure of it. Cree fell asleep in the car . . . and she didn't wake up."

"I don't think I can listen to this anymore," I say. "You people are sick."

"She's the sick one, and I never should've listened to her," Nigel says. "But all that ends now. I'm leaving."

"Leaving? There is no you without me," Cassandra says. "Did you actually think that girl would continue seeing you once she graduated from St. Catherine's? Because if you did, you're more delusional than I thought. You did yourself a favor killing her—saved yourself the heartbreak."

"Be quiet. Don't say another word!"

Cassandra laughs in defiance. "I remember what it was like to be young and beautiful—capturing a man with a single look. But it doesn't last, and she would've wounded you so deeply that you'd be no use to me. And I needed you sharp."

"C'mon, Nigel," I say. "It's like you said—it's over. Call the police. End it for good."

"I told you, Mr. Finnegan, no police."

"Think about what you're saying. Cassandra's your bargaining chip. There's a way out of this for you."

"I've done things . . . Blood is on my hands. So much blood . . . She's right, you know? I am obtuse—weak, afraid. But she's no different than me—right, Cassandra? You feared I'd leave you, and you'd have nothing, and now your fear has come true. Everything you've built with me by your side will crumble today."

Cassandra's nearly hyperventilating, drawing air in fast gulps. "All for a co-ed from Utah?" she asks. "She mattered more than what we built? What future could you have possibly had?"

"I could've been happy," he says. "If only for a little while. It would've been worth it."

"Happiness is overpriced," she says. "And overrated."

Nigel presses the pistol to Cassandra's chest. "Leave, Trevor."

I get to my feet, shaky but standing. "You don't have to do this, Nigel. We can make it right."

"The key to your Falcon is on the driver's seat. It's got a full tank."

"Think about this, man. She should see time for what she's done."

"Walk away," he says. "And don't ever come back to Malibu. There's nothing here for you anymore."

"Trevor," Cassandra pleads. "You can't leave me like this . . ."

I study her hard—it's the last time I'll see her, and I need to remember this moment. "Goodbye, Cassandra."

"Trevor! I'm begging you. Please? Please?"

I set off toward the house as fast as my legs will carry me. When I reach the French doors, I look back: Cassandra bellows in the fog, moping; Nigel looms over her, seeming to relish the moment, soaking it up like a sponge. They both look so small and insignificant, and I wonder why I never saw them as anything other than that.

I go inside the house and make my way downstairs to Nigel's

quarters. On his desk is the computer tower I took from Webb's home. I pick it up. It must weigh ten pounds—it's like an anchor to carry. I haul it up to the guest room, where I pack my bag, wipe down all the fixtures to remove any evidence of Pop's and my fingerprints, and then go downstairs, exiting the house through the garage. My car key is on the seat like Nigel said it would be. I pop the trunk, put in the computer tower and duffle, get in, and start the engine. My heart's thumping, and my hands won't stop trembling. But I'm managing the pain better, numbed by the influx of adrenaline and cortisol.

Gunshots echo through the neighborhood. Magpies flee from the surrounding trees. Has Nigel, Cassandra's trusted confidant, ended her life, or maybe, in a twist of fate, has Cassandra managed to end his? There isn't much time to consider the full implications of either of their deaths. When I think of all Cassandra accomplished, how she was believed to have ruled the LA drug scene for over a decade, operating in the shadows, protected by privilege, I know the city is better off without her.

Yet there's a quiet, near-whispering voice in my head that wonders if I'd been able to save one of them. Who might it have been? Cassandra trusted me. She had become like a friend, despite her occupation. It must be how undercover narcs feel after working in consort with drug traffickers. After months of building trust, the traffickers invite the narcs to their family birthday parties. Only for the narc to ensure the trafficker's arrest months or years later. Bonding only makes betrayal sting all the more.

In this neighborhood, two or three loud booms mean a car backfiring, but for those who know gunfire, panic spreads quickly. People are beginning to emerge from their homes in robes and slippers, frenzied and speaking into their cell phones. They stand on their rich lawns amid Christmas decorations: glowing reindeer and an animatronic Santa waving its hand.

I reverse into the street, shift into drive, and floor the car, sending white smoke into the air before turning a corner and leaving the neighborhood, hopeful nobody captured my license plate with their camera phone.

When I reach Highway 1, my thoughts are still on Cassandra.

There's something inherently foul about exploiting a woman's romantic feelings for personal gain. Sure, it happens all the time: men manipulate women without qualms over the damage they inflict. I, too, am guilty, and perhaps what I did to Cassandra pales in comparison to the lives she ruined with drugs and violence, but it doesn't make me feel any better. Even though she was a criminal who poisoned and murdered, I played her, and it showed me what still lingers beneath the surface: a treachery that, when empowered, turns men into snakes. I know that I'm not a good man . . . I'm unsure if there are any *good* men left in the world. Only those trying to be good, and despite it all, trying might be the best thing we've got going for us.

TWENTY-ONE

"Trevor? What are you doing here?" Kimber asks, standing in her doorway. "What happened to you? You look like hell."

"I need your help," I say, standing on her porch, holding the computer tower. Ordinarily, I wouldn't involve her, especially now that our mutual employer, David Bergman, is dead, but maybe that's also why I drove to Kimber's house in Santa Monica, hoping she could help me do what David was so good at—expose the truth.

"Come in," she says. "Are you all right?"

I follow her inside. She's still in bedclothes: blue flannel pajamas and mule slippers. "Can I set this down somewhere?" I ask.

"Yeah, over there," she says, directing me to her kitchen table. The place feels like a college dorm but with slightly nicer furniture—top-tier Ikea that doesn't sway or come apart when moved, like the console table behind her sofa displaying her minora.

"Do you need something?" She eyes my bruises. "Water . . . maybe an ice pack?"

"No, thank you. I'm making do."

"OK—if you say so. What's with the computer?"

"You and the IT girl still together?"

"Yes," she says. "Myra and I worked everything out. She's been a big help, you know? With David's death and everything."

"I'm glad you've got somebody."

Kimber tosses her dark hair over her shoulder and sits on the couch. "So, what's the deal, Trevor? Not that I'm unhappy to see you, but it's morning."

"I need Myra's help," I say. "Any way you can get her over here?"

"What do you need her for?"

I sit next to Kimber. "That computer has sensitive data on it, and I need her to tell me what it is."

"Whose computer is it?"

"All I can tell you is it's not mine."

"Sounds complicated."

"It is."

"But you must have some idea what's on it?"

"Names," I say. "Probably belonging to some very important people. Rich people."

"It's too early for you to be this enigmatic. Can you say more? Because you realize Myra is going to ask the same questions."

"It's related to a homicide case. I got it from a suspect's home."

"Why are *you* taking stuff from a suspect's home and not the police?"

"Please, Kimber. I know how this might seem . . ."

"Shady," she says. "Without a doubt."

"But trust me. I need to know what's on that computer. Can you please call Myra?"

Kimber shrugs. "All right," she says. "Myra, can you come out here, babe?"

"She's here?"

"Doomscrolling in bed," she says. "Her morning ritual."

Myra enters from the hallway. She's a tall, almond-skinned woman with a curly afro. Kimber and Myra's relationship has been off and on for a year. When they first started dating, Kimber bragged that Myra was a former professional volleyball player and one of the only Black females in the sport to have a major endorsement from an apparel company. I don't know how Myra became an IT supervisor at the Department of Water and Power, but I'm grateful for her career change.

"Who's this?" Myra asks, standing in a hoodie and sweatpants. "A little early for company, isn't it?"

"This is Trevor," Kimber says. "We used to work together. You know? Before . . ."

"Oh, right," she says. "Trevor the PI. You basically saved Kimber's life from that maniac cop."

"Boston," Kimber says.

Myra nods. "Yeah, Boston—that shit was insane."

"In a way, Kimber saved my life," I say. "Her split-second distraction made all the difference."

"Welp, I'm glad you did what you did," Myra says. "Otherwise, I don't know what I'd do if something happened to her."

"I appreciate that, babe," Kimber says, unfolding a blanket draped over the couch arm and wrapping it around her shoulders. "Trevor has a computer problem."

"Big or small?"

"I'm not sure," I say. "I'm hoping you can unlock it for me." I point to the tower on the table.

"Unlock? Or break in?" Myra scrutinizes the computer. "Looks old—like 2005 old. Where'd you get this thing?"

"It's part of a case."

"OK," she says. "Let me get my monitor and see what we're working with."

"I should tell you, there may be disturbing shit on it."

"How disturbing?" Myra asks. "Like dead cats disturbing or pedo porn?"

"There may be images of dead people . . . tortured people."

"Shit, Trevor," Kimber says. "You didn't say anything about that."

"I understand if you want to back out."

Kimber looks at Myra as if to read her mind. "And the people responsible, what happens to them?" she asks.

"Thankfully, they're dead," I say. "But I need to uncover the people who backed and supported them, and I think their information is on that computer."

"So we're basically whistleblowing some deranged assholes," Myra says. "I'm good with that—I'll get my stuff."

It takes Myra two hours to bypass the computer's security measures and access the hard drive. Kimber keeps her plied with bowls of sugary cereal in milk and black coffee. I offer to pay Myra for the trouble, but she refuses once she sees what's on the hard drive.

"Damn," Myra says, looking at the pictures of Black women and men in various stages of undress. It's as Baskin described: dozens of victims chained and suffering.

"What the hell is this, Trevor?" Kimber asks. "Who are they?"

"Victims," I say somberly. "Their killers captured their torture in pictures and sold them in online auctions."

"So, all these people are deceased?"

"It's likely, and I need to know who they are so their families can have closure."

"Wait, wait," Myra says. "I've heard about this kind of thing—auctions that happen on the dark web. People who bid on illegal shit with cryptocurrency."

"How do we find out who received these images?" I ask.

"Some of these pictures are fifteen years old," Myra says. "There might be a listserv associated with them." She looks in folders until she finds a spreadsheet of names and email addresses. "I think this is it."

There are pages of entries, but the names read as fictitious—*Maverick*, *Christopher Columbus*, *Moby Dick*. Dollar amounts are in a field next to the email addresses. Some are totaling in the ten-thousands.

"Who spends that kind of money on pictures of people being brutalized?" Kimber asks.

"People with disposable income," I say. "You know what this means, don't you?"

"We have to be smart about who we show this to," Kimber says. "This gets out, and who knows what these people might do?"

Myra rubs her eyes and looks away from the screen. "God, this is really fucked up," she says. "Who are we supposed to tell about this? The cops?"

Kimber begins to pace. "The FBI is the logical choice."

"I agree," I say, "but convincing them it's authentic won't be easy. We still have no clue who the buyers are, and the email addresses could be fake or closed by now."

"The FBI has teams for this sort of thing. They could track these people down, but how are you going to get them to believe you? I mean, you can't just call up and say you have a computer with snuff pics that were probably sold to the country's most rich and shameless."

"You're right," I say. "We'll have to legitimize it."

"OK, and how do we do that?"

"I've got a friend, James, at the *LA Times*," Myra says. "He's the best at what he does. If anyone could track down where some of these email addresses lead, it's him."

"So, let's do it," Kimber says. "Get James on the phone."

"Are you sure you want to take this on?" I ask. "I nearly died over what these assholes were doing. Who knows where all this will lead?"

"Times like this, I ask: 'What would David do?' and I think I know the answer," Kimber says. "He'd want us to tell the truth, no matter the cost, and that's what we're going to do."

"Kimber's right," Myra says. "It's like you said, Trevor: we need to know who the victims and the buyers are, and then the entire world needs to know them."

"All right," I say. "Let's get this list to James."

"We're going to need a place to work from," Kimber says. "Trevor, have you checked out the office building yet?"

"No," I say, "but now is as good a time as any to pay it a visit."

TWENTY-TWO

Christmas Day, California Institution for Women

Carolers harmonize "Silent Night" in the prisoner's visiting room. They're poor singers, but it's a volunteer gig, so inmates and their families look on with half-smiles and clap at the end of every mediocre song.

"Merry Christmas, Sally," I say, handing her a shoebox. I didn't bother wrapping it since the guards would've torn it apart anyway.

She opens the box. "Not sure what to say . . ." She holds up a king-size package of Lifesavers Gummies.

"I remember you loved these things. The entire Crown Vic smelled like tropical fruit."

She grins. "Thanks, Finn."

"You got it."

"I know you didn't come here to give me Christmas candy."

"I guess not," I say. "Have you signed the prosecutor's deal yet?"

"They were supposed to have it drafted three days ago, but I haven't heard anything. Why?"

"I've been trying to find the best way to tell you this, thought it'd be best face to face . . ."

"Just spill it."

"Cassandra Boyle is dead."

"What?" Sally slaps her palms on the table. "Dead? How?"

"Shot to death by a man who worked for her."

"Like her business partner?"

"Kind of, yeah."

"How the hell do you know this?"

"News of it broke last night. When her daughters couldn't get in touch with her, they called sheriff's deputies to her home. She was found dead in her greenhouse."

"And the shooter?"

"His name's Nigel," I say. "And he's in the wind."

"Nigel, huh? Seems like you've got the rundown."

"There's more to the shooting."

"Like what?"

"I was there. Witnessed the entire thing. Well, not all of the shooting part. I wasn't sure if Cassandra survived or not until I saw the news."

"How exactly does your being there happen?"

"I'd been staying at Cassandra's home while working Avery's case."

"You were staying at that woman's house? Since when do drug traffickers host Airbnbs?"

"It's complicated."

"Do you know what this means?" she asks. "Are you even grasping what you're telling me?"

"I know what it means."

"It means I'm fucked, Finn. Do you get that? Cassandra's dead, so there isn't going to be a deal. My ticket out of here died with that bitch."

"I'm sorry—"

"Sorry? The best you can say is *sorry*?"

"I tried, Sally . . ."

"What do you mean you tried? You're not the one who killed her."

"But I tried to stop it. If I'd only had my piece . . ."

"So, you're telling me I have to spend fifteen years minimum in here because you didn't think to have your gun around a murderer?" She clenches her fists and looks to the guard. "You were in this woman's house, and you never once thought to tell me? Did you bother telling any law enforcement agency?"

"No."

"Of course you didn't," she says. "Cops have died trying to get that kind of access to her, and you get it, walk away with nothing, and she ends up dead."

"I'm not a cop anymore, Sally. You know that."

"But it's my ass on the line, Finn. I mean, what the hell were you doing with her in that house?"

"I needed her resources," I say. "But I know I messed up."

"Damn right, you did. Just go—get the fuck out of here."

"Sally—"

"Go before I do something we both will regret."

I stand up. "I'll make it right."

"No, you won't. Everything you touch goes to shit. So please, I'm begging you: don't try to help me. I'd rather rot in here without having to think that you're out there ruining any chance I might have at getting out."

"I was gathering intel . . . I was close."

"Close only counts in horseshoes, remember?"

"C'mon, Sally. You're angry. I get that. But I'm the only chance you've got. You can't banish me now."

"Oh, but I can, Finn. I never want to see you again, and I mean it this time with every fiber of my being."

"I'm not the reason you're in here. Don't forget that."

"You think I'll forget how I ended up in here? I live with it every second of every day behind these walls . . . and the little bit of hope I held out—that maybe I'd get a deal, and some judge would have mercy on me—is gone. I'm not a bad person—I know that. It was a mistake taking Cassandra's money, but I listened to you and turned myself in, and I got nothing for it. No leniency. No consideration. I should've taken my chances in Oaxaca."

"You two done here?" the guard asks.

"Take me back to my cell," Sally says, offering her wrists for the guard to shackle.

"OK, I get it, Sally. I'm gone."

"Good," she says. "And Merry fucking Christmas."

It's cold and raining. It hasn't rained on Christmas in years. I stand outside Tori's apartment building waiting for the landlord to buzz me in. Pop sits in the Falcon, slumped in the passenger seat, dapper in his suit—gray pinstripe, red tie embossed with glittering snowflakes, and a dark green pocket square. He left the treatment facility on a day-pass, something they reserve for holidays. Given the last time he left, he finished a half bottle of wine, I'll be more vigilant.

The landlord lets me through the gate, and I walk upstairs to Tori's empty apartment. After I told him I was an investigator and an official-sounding story about Tori being willed money from a deceased relative, he agreed for me to see the vacated apartment Tori and Simone once shared.

"Unfortunately, like I said on the phone, she's gone," the landlord says, blowing his nose so hard into a handkerchief I'm surprised the pressure doesn't burst a blood vessel. He has kind eyes and looks to be the sensitive type who is easily moved by a hard-luck story. I'm not surprised he accommodated Tori's decision to break her lease with three months' advance rent to cover his loss. It may seem steep, but many landlords in the city would've demanded five or six months.

"Everything's been cleared out," he says.

"She couldn't have done this all by herself," I say. "Did she have help?"

"Sure, but he wasn't professional-looking. Not like a moving company or anything." He wipes the remaining snot dry. "Just a big guy. Smoked a lot, and his sweat smelled like vodka."

Tori might've gotten help from the ex-boyfriend and supposed stalker Cassandra spoke about. Did she fall back into his snare? Maybe he's the one who paid the landlord to break the lease. I should've seen the signs. Tori wasn't looking for a better life or for me to be a part of raising Simone. She was running away from something, which would matter little to me if she hadn't involved my daughter. Like the domestic violence cases I saw patrolling my beat, an abuser's misdeeds and duplicity lead to a cycle of forgiveness and reoffense—rinse and repeat.

"Did she leave a forwarding address?" I ask, knowing I'd feel more embarrassed if the man knew Tori and I shared a child. What type of father am I that I allowed my daughter to be whisked away to Canada, and I've got no idea where?

"Matter of fact . . ." He digs into his jacket pocket and pulls out Tori's photo. "She asked me to send any mail she got to this address." Written on the back of the headshot from her acting days is a P.O. Box in Burnaby, outside Vancouver.

"Mind if I keep this?"

"Go right ahead. I already took a picture of it on my phone

in case I misplaced it later. Forget my head if it weren't on my shoulders."

I put the headshot in my coat pocket.

"I sure hope you can deliver the money to her," he says. "She looked like she could use it. Not easy being a single mom these days, if ever."

"I appreciate your time."

"Not a problem," he says. "Happy holidays to you."

"Likewise." I walk to the staircase, head down, and go through the gate. The rain begins to pick up. I quickly get inside the car to avoid the downpour.

"How'd it go?" Pop asks.

"She's gone like the landlord said, but she did leave behind an address." I slip out of my raincoat and toss it in the backseat.

"What are you going to do?"

"Not sure."

"Maybe it's time to talk to Sarada," he says. "Get her on board."

"I'm not sure I'm even on board."

"I mean, Cassandra Boyle turned out to be the Queen of Darkness," Pop says. "But if what she said checks out, Tori's living situation isn't good for Simone. If she's back with the guy who's been stalking her, Simone could be in danger. I don't have to tell you how situations like that can turn out."

"Even if I got custody of Simone, what do I know about raising a kid?"

"Nothing," he says. "No more than your mother and me when we started, but we did our best with you," he says. "And as a parent, that's all you can do . . . your best."

"And if my best is shit? What then?"

"You've got a head for it. Not like me when I was your age. I had no idea what I was doing, and had it not been for your mother, who knows how you would have turned out? You'll be fine," Pop says, patting my shoulder. "Besides, what's that Oprah says? It takes a village."

"You're quoting Oprah now?"

"The point is, you won't be alone."

"You're still in rehab, and Sarada's parents are in India. How exactly is that a village?"

"I won't be in rehab forever, got it? Don't worry about me; I'm getting myself together."

"It's just that you've never seemed keen on being a grandfather to Simone."

"The program's helping me see things differently," he says. "I'd like to think I'm changing for the better."

"Tori won't give Simone up without a fight."

"That's expected," he says. "But you can't let that deter you. No matter how long it takes."

"All right, Pop. I'll talk to Sarada about it."

"Good."

I pull away from the curb and start driving toward Sepulveda. Sheets of rain bash the windshield; the wiper blades swat in vain.

Pop sips his gas station coffee from a paper cup. It smells scorched, the way he likes it. "One thing, though," he says, the cup's steam fogging the window. "The Falcon isn't the most practical ride for hauling a kid around."

"C'mon, Pop, you're giving me anxiety."

"I know you love this thing, but you might want to think about something with airbags."

"You won't catch me in a minivan, that's for damn sure."

"I'm with you there, but some of these SUVs aren't bad. Get you something rugged, you know?"

"*Rugged* . . . I'll think about it."

TWENTY-THREE

Folk music plays from the jukebox as Avery downs another shot of bourbon. From the looks of it, he's been drinking since morning. He's in good company. Most people in the dive are drunk, but it's expected on Christmas. Bars do big numbers during the holiday season when self-loathing is at its peak, and there's plenty of cause to get intoxicated.

"Maybe you ought to slow down," Pop says, watching Avery squint from the liquor's burn.

"I'm grown now, old man," he says. "You missed them years when I could've used your advice. I'mma drink as much as I want, for as long as I want."

"Might've been a mistake coming down here," Pop says to me before eying the exit. "Guess we should leave you to it, Avery."

"Nah, stay," he says. "I got you here, so let's air it all out."

"I'm not sure this is the place for that."

"It's the perfect place for it," Avery says. "Look around you. It doesn't get any more depressing than this."

"We've talked about this," Pop says. "I thought you understood."

"Those conversations we had on the phone were just me being cordial. It's 'bout time you met the real Avery so you can see how deep that Finnegan blood runs."

"All right, then," Pop says. "Speak on it."

"For starters, why didn't you want me?"

"I never said I didn't want you."

"Nope . . . nope, but you showed it through your absence. Not once did you come and see me, and why didn't you answer any of the questions in my letters? You only wrote me about how hard it was being a cop. I was trying to get to know you."

"I thought I was giving you a chance to know me."

"I got to know you all right. Saw right through your bullshit,"

Avery says. "How about you just tell me the truth about why you didn't want anything to do with me?"

"Your mom and I were practically strangers. She knew I had a family . . . I didn't want to disappoint you," Pop says. "I knew whatever she told you about me was something I'd fall short of. I couldn't live up to what she wanted me to be."

"Like a father?"

"Yes."

"That's the most cowardly shit I've ever heard. You're a grown man, supposed to be this big bad policeman, and you were scared of what a little boy might think of you?"

"Maybe, but it's the truth, Avery. I didn't think knowing me would be of much use to you, so I sent money. Whatever I could, as often as I could."

"Money can't raise a child. Money can't throw a football or teach a nigga how to balance a checkbook. You can't hug money or talk to it or ask it no kinds of questions."

"You're right. I should've done better. I was immature and selfish, and I'm sorry."

Avery waves to the bartender. "Let me get another bourbon," he says, holding up the empty glass.

"Pop's apologizing," I say. "I know it's not much, but it has to count for something, right?"

"It doesn't have to count for shit, preppy. This is my life, and you two can't come in here with soft apologies expecting us to hug it out."

The bartender arrives tableside, passes Avery another shot, and asks, "On the tab?"

"Yeah," Avery says. "And keep 'em coming. These assholes are paying."

"Afraid that isn't going to happen," I say.

"Figures," Avery says. "You two aren't good for much, are you?"

Pop seems transfixed by the shot glass topped with brown liquor. I nudge him out of his trance. "You good, Pop?"

"Yeah, I'm good," he says. "I've said my piece. Probably best I wait in the car."

I slide out of the booth, allowing Pop room to leave. He

holds for a beat, looks around the bar, and then at Avery. Something's percolating in his head. Nothing good, though. I can see it in his eyes; he wants to say more, and the longer he's in the bar, the greater the temptation.

"It's cool, Pop," I say, giving him the car key. "I'll be right behind you. Just need a couple more minutes here with Avery."

"Ain't that like a Finnegan," Avery says, cutting his eyes as Pop leaves. "Way to dip out, old man. Good talk, though. A real bonding moment."

I sit down and place my hands on the table, worried about how I may use them in the coming moments. "You just had to pick a bar, didn't you?"

"It's not my fault the old man's a drunk."

"He's getting treatment. Maybe that's something you should consider."

"Fuck you, man. I have every reason to be here. I'm the one who lost his girlfriend to mutherfuckin' serial killers, remember? I mean, what are the fucking odds of that happening? So, yeah, I'mma drink till none of this shit matters anymore."

"Doesn't matter how much you drink. You can't undo the past."

"Maybe, but I can sure forget it for a while."

"I'm pretty sure Pop said the same thing once."

"Fuck all that. I'm nothing like you or him. I shouldn't even be sitting here, but you want to know why I am? Because I'm a survivor. I take mine on the chin and keep going. No father—I kept going. Shitty mother—I kept going. Murdered girlfriend—I kept going."

"Yeah, you've had it hard, but you have no idea the things Pop or I have been through. The truth is, we're all alike—us Finnegans are connected not just by blood but trauma."

"So, I drew the short stick, huh? You got the two-parent household and fancy private school. I got the single mom, food stamps, and a revolving door of punks thinking they were my daddy. If you'd been in my shoes, you wouldn't be sitting here feeding me bullshit like some after-school special."

"You're right . . . I can't speak to your pain, but I can speak for Keisha."

"What the hell are you talking about now?"

"The investigation might be focused on Chancellor Webb, Baskin, and Ortiz, but that's only part of this story."

"Man, those guys are guilty as sin, and now the entire world knows it because you gave the photos of them dead people to the press. They put that shit all over the newspapers and internet."

"I did that so the victims' families would know what happened to their loved ones."

"Sure, man, sure," he says. "All I know is the DA dropped the investigation against me, so I guess I should thank you."

"Save your 'thank you,'" I say. "We both know what actually happened that night."

"Yeah, those sick fucks beat Keisha so bad her insides were soup. Even if she didn't trip and bust her head open, she would've died from the hurt they put on her."

"Who told you that?"

"I read about it in the newspaper."

"Well, then, you must have also read that she had plenty of scar tissue from prior injuries long before you two were abducted."

"I don't know nothing about that," he says. "Keisha was hanging with a rough crowd before we got together."

"You're saying you never touched her?"

"Man, if you think that, you're bugging."

"Why don't I believe that?"

"Believe what you want; doesn't matter to me."

"Just like I don't believe you had any intention of getting her help that night she died."

"You need to get your facts straight. I tried to get help. That's what I was doing when you found me. I was flagging down cars." He nestles the shot glass in his palm and thumbs the edge. "You were there . . . saw it with your own eyes. I was damn near dead in the road when you found me. The way I see it, Keisha lucked out. She doesn't have to deal with the aftermath. The nightmares—I can't even sleep."

"Lucked out, huh? You would see it like that, wouldn't you?"

"Think about it. What would life have been like for her if

she had survived? Sucking down meat shakes through a straw? Pissing and shitting into a bag? Every dollar Keisha made was off her body, her looks—it's what she had going for her, and man, did she know it. She brought all the boys to the yard."

"Whether she lived or died wasn't your choice to make."

"Fuck you saying?" He squeezes his hand around the glass, causing the bourbon to spill. Beads of liquor roll over his deformed knuckles, pooling under his palm. "Look what you made me do," he says, wiping the spill with a cocktail napkin.

"She didn't trip and split her skull on a boulder, Avery. It's what Brennan thought all along, and she was right. You bashed her head in, and I think I know why."

Avery chuckles. "You crazy, bro. I didn't kill Keisha. Hell, I was her only shot at surviving."

"A pity," I say, "that Keisha's life depended on a man who only valued his own."

"You don't know shit. I risked it all to get us both to safety."

"Dead weight . . . that's what she was to you."

"Fuck you. I loved her!"

"Yeah, you've said that a lot during this entire investigation. Going on about how much you loved Keisha, and maybe, in your feeble mind, you did. But you didn't bludgeon her out of mercy. You looked at her and knew that if she lived, she'd be a burden to you. You both were surviving off the money *she* made. She was your cash cow, and she gladly forked over her earnings to you out of love, which you gambled away. But you knew what the future held for someone with her injuries, and at that moment, you knew she was worthless to you."

"I ain't the bad guy here. The people who kept us in that basement and tortured us are the monsters."

"You're right, but she trusted you to protect her, and instead, you did the opposite. That makes you the worst kind of monster."

"I've been hearing that shit all my life from my mama," he says. "Protect, protect, protect. Nurture women. Look out for them. And when her boyfriends got drunk and smacked her around, it was me who stepped in. I took those blows so she didn't have to, and what'd I get for it? Not even a 'thank you.'

She'd go on as if nothing happened, and a week later, that same boyfriend would be back in her bed again. I was a kid—who was supposed to look out for me? Protect me? And what did I learn from seeing all that? Some of these bitches don't deserve protection . . . some of them get what's coming to them, but not Keisha. She was special."

"Yeah, well, I can't prove you killed her. The body is post-autopsy, and with LA County's backlog of disregarded and unclaimed corpses, she was cremated days ago . . ."

"How about you take your little allegations and get out of here? Leave me to drink in peace."

I glance over at the two white men sitting near the end of the bar, drinking vodka in shearling-lined leather coats. They've been watching us intently since I sat down, and I give them a subtle nod. "Some people are here to see you," I say.

Avery looks at the men and does a double-take. "What? How'd you—"

The men slide off their barstools and begin walking over. I get out of the booth and stand aside.

"I don't suspect we'll be seeing each other again," I say. "But if we ever cross paths, it won't matter how much DNA we share. I'll bury you."

"So that's how it's going to be, *brother*?" Avery downs the liquor, and the Russians slide into the booth—one next to him, the other across.

"Goodbye, Avery," I say, leaving him alone with the debt collectors. "And Merry Christmas."

Outside, the hard rain has dwindled to a drizzle. I get in the Falcon. Pop stares out the window, watching the raindrops cascade down the glass.

"Took you a while," Pop says. "What'd you say to him?"

"Nothing, really. Just wished him well."

"You think we'll see him again?"

"No, Pop—I don't think so."

"I'm sorry, Trevor."

"For what?"

"Hell, where do I start?"

I turn the key in the ignition. The engine rumbles. "I forgive you, Pop."

"You do?"

"Yes."

"So, we're good, then?"

"Yeah, we're good," I say. "It might not seem like it right now, but everything's going to be all right."

"I sure hope so." Pop's smile is frozen as he looks out the window. "You remember the last time we got rain like this? It's been nonstop for days."

"Can't say for sure, but yeah, it's been a minute."

"It's nothing like when the rain comes down in Palm Springs," he says.

"How's that?"

"I can always see the storm coming miles out. Not like here. It gets cloudy, a little dark, and then the sky opens up. There's so much going on up there in the atmosphere, but most people don't notice until the sun fades and it starts pouring. But there's a comfort in seeing the storm rolling in that makes me feel like things still make sense, you know? Like there's a system at work."

"You getting spiritual on me, now?"

"Oh, I don't know," he says. "Just random thoughts, I guess . . ."

"The desert is starting to grow on you, isn't it?"

"It might be," he says. "I was considering staying out there after my treatment. I priced a few condos with decent square footage. Enough space for the grandkids."

"Grandkids? All this baby talk. Do you know something I don't?"

"Planning for the future, that's all."

"Uh-huh."

"And they say the dry heat is good for the body. Air's probably cleaner, too."

I check my watch. "Sarada's flight will be landing soon."

Pop puts on his seat belt. "Let's roll, then."

"All right, Pop."

"All right, Son."

I put on my seat belt and turn the radio dial to a jazz and blues station playing renditions of Christmas songs. Pop starts grooving, bobbing his head and tapping his foot on the floorboard. We share a knowing glance, and I think about what Sharice said to me in the church, and it begins to make more sense. We have choices in this world: life or death, build or destroy, love or hate. And while I'm choosing love, some people will steadfastly cling to hate, and for them, I have no words, only endless pity.